SACRIFICE

SACRIFICE

a novel by

ANDREW VACHSS

ALFRED A. KNOPF

NEW YORK

1991

THIS IS A BORZOI BOOK
PUBLISHED BY ALFRED A. KNOPF, INC.

ISBN 0-679-40283-7
LC 90-53582

Manufactured in the United States of America
Published June 20, 1991
Reprinted Once
Third Printing, July 1991

for
SHEBA

a warrior who fought blindness
until the last battle closed her eyes

if love would die along with death,
this life wouldn't be so hard

ACKNOWLEDGMENT

Bob Gottlieb

none better, ever

SACRIFICE

1

When you hunt predators, the best camouflage is weakness.

The E train screeched into Forty-second Street. I got to my feet, pulling slightly on the leather handle of the dog's harness. She nosed her way forward, wary. Citizens parted to let me pass. A black teenager wearing an oversized blue jacket with gold raglan sleeves braced one side of the doors with his arm, making sure they wouldn't close as I passed between them. "You okay, man. Step through."

My dark glasses had polarized lenses. The kid's face was gentle. Sad. Someone in his family was blind. I mumbled thanks, stepped off the subway car onto the platform.

I pushed forward on the harness handle, like shifting into gear. The dog headed for the stairs, waited for a clear path, then took me up along the rail.

On the sidewalk, I turned my face toward the sun, feeling the warmth. "Good girl, Sheba," I told the dog. She didn't react, a professional doing her work. I shifted the handle and she went forward, keeping me in the middle of the sidewalk. Away from doors that might open suddenly, maintaining a safe distance from the curb. I closed my eyes, counting steps.

Sheba halted me at the corner of Forty-fourth and Eighth. She didn't watch the traffic signals any more than the other pedestrians did. It's the same rule for everyone here—cross at your own risk.

I made my way carefully along the sidewalk, counting steps, guided by the dog. Found my spot. Tugged slightly backward on the handle—Sheba sat down. I unwrapped the blanket from around my shoulders, knelt, and spread it on the ground. When I stood up, Sheba lay down on the blanket, made herself comfortable. I opened my coat. Inside was a cardboard sign, held around my neck with a loop of string. White cardboard, hand-lettered in black Magic Marker.

PLEASE HELP

I held a metal cup in my hands. Added a few random coins to sweeten the pot.

Waiting.

2

Humans passed around me, a stream breaking over a rock. They didn't look at my face. If they had, they would have seen a couple of rough patches where the blind man had missed with the electric razor. I was wearing high-top running shoes, loosely laced, denim pants, a gray sweatshirt. All under a khaki raincoat that came past my knees. A well-used black fedora on my head.

The local skells were used to me by now. I made it to the same spot every day. Patiently collected coins from passing citizens, face held straight ahead.

I was a piece of scenery, as anonymous as a taxicab.

My eyes swept the street behind the dark lenses.

Sheba settled into her task. An old wolf-shepherd, mostly gray, soft eyes watchful under white eyebrows. She had a warrior's heart and an undertaker's patience.

Hooker's heels sounded on the sidewalk. A bottle blonde, wearing a cheap red dress, short-tight, black fishnet stockings, a hole the size of a half-dollar on the front of one thigh, pale skin poking through the mesh. Low-rent makeup smeared her face. Getting ready to work the lunchtime crowd.

"Your dog's so pretty."

"Thank you."

"Can I pet her?"

"No, she's working."

"Me too . . . I guess you can't tell."

I drew a sharp breath through my nose, inhaling her cheap perfume as greedily as a cokehead. She laughed, bitter and brittle. "Yeah, I guess maybe you can. I seen you before. Standing here."

"I'm here every day."

"I know. I seen you smoke sometimes . . . when someone lights one for you. You want one now?"

"I don't have any."

"I have some . . ." Fumbling in her red vinyl shoulder bag. "You want one now?"

"Please."

She stuck two cigarettes in her mouth, fired them with a cheap butane lighter. Handed one to me.

"It tastes good," I told her, grateful tone in my voice.

"It's menthol."

"The lipstick . . . that's what tastes good."

"Oh. I guess you don't . . . I mean . . ."

"Only my eyes don't work."

She flushed under the heavy makeup. "I didn't mean . . ."

"It's okay. Everybody's missing something."

Her eyes flashed sad. "I had a dog once. Back home."

"And you miss her?"

"Yeah. I miss a lot of things."

"Go home."

"I can't. Not now. You don't understand . . . Home's far away from here. A million miles away."

"What's your name?"

"Debbie."

"These are bad streets, Debbie. Even if you can't go home, you can go away."

"He'd come after me."

I dragged on my cigarette.

"You know what I'm talking about?" she asked, her voice bitter-quiet.

"Yeah. I know."

"No, you don't. He's watching me. Right now. Across the street. I spend much more time out here talking to you, not making any money, I'm gonna get it from him."

Even with my eyes closed, even with her facing me, I could see the coat-hanger marks across her back. Feel them. I shifted my face slightly, let her hear the core to my voice. "Tell him you made a date with me. For later."

"Sure." Melancholy sarcasm.

"Put your hand in my coat pocket. Your left hand."

"Wow! You got some roll in there."

"It's mostly singles, two twenties on the inside. Take one . . . Tell him you asked for half up front."

She glanced over her shoulder, hip-shot, leaned close to me. "I tell him that and he'll be waiting for you later . . . when you go home."

"I know. Tell him the roll was a couple a hundred, it's okay."

"But . . ."

"Just do it, Debbie. You live with him?"

"Yeah . . ."

"You can go home tonight. Away from here."

"How . . . ?"

"Take the money, go do your work. Tell him what I told you."

"Mister . . ."

"Reach in, pull out the roll. Shield it with your body. Take the bill, put the rest back. Pat my dog. Then take off. Tonight, you go home, you understand? Stay out of the bus station—take a train. It'll be okay, Debbie."

She reached in my pocket, knelt down.

"Sheba, it's okay, girl," I said.

The dog made a sweet little noise as Debbie patted her. She straightened up, looked into the lenses of my glasses. "You're sure?"

"Dead sure."

I listened to her heels tap off on the sidewalk. A different rhythm now.

3

It was almost two o'clock before he showed. I recognized him easily by now. In his thirties, close-cropped brown hair, matching mustache, trimmed neat. Wearing a blue windbreaker, jeans, white basketball shoes. Youth worker from one of the Homeless Shelters. Last time he stuffed a dollar bill into my cup. I remember saying, "God bless you."

Watching his smile.

This time he wasn't alone. The kid with him was maybe eight years old. Skinny kid, wearing a brand-new sweatshirt with some cartoon character on the front, munching a hot dog. Having a great time. Probably spent a bunch of quarters in the video arcades first.

They turned into the electronics store a few doors in front of where I was standing—the same place he'd gone into the last time. When he'd come up behind me and put the money in my cup. The same place he always went.

He was inside almost an hour. When he came out, he was alone.

4

He walked past me. Stuffed another dollar in my cup. "May the Lord follow you always," I thanked him. He smiled his smile.

The Prof strolled up to me. A tiny black man, wearing a floor-length raincoat, scuffling along.

"You got him?" I asked.

"Slime can slide, but it can't hide."

"Call McGowan first," I told him, holding his eyes to be sure he got it. McGowan's a cop—he knows what I do, but kids are his beat, not hijackers. "Tell him the freak made a live delivery this time. Tell him to go in the back way—Max is there on the watch."

"I hear what you say—today's the day?"

"The bust will go down soon—they're ready, warrants and all. You find out where the freak goes, where he holes up. They'll take him tomorrow, at work. Then we take our piece out of his apartment. Just the cash—the cops can have the rest."

The Prof took off, disappearing into the crowd. The freak would never see him coming.

5

Time to go. I gently pulled on the harness and Sheba came to her feet. I folded the blanket, wrapped it around my neck, and let the dog pull me forward. I turned the corner, headed down the alley where Max would be waiting.

I spotted Debbie's owner lounging against the alley wall. Tall, slim brownskin man wearing a long black leather coat and a Zorro hat.

Stocky white kid next to him, heavily muscled in a red tank top. A pimp: he needed reinforcements to mug a blind man.

I plodded on ahead, oblivious to them, closing the gap.

The pimp pushed himself languidly off the wall to face me. The muscleman loomed up on the side.

"Hold up, man."

I stopped, pulling on the harness, squeezing the button on the handle that unsnapped the whole apparatus from the dog.

"Wha . . . ?" Fear in my voice.

"Give up the money, man. No point in getting yourself all fucked up, right?"

"I don't have any money," I whined.

I saw the slap coming. Didn't move. Let it rock me to my knees, pulling the harness off as I fell.

"Sheba! Hit him!" I yelled, and the dog sprang forward, burying her wolf's teeth deep into the pimp's thigh. He shrieked something in a high octave just as the muscleman took a step toward me. I heard a crack and the muscleman was down, his head lolling at a chiropractic angle.

Max the Silent stepped into view, his Mongol face expressionless, nostrils flared, eyes on the target. Hands at his side: one fisted to smash, the other knife-edged to chop.

"Sheba! Out!"

The dog backed off, cheated, but acting like a pro. The pimp was holding his thigh, moaning a plea to someone he didn't know.

I squatted next him, patted him down. Found the little two-shot derringer in his belt, popped it open. Loaded. No point warning this dirtbag—he wouldn't be a good listener. I held my hand parallel to the ground, made a flicking motion like I was brushing crumbs off a table. I heard a pop, like cloth snapped open in a gust of wind. The pimp slammed into the wall, eyes glazed. Blood bubbled on his lips. I stuck the derringer back into his belt—it was all the ID he'd need at the hospital.

He wouldn't come home tonight. The rest was up to Debbie.

A putty-colored sedan lumbered into the alley at the far end, bouncing on a bad set of shocks. The cops. Max merged with the shadows. I put on my dark glasses, snapped Sheba's harness, and made my slow way out to the street.

6

The E train let me out at Chambers Street, the downtown end of the line. I found my Plymouth parked at the curb near the World Trade Center. Unlocked the back door, unsnapped Sheba's harness. She leaped lightly to the seat.

I took off the dark glasses and climbed behind the wheel.

None of the watching citizens blinked at the miraculous transformation.

7

I turned the Plymouth toward the West Side Highway, slipped through the Brooklyn-Battery Tunnel, tossed a token in the Exact Change lane, and cruised along the Belt Parkway just ahead of the rush-hour traffic.

Taking Sheba home the back way.

I pulled over to a quiet spot the other side of the Brooklyn Aquarium. Exchanged the running shoes for a pair of boots, the sweatshirt for a turtleneck jersey, the raincoat for a leather jacket. Threw the blind man's props into the trunk.

The Plymouth purred past JFK Airport, its overtorqued engine

muted, well within itself. Sheba slept peacefully on the back seat, pro-
foundly uninterested in where we were going. Just doing her job.

Like me.

I turned off the Van Wyck Expressway onto Queens Boulevard. A
short hop to the City-Wide Special Victims Bureau, sitting in the shadow
of the House of Detention. I found a parking place, snapped Sheba's
harness back on.

The entrance to the Bureau is blocked by a steel gate, guard's desk
to one side, two-passenger elevator to the left of a narrow corridor. An
Oriental woman was at the desk. Pretty face, calmly suspicious eyes.

"Can I help you?"

"I'm here to see Ms. Wolfe."

She handed me a sign-in sheet on a clipboard with a cheap ballpoint
pen attached by a string, but her eyes never left my face. "Your name?"
she asked. The way cops ask.

Sheba jumped up so her front paws were resting on the desk, her
ears up and alert.

"Hi, Sheba!" the Oriental woman said. "I know I've got a treat for
you around here someplace. Let me see . . ." She rummaged in her desk
drawer, came out with a dog biscuit in her left hand. Tossed it at Sheba
while she showed me the pistol in her right.

"Where did you get our dog?" she asked, still calm, much colder.

I moved my hands away from my body. "Ask Wolfe," I told her.

She must have kicked some button under the desk. Wolfe came
around the corner, a cigarette in one hand, a sheaf of papers in the
other.

"What is it, Fan?" She spotted me. "Oh, here you are. Right on
time."

Sheba bounded over to her. Wolfe reached down, scratched behind
the dog's ears. "Sheba, playroom! Go to the playroom." The dog trotted
off.

"He's okay, Fan." Wolfe smiled. The Oriental woman inclined her
head about an inch, put the gun away.

I followed Wolfe back into her office. It looked like it always does: paper all over the place, walls covered with charts and graphs, a computer terminal blinking in one corner. And a white orchid floating in a brandy snifter.

"Where's the beast?" I asked, looking into the corners.

"Bruiser? He's somewhere with Bruno. Everything work out?"

I sat down across from her, lit a smoke of my own. "He brought a kid with him this time. Left him there. When I took off, McGowan's boys were hitting the back door."

She nodded, picked up a phone, pushed a button. A doll-faced young redhead with a pugnacious jaw walked in fast, her spike heels tapping on the hard floor.

"The Kent case, you got the warrants ready?" Wolfe asked her.

"All set," the redhead replied, confident.

"He delivered a kid this afternoon."

"We'll pull him in tonight."

I shook my head slightly. Wolfe caught it, looked up at the redhead. "The warrants . . . you have tap and search?"

"Mail cover too," the redhead said. "The Task Force is on it."

She meant the FBI Pedophile Task Force. They're right down the road from City-Wide. Must be the freak was networked way past the storefront in Times Square—the one thing baby-rapers have in common is enough to link them all over the damn earth.

"Take him tomorrow," Wolfe said, watching my face. I nodded agreement. "At work," she continued. "But start the tap tonight. If he gets a call from the Times Square people, we'll have them hooked in. Execute the search tomorrow night."

"What if he runs tonight?"

"Then grab him. But don't do it unless there's hard evidence that he's fleeing the jurisdiction, you understand?"

"Sure."

The redhead walked out fast, covering ground, her pleated skirt flying around her knees.

Wolfe dragged on her cigarette. "That's the best I can do," she said.

"It's okay. Good enough. I don't think they'll call him . . . degenerates don't work like that. No loyalty."

"A lower class of criminal." She smiled. A lovely, elegant face, framed by glossy dark hair shot through with two wings of white.

Wolfe knew what I was. What I did.

"Sheba was good?" she asked.

"Perfect."

"She's perfect here too. Calms the kids down like no psychiatrist ever could."

"Where'd you get her?"

"You know what happens to Seeing Eye dogs? After they work about ten years, they *retire* them." A soft sneer in her voice. "So their owner won't have to deal with an older dog. You know, they slow up, they get sick easily . . . like that."

"Where do they go?"

"Into cages. That's where I found Sheba. Can you imagine what it must be like . . . to work all your life, be so loyal and true . . . and end up in a cage?"

"Just the last part."

She nodded.

A tall, slender woman came in, sat on the edge of Wolfe's desk, crossed her long legs. An ankle bracelet gleamed. She had a Cleopatra face, long, dark nails. Kept her eyes on me as she talked to Wolfe over her shoulder. "We can't use the shield on Mary Beth. The judge ruled she wasn't a vulnerable witness."

"What does Lily say?" Lily runs SAFE, a treatment center for abused kids, works as a consultant to Wolfe's crew. I've known her forever.

"It'll be close," the tall woman said. "You'll take a look?"

"Yeah." She turned to me. "Want to see?"

"Okay," I told Wolfe. Her beautiful pal acted like I was furniture.

We walked down the hall to the playroom, stood in the doorway. Lily was talking to a little girl. The child had pale white skin, lank blonde hair, thick glasses. She was listening intently to Lily when she looked up, spotted me. Her expression didn't change.

Sheba was standing next to the little girl. I moved a bit too close and she growled, taking a step forward. Our relationship was over.

An angry-looking man in a double-breasted silk suit shouldered his way past me into the room. He had longish dark hair, a thick neck, slight Mediterranean cast to his features.

"You heard?" he asked Wolfe.

"I heard. It's your case?"

"No, it's not my goddamned case. But I'm gonna be there. He wants to watch Mary Beth, okay, we'll see how he likes me watching him."

"Rocco . . ." A warning tone in her voice.

"I know, I know. But . . ."

Wolfe turned to Lily. "How're we doing?"

"We're doing just fine. Aren't we, Mary Beth?"

The little girl's "yes" was a whisper.

I knew what was going on. The judge had ruled the little girl would have to face the perpetrator in court, not testify over closed-circuit TV like they'd wanted. And she was scared. He'd watch her, his eyes warning her, reminding her. Maybe he'd lick his lips, make a little gesture that only she knew. Maybe she'd go mute from terror. Wouldn't act like a kid on TV. A jury of citizen-hypocrites would talk about how normal the defendant looked. And another child molester would be acquitted. Her little face turned slowly, watching everyone in the room.

I stepped back against the wall, feeling her terror radiate—I've been tuned to that station all my life.

I touched Wolfe's hand. Lightly. "Could I try something?" I asked.

"What?"

"She doesn't want to see him, right?"

Wolfe nodded. We all knew who "him" was. There's always a "him" in Mary Beth's kind of nightmares. Or a "her." Sometimes "them." Never a stranger.

Rocco pushed in between us, his nose inches from my face, hoping I'd take offense. "Who're you?"

"This is a private investigator, Rocco," Wolfe told him. "He's worked with me before."

"Private investigators work for whoever pays them."

"Rocco, come over here a minute." Lily's voice.

Lily took him over into a corner. The little girl patted Sheba, watching.

The tall woman stepped next to me, pinning me between her and Wolfe. Listening.

"It doesn't matter what he can see, right?" I asked. "It's what *she* can see."

"Right."

"What's the distance from the witness chair to the defense table?"

"I'm not sure," Wolfe said, looking past me to the tall woman. "You know, Lola?"

"I'll find out," she said, making some gesture at Rocco.

"Wait in my office," Wolfe told me.

8

A chesty thug stepped across Wolfe's threshold. He looked half my height and twice my width, straps from a shoulder holster over his arms. And an annoyed-looking Rottweiler on a heavy chain in his hand.

"I remember you," he said. Some office Wolfe had: the women looked like fashion models, the men looked like a continuing criminal enterprise.

The Rottweiler snarled his acknowledgment—he remembered me too.

"I'm waiting for Wolfe."

"She let you in?"

"Yeah."

"Bruiser, stay!" he snapped at the dog, leaving me alone.

The Rottweiler watched me, praying I'd try to leave.

9

I was on my third smoke when Wolfe and Lola came back. Wolfe smacked the Rottweiler on top of his broad head. "Bruiser, place!"

The thickly muscled beast walked grudgingly over to a far corner, lay down on a slab of carpet. Pinned me with his eyes.

"He gets along with Sheba?" I asked her.

"Not really. They don't mix much. She has her space, Bruiser has his. Sheba, she's the whole Bureau's dog. Even sleeps here. But Bruiser's mine. Aren't you, Bruisey?"

The Rottweiler made a noise between a yawn and a growl.

"The distance between the witness chair and the defense table is about thirty feet, depending on the line of sight," she said. "Why'd you want to know?"

"I got an idea . . . something that might work."

Wolfe flashed her trademark smile—the one that made defense attorneys think about switching to real estate work. "And all you need is the defendant's address, right?"

"You misjudge me," I said, trying for an injured tone. "It's nothing like that."

"What *do* you need?"

"How about a look at the courtroom?"

Wolfe looked across her desk. Lola nodded. "It's after hours," she said.

10

We moved through the marble corridors in a loose diamond-shaped cluster: the thug taking the point, holding Bruiser on his leash. Me to the right, Lily beside me. Wolfe and Lola to the left, Rocco bringing up the rear.

In the center of the diamond, Mary Beth.

Courtroom K-2 was one floor up from the DA's basement. Empty.

Lily escorted Mary Beth to the witness chair. Lola took her place at the prosecutor's table. I sat in the defendant's spot, Rocco next to me. Wolfe stood by the jury box, one hand on the railing. The thug stayed by the door with Bruiser.

"It's your show," Wolfe said.

I took a breath, pulling up the calm, centering . . . so my voice would carry without cutting.

"Hi, Mary Beth," I called out. "Can you hear me?"

She nodded her head. If she said anything, I couldn't catch it.

"Let's play a game, okay?"

Nothing.

"Okay, Mary Beth? Come on, it'll be fun."

Lily leaned over and whispered something to her. The little girl giggled.

Lily nodded at me. I took a roll of bills out of my pocket, handed some singles to Rocco. He took them without a word, going along.

"Now, Mary Beth, my friend Rocco is going to hold something up. If you can guess what it is, you can have it, okay?"

"Okay." Soft, but audible.

"Don't hold up the whole fucking roll," I whispered to him. "One at a time."

He held up a dollar bill.

Mary Beth said something I couldn't hear.

"What was that, baby?" I called out to her.

"Money."

"That's right. You win."

"And you lose," Rocco said, jumping to his feet, walking over to the girl, handing her the cash. Making a production out of it, like a game-show host. Faint trace of a smile on the child's face.

"This is too easy, huh? Okay, Rocco, you stay there. Let's try something harder. Mary Beth, tell me how many fingers I'm holding up and you win again, okay?"

She nodded.

I held up three fingers.

"Three." A little girl's voice, faint.

Rocco bowed deeply, presented her with another dollar.

I tried again.

"One." Her voice stronger now, hint of a giggle underneath.

"Damn! You're good at this, Mary Beth. One more time, okay?"

"Okay." This time, I didn't have to strain to hear her answer. None of us did.

I tried two fingers. She was right on the money. Rocco made the delivery, happy to be spending my cash.

I took a breath. "Mary Beth, take off your glasses, okay? Let's try it that way."

She whispered something to Lily. I saw a grin spill across Wolfe's face and instantly disappear. The glasses came off.

I held up two fingers again.

"I can't see," the child said, her voice clear and firm.

"Try again," I said, holding my hand high above my head.

"I can't see anything."

Wolfe stepped away from the jury box. Walked around until she stood behind me. "Can you see me, honey?" she called.

"No. It's all a blur."

"Then you won't be able to see *him* either, Mary Beth. You won't have to see him, baby!"

The little girl's smile lit up the room.

11

Back in Wolfe's office, waiting for her to come back. Rocco waited with me, suspiciously patient.

"That was a slick trick, man," he finally said. "Where'd you learn stuff like that?"

"From them."

"Who?"

"The freaks. Child molesters, rapists, pain players . . . like that."

"You studied them."

"Up close," I said, giving him my eyes.

Wolfe walked in with Lola, another man next to her. Slim, handsome Spanish guy. Wolfe signaled to Rocco to take off. He acted like he didn't see the gesture—kept his eyes on me. "What's your name, man?"

"Juan Rodriguez."

The Spanish guy laughed. "So where's your cross, homeboy?" he asked me.

I held my hands out, showing him the backs were clean, no tattoos.

Rocco looked over at the Spanish guy. "What is this?"

"This *cholo* is fucking with us, bro'. He was a Mexican, he'd be a pachuco."

Wolfe sat down behind her desk, in command. Lit a cigarette, motioning for everyone to sit down.

"These are my people," she said to me. "I trust them, you understand?"

I nodded, waiting.

"I'm not going to be here forever. Things change, I want them to stay the same, you following me?"

I nodded again. No DA's office is free of politics. Wolfe had made a career of mashing rapists and molesters but she wasn't connected. So she wasn't protected. If she had to go someday, her crew would carry it on. The boss couldn't fire the whole lot of them.

"In or out?" she asked me.

"Do it," I told her.

She dragged on her cigarette. "Mr. Burke," she said, tilting her head in my direction, then toward each member of her crew, "this is Lola, my deputy [Cleopatra with the ankle bracelet], Amanda [the redhead], and Floyd [the Spanish guy]. Rocco's just come with us, a transfer from the Rackets Bureau. You've already met Bruno—he'll be back soon." The Spanish guy nodded in my direction—the others just waited.

The Rottweiler made a noise.

"And Bruiser." She laughed. Nobody else did.

"Mr. Burke has worked with this office in the past. Before some of you came." Looking at Rocco.

He snapped at the bait. "When?"

"Bonnie Browne," Wolfe answered, combing back her thick mane of dark hair with one hand, posture challenging.

I'd been looking for a photograph then. A picture of a little kid. He wanted his soul back. The photo was in a luxurious house in Wolfe's territory, the headquarters of a kiddie-porn ring run by a husband-and-wife team. Wolfe wanted the team—I wanted the picture. Her surveillance crew was on the job the night I went inside. When I left, there was a fire. They found the husband at the bottom of the stairs, his neck broken. The wife was lying on her bed upstairs, still dazed from the ether I'd rubbed into her evil face. The old bitch lived, and she'd ratted out a dozen others. A big case.

Rocco nodded his head. "That was you?" he asked me.

"Mr. Burke assisted in the investigation," Wolfe said, cutting him off. "He has a . . . *limited* relationship with this office. We understand each other."

Rocco wouldn't let it go. "You're a PI?"

"I'm just a working man. Once in a while, like Ms. Wolfe said, our paths cross. That's all there is."

Floyd's eyes found me through the cigarette smoke. "Burke. I heard about you."

"Did you?"

A faint smile played across his mouth. He bowed his head slightly in my direction.

I got up to go. "I'll fill them in," Wolfe said.

12

Balanced. Centered, back to myself. Back from the sweet illusion of family I left in Indiana. No more part of Virgil's family than I was blind.

Illusions can make you jump to conclusions. Like off a bridge.

I have no home. I pitch my tent on rocky ground, a nomad, never planting a crop. I live by poaching. Stinging, scamming, stealing. Always ready to move along when the herd thins out.

I walk the line, but I draw my own. Hit and run. I've been a ground-feeder ever since I got out of prison the last time. A small-stakes gambler in crooked games.

No more hijacking, no more gunfighting. The scores are richer in the penthouse, but it's safer in the basement.

That's what I want—to be safe. When I was younger, I waded in, throwing hooks with both hands, looking for that one shot that would take out the other guy. TKO in the first round. I thought that would give me strength, then. Keep me safe.

But it was me who kept going down. No more. Now all I want is to go the distance, be standing at the end.

Standing up.

13

I nosed the Plymouth into the one-stall garage at the corner of the old factory. The landlord converted it to living lofts years ago. Made himself a nice bundle from sensitive artists with rich parents. I live on the top floor. You look at the building plans, all you'll see is storage space up there. The landlord owed me for something I didn't do—my office is the price.

He could always start charging rent—make me homeless. I could always make a phone call, whisper an address—and the people his coke-loving son sold to the *federales* would make the little rat room temperature.

Pansy wasn't at her post when I let myself in the door. The beast was lazing on the couch, one massive paw draped over the edge, 140 pounds of brick-brained muscle, her light gray eyes flickering with just a trace of contempt.

"You glad to see me, girl?" I asked the Neapolitan mastiff.

She made a sniffing noise, like she smelled something bad on me. If I didn't know better, I would have thought the bitch copped an attitude because I'd worked with another woman.

"You want to go out?" I asked her, opening the back door to the office. Outside, a small iron fire escape, rusty and gnarled with age and neglect. From there, a shaky set of stairs to the roof. She ambled over and climbed up to her yard, ignoring me.

When she came back inside, I reached in my jacket pocket. Took out four orders of shish kebob in pita bread, individually wrapped in foil. They sell them on the street here. Along with watches, jeans, radios, necklaces, logo'd sweatshirts, street maps, handguns, videotapes, books, hot dogs, cocaine, flesh, and artwork. Pansy immediately whipped into a sitting position, slobber erupting from both sides of her gaping maw, watching me toss away the foil, squeeze the whole thing into a giant smelly, greasy ball.

"Still mad at me?" I asked her, holding the prize right in front of her snout.

She didn't move, rigid as a fundamentalist.

"Speak!" I told her, tossing it in her direction. Her first snap sent pieces flying all over the room. Her tail wagged madly as she chased down and devoured every last scrap.

I sat at the desk and watched her. When she was finished, she came over to me, put her bowling-ball-sized head in my lap, making gentle noises as I scratched behind her ears, blissed out.

They're all alike.

Sure.

14

I leafed through my mail. It's not delivered here—I keep PO boxes all over the city, open new ones all the time. I'd never go back to the latest group once this collection of scores was done.

A dozen or so responses to my latest ad in the freak sheets. Darla's only ten years old, but she's real pretty. She loves to have her picture taken, and her daddy's real good at it. You tell Daddy how you want to see Darla posed, and he'll send along some really delicious Polaroids. Five hundred bucks gets you a set of four—custom work is expensive. No checks.

The first loving correspondent wanted Darla in pink ribbons—and nothing else. Another wanted to see Darla disciplined. I didn't read the rest, just carefully separated the money orders, put them in a neat stack to one side.

I mail the original letters to a Customs agent I know in Chicago.

He doesn't know me—I'm his mystery pal. A concerned citizen. The Customs people mail some porno they have lying around to the letter-writers. Then they bust them for possession. I keep the money orders for my trouble. Like a bounty.

Another batch of letters responding to my mercenary recruitment service.

More mail: applicants for membership in the Warriors of the White Night. One human handwrote a long letter along with his entry form. Told the Central Committee how eager he was to link up with real urban guerrillas who knew how to deal with the Nigger Menace. He sent cash—didn't want to wait the customary four weeks for processing.

There's a check-cashing joint in the Bronx that converts the money orders for me. Somebody comes around, they'll describe me to perfection. Black, about six foot four, 230 pounds, shaved head, razor scar down one cheek. Driving a gold Cadillac with Florida plates.

15

Not all my mail comes to PO boxes. My personal drop is over in Jersey. One of Mama's drivers picks it up for me every couple of weeks, brings it to her restaurant. Max takes it from there, stores it at his temple until I come around. It takes longer, but it's safer.

That was the only address Flood had. For years after she left, I waited for a letter. I don't do that anymore.

Michelle's last letter was still on the desk. Shell-pink stationery, a fragrance to the ink.

It's not going to happen here, baby. You're the only one I can tell this to. I'll deal with Terry and the Mole when I make up my mind. Sorry if this sounds incoherent but it looks like your baby sister stayed too long at the fair, honey. I had the money. I still have it—they won't take it. All those years of scheming, risking . . .

I got myself a lovely apartment, right near the hospital complex. At least it's lovely now, once I got through with it. The psychological screening wasn't much of anything. I mean, I didn't tell one single lie until it got to the part about how I've been living these past years, do I have significant family support for sex reassignment surgery?—you know how they do.

I've been living as a woman. That's what they say they wanted, the hypocrites! But I've been a hustler all my life, ever since I escaped. And I didn't always work dry. I told a psychiatrist about my biological family once. I won't ever do that again.

Anyway, it all looked good. What happened is I failed the medical. I've been on the hormones too long, and those bootleggers I dealt with, they must have mixed and matched too many times. I remember how much it hurt when I started, how I got cramps I wouldn't wish on any of my sisters.

The doctor I asked back then, he said it was purely psychological, the pain—all in my head. Of course, he was a male.

Anyway, estrogens can contribute to clotting, they said, and I'd have to come off them before surgery. But if I stop now, stop the hormones, they said I could crash. I've been on them too long, with too heavy doses.

And when they asked me who did my breasts, I wouldn't tell them. The silicon's still holding up . . . I'm as beautiful as ever. But I was crazy once. Before you knew me. When I was so young and headstrong. I played around with some other hormones then. I wanted these poor boobs of mine to lactate, and I had to have *more* surgery.

Bottom line, baby: they won't do it! Too high a risk, they said. I'm all a mess inside.

God, like I needed some fool in a white coat to tell me that.

So here's my choices. I can come back, like I am. Keep taking the hormones. Even get psychotherapy if I want it. Above the table. That's one thing they gave me, I'm official now, the diagnosis is on paper. Pre-op transsexual.

But I learned some things from this. And there's one thing I know, baby, I can never go to jail. Not ever. I'd die first. So how do I live?

I'm trapped, and they won't fix me here. I can go overseas. One of my shadow-sisters gave me a name of a hospital in Brussels, and I know it can get done in Morocco too. Casablanca. Only there's no Bogart for me.

I went through the hormones, the electrolysis, everything. All I wanted from these people was the final chop and some reconstruction. I don't need their simpleminded therapy. In my heart and my soul, I'm a woman. Your sister. Terry's mother.

I need some time. To see what's important to me. I'll let you know.

Watch out over my boy.

I love you.

16

The next morning, I took a short walk. Brought back the newspapers and a bag full of bakery for Pansy. Took my time, stretched things out. I read the paper the way I used to in prison, sucking every ounce of juice from the pages. It didn't bother Pansy—she has a dog's sense of time. Only two limits for her: never and forever.

It was almost ten by the time I entered the garage from the back stairs. A piece of paper torn from a yellow legal pad floated under the windshield wiper. Two broad slashes with a heavy black felt-tip pen, running parallel to a small circle at their base. The number 7 to one side.

Max. Telling me I should come see him right away. Telling me where. Not a sign of forced entrance to the garage. I'd offered him a key once—he thought that was funny. Max the Silent doesn't speak. Doesn't make any noise at all.

I found a parking place in Chinatown, just off the Bowery. Made my way to one of the movie houses standing under the shadow of the Manhattan Bridge. Narrow alley along the side. Back door, dull green paint streaked with rust. I turned the knob, not surprised to find it unlocked. Metal stairs to my left, winding up in a Z pattern. I put a hand on the bannister and two Orientals materialized. They didn't say anything. They worked it together: one watched my hands, the other my eyes.

"Max?" I offered.

They were as silent as he is.

"Burke," I said, pointing at myself.

One moved to me, ran his hands over my body, a light, spider's touch. He wasn't looking for a knife . . . anything less than a machine gun wouldn't do much good where I was going.

They stepped aside. I climbed to the landing, found another door, entered. Followed more stairs, this time up.

Another door. I opened it to a long, narrow room with a high ceiling, lit by suspended fluorescent fixtures. I was facing a row of windows, pebble-glassed, caked with a hundred years' worth of yellowing cigarette smoke. The floor was broken into sections with neatly painted areas: a square, a rectangle, a circle. One wall was lined with weapons: Japanese katanas, Thai fighting sticks, Korean numchuks, throwing stars, kongos. It wasn't for show—in this joint, you checked your carry-weapons at the door. The other wall was mostly Orientals with a light sprinkling of roundeyes, black, brown, and white. Men and women, young and old. No mirrors, no mats, no stretching bars. A combat dojo—bring your own style.

Max moved in next to me, his hand on my forearm. I followed his lead to an empty space along the wall. A short, fat man stood in the center of the rectangle, bent at the waist, the back of his right hand at his hip, the other extended, wrist limp, fingers softly playing as if in response to air currents, almost a parody of effeminacy. He looked like a soft dumpling—nobody'd step aside for him on the street.

A slightly built young man stepped onto the floor. Bowed to the fat man. Moved in small, delicate circles, his body folding into a cat stance, front leg slightly off the floor, pawing. Testing the water.

The fat man stood rooted, only his extended fingers in motion, as though connected to the younger man by invisible wires. All balance centered deep within his abdomen, keeping his point.

The young man faked a sweep with his leading foot, flashed it to a plant, firing off a back kick with the other leg. The fat man made a whisking motion and the kick went off the mark—a motion-block too fast for me to see.

The fat man was back inside himself before his opponent recovered. He waited—the sapling facing the wind.

The young man tried again . . . drew blanks. He threw kicks from every angle, went airborne once . . . but the fat man deflected every attack with the extended hand, never moving from his spot.

The younger man bowed. Stepped off the floor.

An ancient man in a blue embroidered robe stepped to the border of the rectangle. Barked out something in a language I'd never heard before. I didn't need a translator: "Who's next?"

I glanced at Max. He put three fingers against my forearm. The young man hadn't been the first to try and penetrate the fat man's crane-style defense.

I held my left hand at an angle, parallel to my shoulders, in the middle of my chest. Moved my right hand into a fist, swept the left hand aside, smacked the fist against my chest off the carom. Opened my hands in a "why not?" gesture.

The warrior's mouth twitched a fraction, quick flash of teeth behind the thin lips. Pointed toward the floor.

A behemoth stepped into the rectangle, his glossy black hair woven into the elaborate set of the sumo wrestler. Looked like an old oak tree, sawed off halfway up. He bowed to the fat man, dwarfing his opponent. The knife hadn't worked—they were going to the club.

The sumo crouched, snorted a deep breath through his nose, trumpeted his battle cry, and charged. The fat man flicked his extended wrist, spun in place with the rush, and lashed the back of the sumo's head with an elbow as he went past, driving him into the far wall.

The wall survived the impact.

The sumo rolled his shoulders, waiting for the battle music in his head to reach crescendo. His eyes turned inward and he charged again. The fat man's left hand fluttered, a butterfly against an onrushing truck, extended fingers darting at the sumo's eyes. The sumo's fists shot up toward the fat man's face just as the fat man's right hand came off his hip, a jet stream striking the sumo's sternum. The bigger man stopped like he'd hit the wall again. The fat man fired two side kicks into the same spot, snapped back into the circle stance before the sumo could react.

The sumo bowed to the fat man. All around the room, everyone was doing the same.

A dozen languages bubbled in a rich broth. I couldn't understand any of them. Max couldn't hear them. But we both got the message. The ancient man stepped forward again. Said something, pointing to Max.

The Mongolian folded his arms, eyes sweeping the room, measuring. He nodded his head a bare fraction. It was enough. The room went quiet as Max walked into the rectangle.

He was wearing loose, flowing dark cotton pants and a black T-shirt. He bent at the waist, pulled off the thin-soled shoes he always wore, no socks. Bowed to the fat man.

Max stood rigid as steel, vectoring in. The fat man was a master of some form of aikido. He would not attack. Balanced in harmony, he would only complete the circle.

Max bowed again. Extended his own hand, fingertips out. *Ki* to *Ki*.

The hair on my forearms stood straight up from the fallout.

Max slid forward into a slight open crouch, rolling his head on the column of his neck. The fat man waggled his fingers, still into his stance, waiting. Max stepped forward as if walking on rice paper, working his way into the zone. He moved to his left, testing. The fat man's hips were ball bearings—he tracked Max, locked on to the target.

In the space between two heartbeats, Max dove at the fat man's feet, twisting into a perfect forward roll even as the fat man flowed backward—too late. Max was on his back, both feet piston-driving in a bracket at the fat man's body. One missed, the other was a direct hit to the belly. The fat man staggered as Max rolled to his feet, the Mongolian's right fist hooking inside the fat man's extended hand, driving through, spinning, his back against the fat man's chest as he turned, launching the left, chopping down into the exposed neck.

It was over. The fat man held his hand against the strike-point, rubbing the feeling back into his neck. It wasn't broken—Max had pulled the shot.

They bowed to each other. Barks of approval from the crowd. Max pointed to the fat man. Held up his hand, fingers splayed. Touched his thumb, pointed to the fat man. Then his index finger. Same thing. He did each finger in turn, until he came to the little finger. Pointed at himself. Held his chest, panted heavily. Pointed at himself again—held up the thumb. Pointed at the fat man. Held his opponent's hand in the air. Telling the crowd that the fat man had fought four men before Max had his chance—if Max had gone first, the fat man would have won.

I was proud of the lie—so proud to be his brother.

17

Nobody clapped Max on the back on the way out of the dojo. It wasn't that kind of joint.

The warrior touched the face of my wristwatch, moved his hand in a "come on" gesture. Wherever we were going, we were running close.

In the car, Max made the sign for SAFE. Lily's joint on the edge of the Village.

I made a "what's going on?" sign. He held up one finger. Patience.

We motored through Chatham Square. A flock of gray pigeons clustered around the monument set in a tiny triangle of concrete at the intersection of East Broadway and the Bowery. A white pigeon landed in their midst, bulling his way through to the best scavenging. A hard bird, honed by the stress of survival in a world where his color marked him.

18

I stashed the Plymouth in back of Lily's place, followed Max inside. Her office is at the far end of the joint. The door was open. Lily was at her desk, her Madonna's face framed by the long black hair. Another woman was with her, a young woman with dirty-blonde hair, big eyes, a sarcastic mouth. Sitting straight in her chair with an athlete's posture. Maybe eight months pregnant. They were deep in conversation. Max clapped his hands—they looked up.

Max bowed to the women, they returned his greeting. He held up my wrist so they could see the watch.

"Thank you, Max," Lily said. "Right on time."

"What is this?" I asked Lily.

She ignored my question. "You know Storm, right, Burke?"

"Sure." Storm was the head of the Rape Crisis Unit at the downtown hospital. Another of the warrior women who made up Lily's tribe. They come in all shapes, sizes, and colors. They're all some kind of sweet, and they can all draw blood.

"You really want to know?" Lily asked Storm. "You're absolutely sure? Burke's never wrong . . . about this."

Storm nodded.

"Show him," Lily said. Storm extended her hand, palm up.

I sat on the desk, held her palm in my hands. "This is the hand you write with?" I asked her.

"Yes."

I looked closely. Saw the clear triangles emerging from the lines. Like the gypsy woman told me a long time ago. Intersecting triangles for female, open spikes for male.

"It'll be a girl," I told her.

"Good!" Storm said. Then: "Thank you. I didn't want the amnio, but Lily just had to know. It was making her crazy."

I lit a cigarette. Lily made a face. Storm smiled. She smokes too. One cigarette a day, usually right after supper. No more, no less.

"What's the rest of it?" I asked Lily.

"How do you know there's more? Don't you think Storm's question was important?"

"*Storm* doesn't even think it's important," I said. Watching her eyes, knowing I was telling the truth. "And Max wouldn't have a tight time limit for what I just did."

"I'll show you," Lily said.

19

The small playroom has a window of one-way glass—it's a mirror on the inside. I looked through it and saw Immaculata, her long hair done up in a severe bun, wearing a bright orange smock. Max's woman, part Vietnamese, part she'll-never-know. I was there when they met. In the fallout from combat. A chubby baby crawled on the carpet in one corner. Flower, their little girl. Named for another little girl. One who hadn't survived. A tribute to Flood, the little blonde *karateka* who fought to avenge the baby's death. And left when her work was done.

Left me.

Half a dozen kids in the playroom. Running, jumping, scrawling with crayons on a giant piece of white poster board.

"That's him," Lily said at my side. "He's talking to Mac now. Luke, his name is."

The boy looked about eight. Light brown hair, thin face, dark eyes. He was holding a pocket calculator in one hand, pointing at the display window, like he was explaining something.

I felt Storm slide in next to me on my other side. "The police found him. In a room with his baby brother. Two years old. The baby had been hacked to death with a butcher knife. There was blood all over Luke, but he hadn't been touched, just a few surface scratches."

"His parents?"

"They weren't home. Left him in charge of his brother. Said they were only gone a few minutes."

"Anyone popped for it?"

"No. No arrests. No suspects, even."

"We don't treat only direct child abuse victims here," Lily put in, anger edging her voice, like I was a politician questioning her program. "Children who've witnessed horrible violence to a loved one . . . a rape, a murder . . . they're as traumatized by it as if it happened to them. That's why Luke's here."

"He lives at home?"

Storm answered me. "No. His parents were convicted of inadequate guardianship. Turns out they were gone almost two days, not a few minutes like they'd said. And they were very secretive, hostile. Wolfe's unit found out the dead baby wasn't really theirs. Not legally theirs. One of those private placement adoptions, but it never went to a court. The lawyer who handled it got indicted for baby-selling. Luke's been in foster care for about two months."

"And you still don't know who killed the baby?"

"Wolfe says she knows." Something in Lily's voice.

"So what's for me?"

"Last week, we had a TV crew here. They were filming a documentary about child abuse. We gave them permission, under strict conditions. Told them which rooms they could work in, which rooms to stay out of. One of them, this real smart young man, some producer-something-or-other, he took a cameraman into the back, where Luke was playing. When Luke saw the camera, he went catatonic. Froze. The paramedics stuck a hypo in his arm and he didn't even flinch."

"What happened?"

"He came out of it. Maybe an hour later. When I told him he'd been in a trance, he got very angry. Denied the whole thing. Even told us what he'd been doing during that time. Like it never happened."

I watched the kid, adding it up.

"Burke, you know what it means, don't you?" Lily asked.

I ignored her question. "Can I talk to him?"

"Let's try," she said, opening the door to the playroom.

20

They worked it like a drill team. Lily flashed something to Immaculata, who immediately drew Luke close to her as Storm muscled the other kids out of the room.

"Hi, Mac," I said. "Who's your pal?"

"This is Luke," she said gravely, one hand on his shoulder, the long, lacquered nails spilling against his chest. Talons, guarding.

The kid's eyes were pearly darkness. "What's your name?" he asked me, trembly thread in his voice.

"Burke."

"How do you spell that?"

I told him.

The kid's eyes went thoughtful, rolled up into his head, snapped right back. "Our names are linked," he said.

"What do you mean?"

"They have the same letters. U. K. E. In both our names. Maybe they have the same root. Mine is from the Bible. Is there a Burke in the Bible?"

"Not by that name."

"Are you Immaculata's friend?"

"She is my brother's wife."

"Max is your brother?"

"Yes."

"It's true," Mac assured him.

"Immaculata is my friend."

"I know. That means you're my friend too."

His eyes flickered again, straightened. "Do you know any monsters?"

I hunkered down next to him, getting my eyes on the same level. "Yeah, I know some."

"Do you fight them?"

"I have."

"Do you win?"

"Sometimes."

"Are you scared . . . when you fight them?"

I held his eyes, willing them to stay on mine. "Yes," I told him. "Yes, I'm scared."

He held out his hand to me, a soft child's hand. "Don't be scared. If you're my friend, you don't have to be scared."

"I'm not scared now."

His eyes rolled again. Came back slower this time. "Burke?" he asked. Like he was seeing me for the first time, waking up from a dream.

"Yeah?"

"If we put our names together, you and me, do you know what they would be?"

"No. What?"

"Burke and Luke. Together it would be Lurk. What do you think?"

"I think you're right." Watching his eyes, holding them steady. Tiny lights dancing in them now—candlepoints in the night.

I got to my feet.

"Are you coming back?" he asked.

"Count on it," I told him.

21

Back in Lily's office. I lit another smoke, waiting.

"He's got a genius IQ," Lily said. "Tests right off the scale."

"I could tell."

"What else can you tell?"

"He's video-phobic, right? Somebody photographed him, maybe videotaped. While something ugly was going on . . . maybe to him. You see the same reaction from some kids when a flashbulb goes off."

Storm edged forward. "He was examined at our hospital. After the attack on his baby brother. They found something besides the knife scratches."

I turned my face to her, waiting.

"A prolapsed rectum," she said, icy hate in her soft voice.

"The parents?"

"Wolfe thinks so," Lily said, something standoffish in the way she said it. I wasn't going to let it go by twice.

"Wolfe is your pal, right?"

"Sure."

"Your sister?"

"What's your point?"

"What's yours?"

She looked across the desk to Storm. Shrugged her shoulders. "Luke's been sexually abused. Wolfe should be right on top of it—she knows what we know. But she's waiting . . . like there's something more."

"And she doesn't like him." Immaculata's voice, stepping into the room.

"How do you know?" I asked over my shoulder.

"Luke knows. He told me."

Immaculata had a baby. Lily had a glowing teenager named Noelle. Storm was pregnant. Wolfe had no children. I never would. I glanced at Storm's swelling belly. "You're sure you're not . . . ?"

Lily caught my look. "No, it's not that. Wolfe is just like us. She adores Noelle. And Flower. She *knows* something."

"And you want . . . ?"

"We have to protect the child," Immaculata said. "That's what we do here."

"Wolfe won't talk to me," I said.

Lily smiled her Madonna's smile. "She might . . . she likes you."

Storm giggled.

Women. "I'll take a look," I told them. Immaculata kissed me on the cheek.

22

Max and I motored over to West Street, took it north past the triangular wedge of the short-stay motel at Fourteenth Street, hooked a U-turn, and headed back downtown. Horatio Street runs through the Village, a nice block, brownstones, well kept. On the other side of the highway, it's a deadend street, runs right up against the filthy Hudson River.

The Prof was there, wrapped in his long overcoat, a flaming red silk scarf around his neck, the ends trailing almost to his feet.

Midafternoon now. When it turns dark, the long parking lot parallel to the river becomes a hustler's strip. Boys work the pavement, competing for the attention of the cars that slowly cruise the circuit. Manicured fingers push buttons—tinted glass slithers down. Young faces ravaged by the acid of their lives appear in the opening, auditioning on a private TV screen. The winners get to climb in the front seat and open their mouths. They usually finish at the end of the concrete strip—it doesn't take long. The kids get out of the cars and wait for the next customer. Sometimes a dark posse car comes by, loaded with cold-eyed blacks fondling automatic weapons. The crack express. Then the kids become customers themselves.

Out here, the winners go to jail. The losers get dead. Freaks don't like their little boys covered with condoms, but they don't mind a shroud.

We got out of the car, standing side by side. The Prof stepped into the space between us.

"There was more to the score," the little man said.

"You have enough time?" I asked him.

"I didn't Hoover the place, Ace. You never know when the maid's gonna show."

The Prof had graduated from shotgun bandit to hotel burglar, one of the very best. Worked with a shoeshine box over his shoulder, no nerves. But he wasn't perfect—I'd met him in prison. Every wheel has a double zero someplace, you spin it long enough.

I barely felt the little man's touch as something slipped into my coat pocket. We worked this 50-50. The Prof got half for taking the up-front risk of going inside—I split my half with Max.

"The cash ain't wrapped in trash, bro'. The freak had a Xerox in his pad. I made you some copies."

I fingered a roll of paper. The money would be inside.

"Pictures?" I asked.

"The Yellow Pages, man."

A pedophile's address book. Maybe worth more than the cash.

Traffic noise at a distance. Safe and quiet where we were. Little knots of people all around, dealing. Nobody looked too close.

"Drop you anywhere?"

"I'm cribbed up north, 'home. Get me to the tunnels, I'll ride the rails."

We dropped him off at Fourteenth and Eighth. Headed back downtown.

23

The white dragon tapestry was barely visible in the streaked window of Mama's restaurant. All clear. We parked in the alley behind the joint, entered through the unmarked steel door. The kitchen crew nodded to us, eyes over our shoulders in case we hadn't come alone.

We took my table in the back. I held my hand at stomach height, indicating a child. Then I went rigid, holding my arms out so tight they trembled. Pointed at Max, a question on my face.

He nodded. Taking me to see Luke had been his idea.

Mama stood between us—I hadn't seen her approach. She bowed to Max, to me. We returned her greeting. She snapped something at the young Chinese pretending to be a waiter. I should know the Cantonese words for hot and sour soup by now, but Mama never seems to say the same thing twice.

The tureen of soup came. Mama served Max first, then me, then herself.

Max took a sip. Made the sign of a flower opening itself to the sun. I told her it was the best she ever made. Mama nodded curtly—any lesser praise would be a grievous insult.

Mama toyed with her soup, hawk-watching me and Max to make sure we emptied our bowls. Refilled them without being asked.

The waiter cleared the table, put glasses of clear water before us, a small porcelain ashtray.

I pulled the Prof's package out of my jacket, unwrapped it carefully. Separated the cash from the paper, put the paper back inside my pocket.

Mama riffled through the money, counting it quicker than any machine could. Almost six grand. She cut it in half, pushed one pile to me, one to Max. We each separated a piece, handed it back to her. Mama was my banker, holding a piece of every score, keeping ten percent off the top for herself.

She held up the bills Max handed her. "For baby," she said, not bothering with sign language. Max didn't argue with her—he wasn't tough enough for that. He lit himself a smoke from my pack.

"Everything good now," Mama said. "Back to old ways."

24

When Mama got up to attend to her business, I made the sign for Luke again, telling Max I wanted to know why he was pulling me into this.

The warrior opened his eyes wide, pointed to them. He'd seen it too.

Nothing more to say.

I needed an excuse to see Wolfe again. It would come to me. Max and I went through the Harness Lines, but I couldn't find a horse that appealed to me.

I thought about the racetrack. About going there with Belle, watching as the big girl so deeply identified with a game mare who came from off the pace. Bouncing in her seat, yelling, "Come on!" Her battle cry.

The last words she screamed at the police before they cut her down.

If love would die along with death, this life wouldn't be so hard.

A tap on my shoulder. Mama. The bench opposite me was empty. My watch said four-thirty. I must have gone somewhere else, losing track of time.

"Call for you. Island man."

I picked up the pay phone, one of several standing in a bank between the dining room and the kitchen.

"Yeah?"

"Greetings, mahn. I have some work for you."

It was Jacques, a sunny-voiced gun dealer who worked the border between Queens and Brooklyn. Firepower to go, wholesale lots, cash and carry.

"I got plenty of work now."

"This *is* your work, mahn."

"I don't do deliveries anymore."

"Your true work, mahn. Everybody knows. Come see about me."

"In a couple of hours," I told him, and hung up.

25

My true work. Wesley said it was a bull's-eye painted on my back. But he was gone, hunting the devil, not even leaving the cops a scrap of flesh to put under their microscopes. Wesley, the stalking sociopath. The perfect hunter-killer. We'd come up together, practiced the same religion when we were kids. But the ice-god had come into his soul until he wasn't human anymore.

In the dark part of the streets, people whispered he wasn't really dead.

The sun dropped behind me as I drove along Atlantic Avenue toward deeper pockets of darkness. Turned into a narrow driveway, flashed my high beams twice.

A barge-sized old Chrysler rolled slowly across my field of vision in the rearview mirror. It came to a stop, blocking my Plymouth from the street. I looked straight ahead, waiting. Heard the icy dry sound of a pistol being cocked.

"Come on out of your car, nice and slow. Leave the keys." West Indian voice, not Jacques's.

I did what the voice said. He was a slim young man, hair cropped close, prominent cheekbones dominating a pretty face, tiny, lobeless ears pinned flat to his skull, big eyes with a bluish cast in the night light, long lashes shadowing. Reddish highlights dominating mahogany skin. Wearing a dark green Ban-Lon long-sleeved shirt buttoned to the neck over dark slacks. Looked like the kind of kid the wolves would jump on as soon as he hit the prison yard. They wouldn't know what they were dealing with until the guards came. With the body bags.

He stepped to one side, the gun tracking me, waist high. I walked straight ahead. A door opened. I heard the Plymouth's engine kick over.

Down a flight of metal steps. Felt the young man behind me, heard the door close, bolts snap home.

Horseshoe-shaped table, the midpoint against the wall. Jacques in the center, an old woman on his left. One man sat on each wing. I stepped into the open space, waiting.

"So you came, my friend." A faint light glinted on Jacques's high cheekbones.

"Like you asked."

Another man stepped out of the shadows. Patted me down, neck to ankles. I stood still for it—every church has its own ceremonies.

The man stepped back. Returned with a straight-backed chair. I sat down.

"Anything you want, mahn? A drink, maybe? Some fine rum we have here."

"A cigarette?"

"You don't have any?"

"I came empty."

A smile bloomed on the Islander's noble face. I'd shown him respect by walking in with empty pockets. He knew what you could fit in a pack of cigarettes—he was in the business. Jacques nodded at one of the men on the table's wing. "Get my friend cigarettes."

The man got up, extended a pack to me.

Jacques's voice was soft. "Mahn, that is not what you do. My friend does not want *your* cigarettes, he wants his own."

"How I know what he smokes?" the man said sullenly.

Jacques's voice went chilly. "You *ask* him, mahn. Ask him nicely. Then you go out and you get what he wants. A fresh, new pack. Is that so hard, now?"

"What you smoke?" he asked me.

I told him. He walked away.

Jacques shrugged his shoulders. "Young boys, Burke. All hot blood. Better they learn from a gentle man like me, huh?"

"Yeah."

"This lady has a problem, my friend. I would like for her to tell you. All right?"

"Sure."

He turned to the old lady. "You tell the man now, missus."

"He look like the police to me," the woman said.

Jacques chuckled. "Don't let that ugly white face fool you, lady. This is a very bad man."

"He gonna help me?"

"We will see. First, you tell him what you tell me. Come on now."

The old lady gathered herself, her face turned toward me, her eyes somewhere else.

"I got a grandson. Derrick. My daughter's child. He almost four years old. My daughter on the Welfare, lives in that hotel out by the airport. Her man is a vicious beast. Beat her all the time, take her check. He beat my grandson too. For nothin'. Right in front of my eyes. I go to stop him once, an' he punch me right in my face. Broke this bone, right here." Touching her face, eyes focusing on me now.

"Monday my daughter calls me. Says her baby run away. I tell her, how could that be?—he too small to run away. She cryin' and all, says the police there. Ain't nobody seen her man. My Derrick is gone."

A tap on my shoulder. Jacques's man, handing me a pack of cigarettes. I slit the cellophane, took one out. The man handed me a paper packet of matches—I fired one up.

Jacques leaned forward. "We found the man, Burke. Talked to him. He say he knows nothing. Okay. We talk to the girl too. Same story. It *is* a story, mahn. Finally, she tells us the man took the baby out of there, said he's going to give the child to another woman of his."

I dragged deep on the smoke. Still waiting.

"What we need is a man to look, Burke. Look around."

"Why me?"

"It's what you do, mahn. Your work, like I said. People know, word on the street—Burke looks for runaways, yes?"

"The baby didn't run away."

"I know. This good lady here, she is one of us. Like a mother, always to help, that is the way she is. She wants her grandson back."

"Why don't you ask the man? Ask him again."

"He has vanished, mahn. We are looking for him, but . . . for now, until we find him . . ."

"It's a long shot."

"I know, mahn, but . . ."

"Obeah," the old woman said. Like it explained everything.

"Why do you say that, ma'am?" I asked her.

"That is what I heard, white man. You know them?"

"No."

"Her man, Emerson, that is his name. He is with those people. I think that is where he take my grandson. To be with them too."

"You take a look, mahn?" A soft undertone in Jacques's voice, the sun banked.

"A quick look," I warned him.

"Clarence will go with you," he said, nodding at the young man who met me in the parking lot. "In case there is a problem with any of our people, yes?"

"So long as he listens."

"Clarence, for this work, Burke is your boss, you understand? Like it was me talking. I told you about this guy. You listen, and you learn."

The slim young man nodded agreement.

"We have anything else to discuss?" he asked. Meaning: how much?

"We'll settle at the end," I told him. "No guarantees. Clarence has all the information?"

"I have it all." Clarence's voice, gentle and calm.

"Let's do it, then," I said.

26

"We'll take my ride," Clarence said, standing in the parking lot.

"I'm not hitting Queens in a posse car, son."

"Posse? No, mahn, we will go in my car. A true West Indian car. Wait here."

He pulled up in an immaculate Rover 2000 TC, British Racing Green. I climbed inside. The black leather smelled new, the walnut trim gleamed. Clean and spare, letting the craftsmanship show.

"Very fine," I congratulated him.

"This is my baby," he said, flashing a quick smile.

27

On the way over, I read through the contents of a thick manila envelope Clarence handed me. All the police reports, a complete package, even the SSC records. SSC, Special Services for Children, the agency that investigates child abuse. It used to be called BCW, Bureau of Child Welfare. Now they call it CWA, the Child Welfare Agency. That's a politician's idea of social change—change the names. You can tell when someone first got stuck in the net by the name they call it. Same way you can tell how long a man's been in jail by his prison number. I didn't ask where Jacques got the records.

SACRIFICE

We took Atlantic all the way through East New York, turned left on Pennsylvania to the Interborough, found the Grand Central. Clarence pointed the Rover's nose to La Guardia.

We exited at Ninety-fourth Street, crossed over the highway. The hotel was a long, thin rectangle, the narrow piece fronting the service road to the highway. Clarence pulled in the back way. Plenty of parking.

"She's inside. Still lives here. You want to start with talking to her?"

They don't let you stay in those hotels once you lose your meal ticket—maybe the Sherlocks at SSC thought the baby really had run away on his own. "Let's wait a minute," I told him. "Get the smell."

He nodded agreement. I lit a cigarette—Clarence tensed, like something was going down. I pulled out the ashtray—it was a virgin. I rolled down the window, blew the smoke outside, felt him relax.

A corroding van sat diagonally across from us, grounded on four flat tires, an indistinct figure behind the wheel. An orange BMW approached. Stopped. Man on the passenger side stepped out, went over to the van. Money showed. A hand extended out of the van, a Ziploc bag held aloft. The streetlights caught the vials of crack inside, sparkling. Street diamonds.

"Rastas," Clarence said. Yeah. Ganja for fun, hard stuff for money.

A dog barked, close by.

A woman staggered out the side door, high-yellow complexion, wearing white shorts and white spike heels, her makeup as sloppy as the cheap wig sitting lopsided on her head. She stumbled, one hand against the wall to guide her.

"Crack whore." Clarence's flat, uninflected tour guide voice.

Four boys came out the same door, wearing black vinyl jackets draped to their knees. They swept the street with hard looks, challenging. The leader crossed over to us, the others flanking out behind. He stopped in the street, waiting. Clarence watched him the way a gorilla watches a jackal. I'm a vegetarian, you understand, but if you insist . . .

The leader veered to his right, moving off, shooting a last warning look.

Clarence held the automatic calmly against his thigh, looking nowhere special.

28

The security guard at the door was a careful man, watchful that no visitor meant him harm. The tenants had to look out for themselves.

"Room 409," Clarence said, letting me lead the way. The same way you did in the jungle: point man on the alert, next man up with the heaviest firepower.

The stairs smelled of human waste. A large pile of it was on the second landing, wearing a blue-and-orange Mets baseball cap with matching jacket. He completed the ensemble with a regulation Louisville Slugger.

"What you want here, whitey?"

Clarence slid in next to me, pointed his 9mm automatic at the pile's face. "Business," he said, soft-voiced. "Maybe business with you. What you say, mahn?"

The bat clattered as it bounced on the concrete floor. The waste pile backed away, mumbling something.

Carpet runner on the corridor floor as thin as stockbroker's ethics. The walls were beige filth, the doors the color of starving roses. Numbers scrawled on their faces with black grease pencil. Murky light fell in spotty pools, most of the overhead fixtures wrecked—pre-mugging preparation.

We found the room near the end of the corridor. "When we get inside, follow my lead," I told Clarence, motioning him to one side in case they answered my knock cowboy-style. I put my back against the wall, reached over, and rapped lightly on the door.

Nothing.

I rapped again, hard. The door opened a crack.

"Who is it?" Woman's voice, phlegm-clogged.

Clarence answered her. "We come from your mother, Miz Barclay . . . she sent us. We have something for you."

"Emerson, he ain't here. I *tole* you."

Clarence pushed the door with his palm, gently. I followed him into the room. The woman walked ahead of us. Sat down on the bed. The room was long and narrow, dominated by a double bed. Bathroom door stood open to the right, Hollywood refrigerator against the other wall, two-burner hot plate on a shelf. A small color TV set sat on a black metal stand, complicated arrangement of antenna loops on top, looked like a model of the solar system. On the screen, cops wearing suits they would have had to explain to Internal Affairs were chasing drug dealers in their Ferrari.

"We need to ask you some questions, ma'am. This guy, he is from Jacques. Understand?"

"Yeah." She never took her eyes from the screen.

I walked over, turned it off. Anger flickered in her eyes—she wasn't drunk.

Clarence drifted over to where he could watch the door, hand in his pocket. The woman lit a cigarette, retreating into dullness.

"The night Derrick disappeared," I asked her, "tell me when you first noticed him missing."

"I dunno. Maybe nine o'clock, ten."

"What did you do?"

"We . . . I went lookin' for him. Asked everybody. You ask them, they'll tell you."

"And then . . . ?"

"We couldn't find him. So I called the cops."

"What time was that?"

"I dunno . . . maybe midnight."

The 911 call had been logged at 3:28 a.m.

"Where was Emerson?"

"Emerson don't stay here, mistah."

"Where was Emerson that night?"

"He wasn't here. I tole the cops. He wasn't here."

She wasn't going to tell us anything. Years of dealing with Welfare and Child Protective Services had perfected the sullen-hostile-stupid routine. The cops had already threatened her with a murder rap if she was shielding Emerson. She didn't look afraid of anything society had to offer.

"You got a silencer for that pistol?" I asked Clarence.

"I got this, mahn," he ice-whispered, taking a straight razor from his pocket.

"That'll do. Start on her arms—it'll just look like more tracks when they find the body."

She was off the bed, opening her mouth to scream as Clarence slammed her back down, driving his shoulder into her chest, stuffing a handful of the ratty bedspread into her mouth. He pinned her flat with one knee. The razor gathered light as if it were a crystallized gem, waving hypnotically before her eyes. Snot bubbled in her nose as she fought for breath.

I leaned over her. "You want to tell us, now? Before we start cutting?"

Her head nodded hard enough to snap her neck. Clarence pulled the bedspread from her mouth, shifted his hand to the back of her head, pulling hard on the hair to expose her throat. The razor was ready.

"You scream, it's your last one," I said.

"Emerson took him—I didn't do nothin'."

"I know. Tell me what happened."

"Derrick was bad. Emerson and me was . . . in the bed. Derrick wouldn't be quiet, so Emerson picked him up to give him a slap. Derrick wet on Emerson and Emerson punched him in the chest. When we got done . . . in the bed, Derrick, he was still layin' there. We couldn't do nothin' with him. Emerson put him in one of the bags."

"What bags?"

"Over there," she said, gesturing with her eyes. In the corner, a box of green plastic Hefty bags.

"Then what?"

"Emerson, he went out."

"What did he say when he came back?" I asked her, guessing.

"He say, nobody ever find Derrick. It's okay."

"How long was he gone?"

"I dunno."

Her theme song—but I believed her this time.

"Why'd you call the cops?"

"SSC was comin' the next day. To check on the baby. They took him away before."

"And cut your check, right?"

"Yeah."

"Does Emerson have a car?"

"No, he ain't got no car. He had a car, but . . ."

"Never mind. He calls you, right?"

"I ain't got no phone here."

"There's pay phones downstairs."

"He don't never call me. Sometimes, he come by."

"On check day?"

"Yeah."

I signaled to Clarence. He stepped away from her, wrinkling his nose at the smell.

My eyes caught a color photograph on the dresser, propped up in a goldtone frame. I walked over to it. The woman, standing next to a tall, sheik-handsome man with a mustache, wearing a cream-colored suit, panama hat.

I held it up. "This Emerson?"

She nodded.

I popped the picture out of the frame. "Fix it," I told Clarence. His razor sliced surgically, leaving me just the man's photo. I slipped it into my pocket.

"What gonna happen to me?" the woman asked.

"Nothing. You're okay."

"I'm pregnant, mistah," she said as we stepped out the door.

29

We exited the hotel into a blanket of misty rain. Clarence started to cross the street. I patted his arm to halt him.

"The car's over there, mahn."

"Emerson didn't have a car."

"So what we do?"

"What he did. Come on."

30

We walked down the block, heading for the lights of La Guardia Airport to the north. Pitch dark now, but the block was choked with humans. Wheeling, dealing, stealing.

"Too many eyes," I said to myself. We crossed the service road— stood on the other side. To our left, the bridge to the airport. A deep ravine underneath, cut down the middle by the Grand Central Parkway.

"Let's try down there," I told Clarence.

We stepped in carefully. The underbrush was so thick you couldn't see the ground. We worked our way downhill. I spotted a refrigerator crate lying on its side against a tree, motioned Clarence to be quiet. A man crawled out of the crate, shuffled off into the darkness. We followed a narrow dirt trail toward the highway. On both sides, humans. A whole colony of homeless, living in the jungle. I could feel the watching. No way Emerson buried a baby here without being seen.

We reached the highway, turned left, in the direction of Manhattan. Cars shot by only a couple of dozen feet away—we were invisible.

"How we gonna find anything out here, mahn?"

"Keep quiet, Clarence. Let me work."

The monster's work. Being him. He didn't have a car. He had a body. He didn't have time.

Feeling my way.

Moonlight glinted on tree branches. Taking me back to the jungle in Biafra a long time ago. This time, hunting. Then, I was the prey.

Voices. Chanting sound from above us, high on the rise. We started up the hill. I looked back at Clarence—the pistol was in his hand, face set.

We stepped into a clearing. The moonlight slanted, pulling my eyes to a gnarled tree growing on a sharp angle out of the sloping ground. Something . . . I looked closer. Suspended from a rope, a leather bag, maybe two feet long, banana-shaped. The seam was closed with heavy stitches, crosshatched with long pins, pearly red and white heads in an alternating pattern. The bag swung gently in the night, like a lynched man. I felt the fear imploding in my gut. My hands shook.

Clarence saw it too. "Juju," he whispered. "Very bad, mahn. This is an evil place."

We skirted the tree, climbing toward the top. The chanting came closer. Then we saw them. A phalanx of black males, standing in a wedge formation. Wearing long white shirts with little round collars, black pants. Looking out over the rise, the leather bag swinging down below them. Clarence raised the pistol, sighting in.

I whispered, "No!" Tugged at his sleeve, pointing to our right. He shuddered, his whole body shaking.

I took the lead. We worked our way about another quarter mile in the direction I'd pointed, climbed down to the highway.

"He couldn't go that way," I said, pointing back to where the chanters worshiped the leather bag. "We've got to cross the road. Ready?"

Clarence nodded. We waited for a break in traffic. Made a dash for it. Waited on the highway divider for another break, charged across to the other side.

We skirted the airport, the giant planes fog-shrouded, only their lights visible, following the chain link fence. No place to hide a body.

We came to a residential block running parallel to the airport. Turned right.

"What you looking for now, mahn?"

"Water," I told him. Thinking back to prison. Watching and learning. Studying the freaks. They're always magneted to water. I remember asking the Prof about it, one cold day on the yard, trying conversation to keep warm.

"How come the skinners always work near water, Prof?"

"It's astrology, schoolboy. The stars in the sky never tell a lie—you know what they say, you can find your way."

"Astrology is bullshit."

"No, bro', here's what I know. The true clue—the real deal. Inside, a man's not blood, he's water. That's what we are, mostly water. The moon pulls the water, the tide takes the ride. Same moon pulls on us."

"So how come the freaks . . . ?"

"The moon's for seekers, schoolboy. Some it pulls strong, some it pulls wrong."

I knew there was water out there. Rikers Island stands just to the west of the airport. Nice name for a jail. I remembered hearing the water from my cell window. Emerson must have done time, must have been there too. He'd know.

The chain link fence made a ninety degree left turn. I looked up at the street sign. Nineteenth Avenue.

Big white metal panel on the fence, red and black letters: NO TRESPASSING.

"In there," I told Clarence, pointing.

The bottom of the fence had been pulled loose. Clarence held it up like a blanket off the ground. I slid through on my belly. He lay on his back, bench-pressed the fence off his chest, used his legs to push him under.

The jungle was thick on the other side. A clear path to the water, well worn.

Dampness muffled the airport sounds. Behind us, lighted houses, parked cars. Ahead, black water. I knew its name from the maps I'd read in jail—Bowery Bay.

The path disappeared. The undergrowth was belt high, cuppy ground below pulled at my feet. We pushed our way through, reached the edge. Thick wooden posts stood upright between cracked slabs of concrete. Scuffling noises, scratchy sounds. Rats.

"I don't like it here, mahn."

The Rock was straight ahead. To our left, the Hazen Street Bridge. The one that carried busloads of humanity every Visiting Day, some hearts full of pain, some mouths full of dope, to be exchanged with that first kiss, contraband-sweet.

We walked to the edge. Looked down. I found a fist-sized stone. Tossed it in. Listened for the sound.

"Deep water." Clarence.

"Deep enough," I said, watching the softly lapping current. Remembering how cons used to study the tide tables like it was the Bible. Rikers Island wasn't Alcatraz—plenty of guys had made it outside the wire, gone into the water and lived to tell about it, usually Upstate.

"This is it," I said to Clarence. "This is where he dumped the baby's body. Derrick's in there."

Clarence looked out into the night. His young man's voice fluttered in the dark mist. "No, mahn. I don't think so. I think maybe the devil has him."

31

My Plymouth was waiting in the side yard of Jacques's joint.

"You'll tell him?" I asked Clarence.

"Don't you want . . . ?"

"Tell Jacques, I'll be around, give him a call."

His mahogany face was set, eyes troubled.

"It's okay," I said. "All over now. We found the truth—if the baby's not in the water, he's in the ground."

"It wasn't the baby's body the old woman wanted, mahn."

"It's all that's left."

"No, my friend, there's one thing left."

"Better ask Jacques about that first."

"Do you know we love children, mahn? Our people?"

"Yes."

"My mother, she was handy with the switch, mahn. A strong woman." His pale tracker's eyes held mine. "And Mother, she had her men friends too. But never, never once, mahn, I tell you, would any of them ever raise a hand to me—it would be worth his life. I started this"—waving his hand panoramically in front of him, the hand so quick to hold an automatic or a straight razor—"for her, mahn. For the money. She is gone now. Every year, on the day of her birth, I honor her."

I sat quietly in the car seat, waiting for the rest. The bitch who raised me had no honor. But she had plenty of hotel rooms. Attica, Auburn, Dannemora . . .

"What would make a woman do that, mahn? Let a man kill her baby in front of her eyes?"

"The answers don't change things."

"What would be justice, then, mahn? So the baby may sleep in peace?"

I shrugged. He was such a young man.

32

I crossed the Brooklyn Bridge into my home country. A small truck rumbled ahead of me, the early sun orange against its quilted aluminum sides. When it parked, the sides would open into a portable coffee shop, serving the mass of humans who work the courthouse district. Morning brings citizens to the street, nervously plucking at the daylight like a protective coat, safe from the vampires for another day. Their city, they tell themselves. Night comes, and they give it back.

I live under the darkness, where it's safe. Safe from things so secret that they have no name. Under the darkness—it's not territory you occupy—you take it with you. It goes where I go—where I've been. The orphanage. Reform school. Prison. Even now.

There's others like me. Children of the Secret. Raised by so many different humans. Those who ignored us, those who tortured us. No place to run, so survival becomes all. For us, a religion. Nourished on lies so that we alone know the truth. An army of us. You can't see us, but we find each other. Like a special breed of damaged dog, responding only to the silent whistle.

All things come to those who wait.

Some of us wait in ambush.

Burke isn't my name. It was my mother's, I think. Baby Boy Burke it said on my birth certificate. Weighed 7 pounds 9 ounces, born 3:03 a.m. Mother's age at birth: 16. Father: Unknown. Number of children born alive prior to this birth: None.

I never looked for her, my mother. Never wondered if she believed she was doing the right thing by giving me up.

I have plenty of birth certificates now—you need one to get a passport.

Juan Rodriguez is the name on my driver's license. Juan's a citizen:

pays his taxes, contributes to Social Security. He gets a parking ticket, he takes care of it.

Juan owns property too, but nobody knows. A piece of a junkyard in the Bronx—not the Mole's joint, a little slab of dirt not far from Yankee Stadium. The deal is this: The guy who runs it pays me a salary. I endorse the checks and he turns them into cash. Keeps a piece of each check himself for his trouble. Kicks out a W-2 form for me every year, pays the Workmen's Comp, the Unemployment, all that. You can hide your sins, but the IRS will find the paper.

Mama is my bank account. She doesn't pay interest, but she doesn't make bad loans to politically protected looters either, so my money is safe. Most of the cash gets converted into hard currency: gold, diamonds, like that.

In case I have to use one of my passports someday.

33

Pansy's ice-water eyes flickered disappointment as I let myself in. She always looks like that when I'm alone—she was born to war.

The phone on my desk never rings, at least not for me. It's not mine—the Mole wired it up from the loft downstairs. I can call out, as long as I do it early in the morning when the delicate souls who live below me are still sleeping off last night's chemicals. They can sleep easy, subsidized by their parents, immune to the NEA jihad.

I made Pansy and me some breakfast from the scraps in the tiny refrigerator. Drank a little ginger ale to settle my stomach. Smoked a cigarette while Pansy went up to her roof.

Slept through the day.

34

My sleep was full of refracted dreams. Like trying to read through a diamond.

Belle's red Camaro flying at a wedge of police cars. Gunfire. The Camaro pulled to the side of the road. The big girl got out, hands held high. Prison wouldn't hold her.

Flood bouncing a baby on her knee. A fat little baby. Japanese screen in one corner of the room, daylight pouring in. A hand on her shoulder. Not mine.

Strega on my lap, wearing blue jeans and Elvira's *Zzzzap!* T-shirt. Crying. Me patting her, telling her it would be okay.

The Prof's voice: "Nobody knows where he's going, but everybody knows where he's been."

Candy: "Take the leash. Feel the power."

Me standing over Mortay in the construction site, gun in my hand. Blood-lust shredding the fear in me. Asking the wounded death-dancer: "You still want Max?"

Blossom's face close to mine, covering me with her body, moaning, her copper-estrogen smell filling the shark cage, machine-gun fire in the night.

Lily and Immaculata, walking down the street, each holding one hand of the same little kid, swinging him between them.

I woke up, shaking like the malaria was back.

35

I let Pansy back out to her roof while I took a shower. Dressed slowly, in no rush. Promised Pansy I'd bring her something back from Mama's.

But first, another look. Time to collect a bargaining chip to put on Wolfe's table. I beat the late-afternoon rush-hour traffic out to Queens. Needed daylight to face what I had to do.

The Plymouth rumbled to a stop on the shoulder of the Grand Central, right across from the highway mile marker I remembered from last night. I hit the emergency flashers, positioned the mini hydraulic jack under the frame, pumped the rear end of the big car off the ground, loosened the lug nuts with a T-handled wrench.

I pretended to rummage through the trunk, checking the space around me. Nobody stopped to help—this isn't Iowa. Traffic droned on my left. The jungle waited to my right.

I slipped on a pair of heavy leather gloves. Lined with a thin layer of chain-mail mesh, they'd handle fire or razors. The machete was Velcro'd to the back of the fuel cell, waiting. I took an army blanket-poncho from the trunk, pulled it over my head. One more 360 look around and I was into the jungle.

The leather bag was swinging from the tree, bursting at its seams, the afternoon sun glistening on the hide. It seemed to squirm with life—like a cocoon ready to birth. I climbed the steep slope, reached up. I could just touch the lowest tip—no good. I climbed to higher ground, draped the nylon loop to the machete around my neck, and pulled myself onto the tree. Crawled out a thick limb until I was close enough. Grabbed the rope in one hand and hacked at the knot holding it to the branch. Three hard shots and it came free. I crawled backward off the tree limb, holding the bag in one hand like a fishing line with slimy bait at the end.

I pulled the poncho over my head, wrapped it around the bag.

Carried it in one hand back to the car. Everything went into the trunk.

I merged with the traffic, U-turned at the overpass, headed back to Manhattan.

36

Driving home against the traffic, feeling the heat of the voodoo bag behind me.

"When you're on the road, always look back cold." The Prof. Talking to me on the prison yard years ago. Reminding me how suckers think they have to travel to see what they left at home. Prison even makes you miss hell.

Everything I'd had in Indiana—a short-term lease on belonging—it was gone now. I was home. Driving through the war zone, bombarded by imagery. I flicked on the all-news radio station. A human beat his baby to death, cut the kid up, fed the parts to his German shepherd. The authorities took charge. Killed the dog.

They say when a dog tastes human flesh, it'll always seek more. A dog like that, you have to put it down. When humans get the same way, we give them therapy.

Liberals always know what to name things. To them, graffiti vandals are ghetto expressionists. Probably think mugging is Performance Art too.

The mayor was saying something about the city being a gorgeous mosaic—all the lovely colors. Trying to govern from the fetal position, wearing shades. It looks different from ground zero.

A different rhythm too. Some Oriental kids haunt the libraries—others fondle their automatic weapons and visit the restaurants, asking for contributions. Hispanic hit-men, pretty in pastel, posture like blood-hungry peacocks in the discos while their brothers and sisters work double-shifts in the sweatshops to afford an education for their children that their ancestry will bar them from using. Some white kids plot their privileged futures in prep school while skinheads join the only club that will have them. Black doctors on their way to the hospital walk past children of their color spending their lives on concrete, going to the hoop, the crack-monster patiently waiting for their dreams to die. The baddest of the B-Boys form sidewalk posses, naming themselves after video-game killer-machines. They rat-pack citizens, taking them down like wild dogs, ripping, snatching. Gotta Get Paid. Rustling, they call it. Nitrous oxide and amyl nitrite have parties with never-connected kids who think devil-worship is something you can do part-time.

Only the names change. Nothing deadly ever really dies. Crank makes a comeback at rock concerts—Jello-shots are invited to all the right parties. Fatal fashions.

And the kids go down. Gunfire in the ghettos—cluster suicide in the suburbs.

Welfare hotels: crack dens with security guards, where residents rent out their babies as props to beggars. The older kids can't get library cards from those addresses, but they're welcome in the video arcades in Times Square. Where even the night is bright. And where it's always dark. Like in the subway tunnels, where the rats fear the humans who stalk the platforms, muttering their secret codes, looking for women to push onto the tracks.

Back alleys where abandoned babies in garbage cans are the lucky ones.

The sun shines the same on them all: yuppies on their pristine balconies, working on their tan; below them, winos on their urine-stained cardboard pallets, working on being biodegradable.

This isn't a city—it's a halfway house without a roof. Stressed to critical mass.

I was driving with camera eyes, taking snapshots. Three young men wearing silk T-shirts, their hair cut in elaborate fades, short on the sides, long in back. Lounging against a black Eldorado, the sparkling car resplendent in gold trim right down to the chains framing the license plate. Two decals on the trunk lid . . . USA and Italia. So nobody would mistake their ride for one of the *moolingiane*.

Dark-skinned *vatos* refuse to speak English when they're busted, protecting against the same fatal mistake.

The Chinese have a word for Japanese . . . means something like snake.

Only our blood is all the same color. And you can't see that until it's spilled.

Fear rules. Politicians promise the people an army of blue-coated street-sweepers for a jungle no chemical could defoliate.

And behind the doors, breeder reactors for beasts. The walls of some buildings still tremble with the molecular memory of baby-bashing violence and incestuous terror.

I know all this. And more. But it was the bag in the trunk that shuffled the fear cards in my deck.

37

I stowed it in Mama's basement. She watched me unwrap the poncho.

"You know what this is?" I asked her.

"Spirit bag—bad spirits."

"Yeah. You smell money, Mama?"

"No," she said.

I worked the pay phones upstairs, reaching out my probes for the Prof, leaving word.

38

Driving back, I exited Chinatown, turned right at Pearl Street. A pair of guards stood in their blue vinyl jackets, BOP in yellow letters across the back. Bureau of Prisons. Pistol-grip shotguns on slings over their shoulders. The MCC, the federal jail, sits on that corner. As blank-faced as the guards.

It looks the same inside.

39

I tried Mama from the hippies' phone a little before six the next morning. The Prof had called in, left word to see him anytime before ten.

I found him explaining the scam to Agatha. The Prof has organized more domestics than any union ever could. Newspapers were covered with red circles. I looked over his shoulder. All ads for lawyers. You had a car accident? Slip and fall in front of a supermarket? Your baby born brain-damaged? Give us a call. No fee unless successful. The stuff about "expenses payable at conclusion of case" was in much smaller type. He was running the game down, Agatha nodding her head, focusing, getting her act together.

"You want this to last, you got to move fast," he was saying to Agatha. "Fiona's gonna be at the hospital. Say what you got to say, don't let them play. One call, that's all. Got it?"

She nodded. He gave her a handful of quarters and she waddled off to the pay phones.

I lit a cigarette, sipped the cup of hot chocolate the waitress brought over, waited.

"Here's the slant on the plant, brother. You know Fiona? Works the trucks in the meat market? She's in the hospital. Some psycho chased her right up on the curb with his car. Broke her leg, ripped up some stuff inside. She's gonna need operations for days."

"So she needs a lawyer?"

"For what, man? The citizen who hit her, he disappeared. It'll go as a hit-and-run . . . those ain't no fun."

"Where's the money?"

"Agatha calls up about a dozen of these lawyers . . . the ones who advertise, dig it? She tells each one that Fiona is her daughter, okay? Sixteen years old. Tells them she was hit by an Exxon truck on her way to school. Ain't a shyster in town wouldn't grab that one, right?"

"Right."

"So Agatha tells them some sleazy lawyer got tipped to the case by one of the ER nurses, right? And the lawyer came to the hospital, signed up the case. Now Fiona, she's only sixteen, okay? Agatha wants to know if this is legit, see? She don't like the idea of vultures moving in on her poor baby. Wants a new lawyer."

"So?"

"So the lawyer, he calls the hospital. Verifies that Fiona's a patient, had some real harm done to her, vehicle accident. The boy thinks he got money in the bank. Agatha tells him she'll sign the retainer, no problem. Sweetens the deal a bit—tells the lawyer that Exxon already sent a guy over to the hospital, offered her a hundred grand to sign a release, see?"

"Okay, so she gets fifty different lawyers on the case. So what?"

"Here's where we score. Agatha tells the lawyer she needs some cash to tide her over. Got to quit her job, spend every minute with her baby-child in the hospital, needs cab fare to visit her, buy her some presents, keep her spirits up, all that. Some get the message, some don't."

"So what could she get, couple a hundred bucks?"

"Yeah. Couple a hundred bucks. Maybe ten, fifteen times before today's over. Not so shabby."

"Does it bounce back on the kid?"

"What kid? Fiona's twenty-five if she's a day. Been turning tricks since she came in from the sticks. They come around, ask her some questions, she don't know nobody named Agatha. Her poor mama's been dead a long time."

"It's a lot of work for a little piece of change."

His eyes went sad. "Thought you'd dig the play, man. Stinging lawyers. And no risk."

"Yeah, but . . ."

"Maybe you got a better plan, 'home? Let's see now, what would a big-time thief like you need for a major-league take? How about a pistol and a getaway driver . . . then all you'd need is a liquor store."

"I wasn't downing your play, Prof."

"You ain't got the bail, you stay in jail, chump. You know why they call some plans foolproof, schoolboy? 'Cause even fools like you couldn't fuck it up."

"I got something else now."

"I wasn't offerin' to cut you in, Jim."

"Hey, I'm sorry, okay? It's a good plan."

His eyes held mine, alert now, homing in on the target. "You not getting a touch of that fever again?"

"What fever?"

"Monster fever, man. A kid gets done, it's just fuel for your duel, fool. You hear the bell, you go to hell. Like before that mad dog Wesley checked out. When you almost jumped the track."

I lit a smoke, cupping the match even though we were indoors. "I'm done with that," I said quietly.

After Belle died, I was heart-torn sad for a while. Missing what I'd lost. When I learned the truth . . . that it had all been for nothing . . . I lost myself. I'd hunted Mortay and it cost me Belle. And while I was stalking, scared, another hunter was in the shadows. Wesley.

Wesley never missed. He was a heat-seeking missile—he took your money, you got a body. Every time. If I'd just waited, stayed down, kept clear . . .

After that, I stopped being myself for a while. Needed a regular shot of risk-driven adrenaline to keep me alive. It almost made me dead.

"That's finished," I told him.

He held my eyes long enough to satisfy himself. Nodded. "What is it, then, schoolboy? You got something on?"

"Maybe." I brought him up to date, weaving the threads I'd gathered into a tapestry. Keeping it short and clipped, watching his face. He'd raise an eyebrow if I dropped a stitch.

He lit a cigarette from my pack, letting the smoke bubble softly from his mouth, stroking his chin.

"The bag plays like juju, but the sound don't tie it down. It's all got two sides . . . Mojo hand, Little John the Conqueroo, black cat bone, working roots . . . that's why fools call some of it black magic . . . not just 'cause my people started it, but 'cause there's another kind. Some of it's like a church, but there's things you can't ask the Lord for, see?"

"You don't think it's connected?"

"No way to know, bro'. How big is the bag?"

I showed him with my hands.

"Big enough," he said.

40

I found a pay phone on the Upper West Side, called Wolfe on her private line.

"Yes?"

"It's me . . . you recognize my voice?"

"No. You must have the wrong number."

The phone slammed down.

41

I threw in another quarter, dialed Storm's number.

"Rape Crisis Unit."

I asked for her.

"Hello?"

"How's your little girl coming along?"

"My . . . Oh! Hi, Burke!"

Citizens don't think about security. "I just called Wolfe. She hung up on me."

"Now why would she . . . ?"

"That's what I want to know."

"You didn't call on the private line, did you?"

"Yeah, I did."

"Oh. Well, Wolfe's been acting strange lately, like we told you. She told Lily she thinks that line is tapped."

"So how do you talk to her? Only in person?"

"No, we call the switchboard. Wolfe says they can't run a tap on all the incoming calls without a live operator in place."

"Thanks."

42

"Special Victims Bureau."

"May I speak to Ms. Wolfe, please?"

"Who shall I tell her is calling?"

"Juan Rodriguez. I'm a federal parole agent."

"Please hold."

A flat, uninflected voice came on the line. "This is Wolfe."

"It's me again."

"How can I help you?" Same tone.

"I have something I'd like to show you. Something that may relate to a pending investigation."

"Bring it in."

"It's not that easy."

"You know the Four Flags diner on Queens Boulevard? Right next to the motel on the south side?"

"Yes."

"I eat lunch there around one-fifteen most days."

"Today?"

"That's my plan. In this bureau, you never know . . . emergencies and all . . ."

43

Wolfe's battered Audi pulled into the diner's parking lot, jouncing over the speed bumps. The car looked like it had been painted with rust, the windows streaked, front license plate dangling from the one remaining bolt. Lola next to her on the front seat, a dark mass moving in the back. The Rottweiler.

They left the dog in the car—didn't lock the doors.

I lit a smoke, waiting.

A midnight-blue Firebird pulled in behind Wolfe's car. Rocco and Floyd got out, scanned the lot. They seemed to be arguing about something.

I finished my smoke, went inside.

The place was jammed with a lunchtime crowd. The hostess stopped me at the door.

"Smoking or Non-Smoking?"

"I'm meeting some people . . . they're already here."

"Smoking or Non-Smoking?"

"Wherever they're already sitting, okay?" I walked away from her before the tape could recycle. Spotted Wolfe in a far corner, her back against the wall, Lola across from her.

"Mind if I join you ladies?"

"Sure," she said. "Have a seat. We haven't ordered yet."

The waitress came by. They ordered chef's salad. I did too. Listened to them talk until the food came . . . the waitress would be too busy to stop back after that.

"Sorry about the call earlier."

"The private line is tapped," Wolfe said, no expression in her voice. Like she was giving me a weather report.

"The only one who could do that is . . ."

"Yes. It's not your affair. What do you want to show me?"

"You're looking for a baby. Derrick is his name, right? Disappeared from the Welfare hotel over by La Guardia?"

Wolfe looked at Lola, nodded.

"Somebody asked me to look for him too."

"And?"

"I think I know where he is."

"Alive?"

"No."

"You've seen the body?"

"No."

"Is there anything to connect this to . . . ?"

"Emerson?"

She nodded again.

"Emerson beat the baby to death. In that room. Right in front of the mother. Then he went out to get rid of the body."

"How do you know this?"

"Just a guess. But if you found the body, it would be enough?"

"Depending on what shape it was in . . ."

"You got wants out for Emerson?"

"No."

"How come? Don't you even want to talk to him about this?"

Wolfe lit a smoke. I felt Lola's body shift next to me. "He's locked up," Wolfe said. "On another charge. In the Bronx."

"So you can't question him?"

"His lawyer says no."

"Or her?"

"She hasn't been arrested." Meaning she *could* talk to her, but she didn't have enough ammo to do it yet.

"Let's say, just to be talking about it, that you knew he left the hotel room with the baby's body . . . came back in an hour or two, what would that tell you?"

"Nothing much. You can cover a lot of ground in a couple of hours."

"And if he didn't have a car . . . or access to one?"

"Okay. You going to give us a nice sworn-to-under-oath affidavit about this? Be a confidential informant?"

"I can't do that . . . I don't know anything, see? I'm just talking about a theory."

"We can't get a search warrant on a theory," Lola tossed in, trace of a Brooklyn accent coming through for the first time.

"You don't need a warrant to search some places."

Wolfe's eyebrows rose.

"Public places," I said.

Wolfe leaned forward. "What do you have to show us?"

"It's in my car."

We finished our meal. They spent the time talking about Lola's new boyfriend. Sounded like he wouldn't be around long.

They picked up my check.

44

"I'm parked against the back fence. An old Plymouth. Pull your car next to mine, open your trunk."

I caught Rocco and Floyd in the edge of my vision. Wolfe's Audi pulled in. Lola went around the back to open the trunk. Wolfe snapped a lead on the Rottweiler, walked him over to my car.

"Bruiser, stay!" The beast dropped into a sitting position the way a sprinter settles into the starting blocks, eyes only for me.

I opened the duffel bag in the trunk, pulled out the blanket inside. Uncovered the leather bag.

"You know what this is?" I asked.

Neither of them said anything.

"I traced Emerson's path from the hotel. Found this along the way."

"The way to where?"

I told them about the dark water surrounding Rikers Island. Step by step.

"You think the baby's in that bag?" Wolfe.

"Maybe some pieces of him, but I doubt it. I think he's in the water. You can get divers without a warrant, right?"

"Yes. But it's a long shot. Unless he weighted it down, it could be anywhere."

"Worth a try."

"Sure."

"I'll put the bag in your trunk. The coroner will tell you the rest."

"And how did we come by the bag?"

"I figure, maybe Rocco and Floyd were doing some investigating, ran across it, cut it down. Tagged it in an evidence sack, all the right stuff."

"When would they have done this?"

"Why don't you ask them," I said, flicking a glance to my left.

Wolfe spotted them. "Get over here!" she shouted. Lola giggled.

They walked over, looking everyplace but at Wolfe.

"One of you two clowns put this in my trunk," Wolfe said, pointing at the bag.

"What is it?" Rocco.

"We don't know yet. You and Floyd found it last night."

"Huh?"

"Shut up and do it. I'll talk to you two when we get back to the office."

"We just thought we'd . . ." Floyd.

He caught a warning look from Lola, cut it short.

Rocco took the bag in his hands. An ugly low snarl came from Bruiser.

"No!" Wolfe barked back at him.

"I'll call you," I said to Wolfe.

She stepped close to me. The breeze ruffled her hair. Orchid perfume. "Give me a number. I'll call you."

I gave her Mama's number. She didn't write it down.

"I'm not there much. Leave a message."

"I know," she said.

They were all still standing in the parking lot as I pulled out.

45

I made my rounds the next few days. Patternless, like always, in case anybody was interested. Somebody left a message for me at the poolroom. Wanted to buy guns. A lot of guns, full-auto only. Probably the ATF, checking to see if I was still in business.

Dropped by the clinic in Brooklyn where they buy blood. I buy in small lots, but I outbid the Red Cross every time. The blood goes into small clear plastic packets. The way it works is this: The team hits a bank. One guy vaults the counter to grab the money while the others hold everyone down at gunpoint. The counter-vaulter cuts his hand going over, curses real loud, like it hurt. When the cops come, they send the lab for the spot where the blood spilled. DNA fingerprinting. They ever catch the robbers, the blood sample won't match. That's why rapists are the only humans you can count on to wear condoms in this town.

I collect matchbooks too. From restaurants I've never visited. They make good souvenirs to leave behind at a crime scene.

I never supply ideas, just equipment. Not a middleman, never in the middle.

There's also good money in body parts. Any part. I once saw an ad for a kidney. One hundred grand cash, jump right over that long waiting list. Sometimes, people are poor enough and cold enough to pop out a kid's eye, make him a more pitiful sight. A better beggar. Predatory anthropologists figured it out—offered the same service but with full hospitalization for the kid. Even threw in a few bucks. And they sell the eyes over here. Everybody wins. Fetal tissue is the perfect transplant material—it'll bond to anything and the body won't reject it. I wonder if the "pro-life" mob knows an abortion could save more lives than the mother's.

46

Some women have beautiful eyes. Their girlfriends tell them it's their best feature. So they wear a ton of eyeliner, mascara . . . like that.

Bonita bent over a lot.

She works in a joint that serves food and wine, little stage in the back, performances every night. Stand-up comics, singers, short dramatic pieces.

Bonita's an actress. Between jobs just now.

I found a table against the side wall. Smoking section. I wonder if they have them in prison now.

"Hello, stranger."

"Hi, Bonita." She was all in black: a tube skirt over a body stocking, spike heels.

"I called you a couple of times. Didn't that Chinese woman give you the message?"

"Here I am."

"Why didn't you *call*?"

"I did. Got your answering machine."

"So why didn't you leave a *message*?"

"What's the point? You already have my number."

"But then I'd know you *called*, honey."

The girl couldn't act but she could read an audience. Just as I was asking myself why I came, she switched away to get me some ice water, shaking it hard enough to blow out the candles on the tables.

"I'm on my break soon," she said when she came back. "We can watch the show together."

"What show?" I asked her, barely controlling my enthusiasm.

"Oh, it's *so* good. It's like a play, or something. Just wait. That's why it's so full tonight."

I crunched a flaky croissant between my teeth, sipped the ice water. She left the little glass bottle on the table. I wondered if trendoid B-girls drank tap water when they hustled salad-bar customers for drinks.

Bonita came back. Sat down just as the lights dimmed. I could see a couple of men setting up the stage. The lights came up. Tall, big-shouldered man was facing the audience, a Doberman lying at his feet. Looked like one of those Pacific Northwest lumberjacks, long brown hair, ropy muscle all along his forearms. He had a power drill in his hands.

"I know how things work," he told the audience, mouth a thin line. "When they get broke, I fix them."

The big man had a straight-ahead stare. Empty and flat, not challenging, not backing off either. Talking like it was coming from inside his head.

He lived in the basement, he told the audience. Janitor. Lived in a lot of places, some of them not so nice. And he did some things in those places, not nice things. Now he just wants to live in his basement, fix whatever's broke. The crowd was quiet, listening to his story.

The dog didn't bark, he told us. Some freak had carved him up when he was a puppy, cut into his throat. "But he still works," the man said. His voice had life in it, but subdued, an undertone of Wesley's dead-robot sound.

There was a kid who lived in his building. Slow in the head, but a sweet boy. He was scared of monsters coming for him in the night, so the man made him a machine. Just a bunch of flashing lights on a box with a toggle switch. The kid liked the machine. Slept good for the first time.

The kid went to a special school. His teacher, Dr. English, told the mother that the machine was a placebo. A fake, but one the kid believed in.

One night, the kid started screaming and he didn't stop. An ambulance took him away. The man visited him in the hospital. The kid told him the machine wasn't any good anymore.

The man said he was sorry—he'd build him a better one.

The man said he knew how things worked. Did some checking. Seems this Dr. English used to work at another school up North. The school had been closed behind some sex abuse scandal. Some teachers indicted, Dr. English resigned. The man called the kid's school. Dr. English was out. Broke his arm in a ski accident. Funny, the lady on the phone said, Dr. English only came to their school from his old job because he hated the cold weather.

The boy lived on the second floor. There was a fire escape leading to the ground.

We watched, listened as the man put it all together. Watched as he painstakingly drilled holes through the center of two hard rubber balls, strung a loop of piano wire between them. Tested it by snapping it in his hands.

The man was getting dressed. Dark jacket, pair of gloves, a black watch cap on his head. When he pulled it down, it turned into a ski mask. "Tonight, when it gets dark, I'm going to show this Dr. English a machine that works."

The stage went dark. Somebody gasped in the audience. Then the applause started. Built to a peak. Stayed there.

The man came back out. The announcer took the mike, called his name. David Joe Wirth. A pretty girl at a front table stood up, waved a fist at him, her dark ponytail bouncing. He smiled. They left the front together.

I watched the crowd. Wondered how many of them shared the Secret.

47

Later, in Bonita's studio apartment on the fringe of the Village.

"My roommate will be back soon," she whispered, sliding the tube skirt down over her hips.

Later, at her kitchen table. "Did you get it?" she asked me.

"Get what?"

"The *play*. The one we saw tonight. I didn't, the first time he did it. See, the teacher at the school, he was molesting that little boy. And the boy's mother, she *trusted* him. That's why the machine didn't work . . . the one the janitor made for him . . . the monsters weren't all in his head like they thought."

"Yeah, I got it."

"Isn't it *disgusting* . . . what some people do?"

"Yeah."

"I wonder where she is, Tawny. I thought she'd be home by now."

"It's okay, I gotta take off myself."

"She's going away next weekend. You could spend the night . . ."

"If I don't have to work, I'll call you."

"You *better*," sitting in my lap now, squirming.

"Bonita, I feel pretty stupid about this, but . . ."

"What?"

"Well, I wanted to buy you a present . . . just to show you how much I care and all. A charm for your bracelet . . . I saw one I really liked . . . a little gold heart . . ."

"Un-huh . . ."

"Yeah, but by the time I got to the store, tonight, it was closed. So, I was wondering . . . I don't mean to be crude or anything . . . you know the crazy hours I work . . . Could I give you the money, let you pick it up for yourself? . . . I mean . . ."

"Oh, you're so *sweet*, honey. I don't mind at all."

I handed her five fifty-dollar bills, folded in half. She put them on the table without looking.

"You have to go right *now?*" she purred, squirming some more.

Maybe she wasn't *such* a lousy actress.

48

I cut myself shaving the next morning. Took a plump leaf from the aloe plant on the windowsill, punctured it with my thumbnail, smeared it on, watching Pansy sneer at my clumsiness. Thinking of Blossom and her goddamned health advice.

Ate slowly. A rosette of michetta roll, hard crust, hollow inside. Only place you can get them in New York is this Milanese bakery in Brooklyn, on the Bushwick border. Real Italians. I'd been going there for years—never heard them say Mamma Mia once. I smeared cream cheese on each piece as I snapped it off. Drank my ice water, swallowed the beta carotene and vitamin C.

Blossom again.

If I ever went over her back fence one night, I wouldn't need cash. Or lies.

I snapped out of it, looked over to the couch. "Want to go for a ride, girl?"

Pansy's tail thumped happily.

Saturday morning, bright and clear. We took the Willis Avenue Bridge to the Hutch, headed north. All the way to the wilds of Dutchess County, almost a two-hour drive.

Teenage girl hitching by the side of the road. I thought of a maggot who picked up a girl like that in California. Raped her, chopped her hands off so there wouldn't be fingerprints, and dumped her in a culvert. The little girl lived, somehow. The maggot's already been paroled—it's not like he robbed a bank or anything. I read he got arrested again in Florida. For shoplifting. The paper said he stole a hat, but he'd paid for another item he had in a bag. A box of diapers.

I knew I was close when I saw the clapboard shacks standing just off the dirt road. A trio of chopped-down Hogs sat outside one shack, ape-hanger handlebars sprouting like stalks from the chromed engines. One of those prefab metal sheds sat behind the shack. They'd be cranking up the heat inside, making meth, choking on the ether fumes. The bikers figured out the dope business a long time ago—the real problem is getting the stuff across the border, so they cook their own right here.

The last house made the others look like Mr. Rogers' neighborhood. Set well back from the road on a winding, narrow approach, it sagged from depression. Tar paper covered most of the windows, missing shingles pockmarked the roof, the whole sorry mess rotting from termites who had long since fled to better pickings. If it burned to the ground, the coroner would call it suicide.

I pulled the Plymouth into the side yard, gunning the engine, sliding on the dirt, letting him know I was there. Turned off the ignition and waited—I wasn't going to jump out too fast.

He came around the side of the house, a tall, rawboned, slope-shouldered man with a doofus mustache. Hair cropped short, wearing tiny round sunglasses. A rifle in one hand, a dog on a chain in the other—a white pit bull with a ring of black fur around one eye and one black ear. The animal didn't look a bit like Spuds McKenzie.

Elroy. He lived back in the woods. Off the land, he said. He'd jack deer by spotlight at night when they came to the salt lick he'd set up. Blow ducks off the water with his shotgun. Anything that had fur, feathers, or scales. He wasn't a hunter, he was an armed consumer.

Even the bikers cut him considerable slack—people said he ate road-kill sandwiches.

I hit the window switch, let him have a good long look.

"Burke!" he boomed out.

"Yeah, it's me. Put the gun down, okay?"

"Sure."

"And tie that animal up."

"Barko wouldn't hurt anyone," he said, sounding insulted.

"I got Pansy in the car," I told him, by way of explanation. I climbed out. The pit bull watched me with only mild interest, but his ears were cocked. He had Pansy's scent, growled a challenge.

We walked around behind the house. Elroy had his own prefab shed too. Maybe they came with the original houses.

"You have the paper?" I asked him.

"What's your hurry?"

"That paper isn't going to move itself, Elroy."

"Come on," he said.

We walked past the shed toward the woods. Two more pit bulls were anchored to metal stakes set in cement. One had an old tire in his alligator jaws, waving it around in triumph as the other watched.

"Aren't they beauties?" Elroy asked.

"They are, for sure. You training them?"

"Yeah! Want to see?'"

"Okay."

"Barko's really my best one. Just wait here, I'll get him."

He came back leading the dog. The other two yapped in anticipation, pawing the ground. A low-slung four-wheeled cart stood on a level patch of ground, piled high with solid-concrete blocks. Elroy took an elaborate leather harness from a hook on a nearby tree. It was lined with some spongelike material. As soon as he took up the harness, Barko began running in little circles, overcome with excitement.

"Come on, boy! Time to work!"

Barko trotted over on his stubby legs and Elroy fitted him up. He attached two short leads from the harness directly to a U-bolt on the front of the cart. Barko stood rigid at attention, waiting.

"Okay, baby . . . *pull!*" Elroy yelled.

The pit bull surged forward, straining against the harness, fighting for traction. When all four legs locked in, he began to inch forward, dragging the cart behind him, foaming a bit at the mouth, Elroy screaming, "Full Pull, Barko! Full Pull!" Soon the little tank was slogging forward, like a man wading through setting cement. Barko never faltered, chugging ahead until Elroy ran to intercept him, kicking a wooden wedge under the cart's wheels. He unsnapped the harness, held the dog high over his head in both hands.

"The winner . . . *Barrrko!*"

I swear the dog grinned.

"*That's* what you're training the dogs for?"

"Sure. You don't think I'm gonna let my dogs *fight*, do you? This is the latest thing. They get ninety seconds to pull the weight fifteen feet—that's a full pull. Barko's going in the middleweight class this fall."

"Pit bull tractor pulls?"

"Yeah, man! You know how much Barko just lugged across the finish line? One half ton, man. A thousand pounds. And that was on grass—the regulation pulls're on a piece of flat carpet. Better traction, smoother roll."

"Unreal."

"He's still working. The record's a little over one full ton, man. Twenty-one hundred pounds."

"What pulled that, a Clydesdale?"

"A pit bull, Burke. A forty-eight-pound bitch, in fact. That's the middleweight class, not the open. Some of those damn Rottweilers, they could pull a house."

"Jesus."

"Yeah, they're amazing, huh?"

Elroy dropped Barko to the ground. I saluted him. He trotted back to the front.

"Pansy's in the car," I reminded him.

"Barko's no dog fighter."

"He's a pit bull."

"It's all in how you raise them, man."

Some of Elroy's receptor sites were burned out, but he knew the truth.

"Let's look at the paper," I said.

49

It was spread out on a long clean table in the shed. Bearer bonds, beautifully engraved. Face value, ten grand each. Elroy had been a counterfeiter, but his last stretch in the pen had cured him of playing with funny money. Now he just worked in small lots: bonds, deeds, certificates. Takes some real skill, and you need specialists to move it, but the risk is lower.

"How many you got?" I asked him, turning the paper over in my hands, admiring the craftsmanship.

"Three point five million, you add it up."

"You know how the quick flip works, Elroy . . . you're looking at maybe a hundred grand your end, tops."

"That's okay. This'll be my last score. I got plans, anyway, do something else to make a living."

I put the bonds into my attaché case, walked out to the car. Barko was lying in the sun, basking in the glow of his recent triumph. Pansy's massive head was framed in the front window of the Plymouth.

"Could I look at her?" he asked.

"Tie your guy up first . . . just in case."

I opened the door and Pansy strolled out. I gave her the hand signal for friends, and she stood patiently while Elroy pawed all over her, even pulled back her lips to check her teeth.

"She's gorgeous, man. True Italian stock, I can tell. The Italians breed them much lower to the ground. It's good you didn't dock her tail."

I lit a cigarette, watching my dog.

"Her hips are like steel," Elroy muttered. "You work her on tree jumping?"

"No, she pretty much exercises herself."

"Burke, I got a great idea."

"What?" Shuddering inside. Elroy had this great idea in the joint once . . . pressurize a bunch of chemicals inside the home-brew the Prof was cooking up, turn the jungle-juice into high octane. The vat exploded, blew a big slab of concrete out of the wall in the kitchen. The Man thought it was an escape attempt and locked the whole place down for two weeks. The Prof hasn't spoken to Elroy since.

"You know what a Bandog is?"

"Not exactly."

"The newspapers, you know how they have those headlines: baby chewed to death by pit bull, Rottweiler mauls toddler . . . like that?"

"Yeah."

"Well, these fucking idiots, they don't understand. It's all in the way you raise them. It's not the dog, it's the owners." The maniac paused for breath, ready to make his pitch. "Anyway, you want to own a pit bull in New York now, you got to have special insurance, register it and all. Same for Rottweilers in England. See, what they really want to do is *ban* the dogs, get it?"

"No."

"You can only ban a dog if it's a particular breed, right? Like a Doberman or a collie."

"So?"

"So some breeders got the idea of *combining* breeds, you see what I mean? Like, if you cross a Doberman with a collie, you ain't got a Doberman, and you ain't got a collie."

I lit a smoke, wondering if he'd ever get to the point. If there was a point.

"So they started with pit bulls, 'cause they was the real targets. There's a lot of so-called Bandogs out there, crossing pits with Rhodesians, with bulldogs, Rotties, all kinds of crazy stuff. But the real thing, the true Bandog, you got to cross a male pit bull with a female Neo. That's the only way to go."

"What do you get?"

"They look like giant pits, man. Run maybe ninety, a hundred and ten pounds. All bone and muscle. And dead game."

"Damn."

"Yeah! Now the way I figure it, we mate my Barko and your Pansy, and we got the foundation stock for the best Bandogs in the world. Maybe get the first dogs to pull a ton and a half. What d'you think?"

"I never bred her, Elroy. Tried a couple of times, but she wasn't having any."

"Can't we at least *try?*"

"I'm not tying her up. She *wants* to do it, and you'll take all the puppies when they're weaned . . . I'll think about it, okay?"

"Yeah! Sure, I mean . . . only if they *like* each other, okay?"

"All right."

"Great! Let's see, okay?"

"Elroy, you psychotic, Pansy's not in heat."

"Just to see if they get along . . . come on, Burke."

"She's dangerous, Elroy. Big and dangerous."

"Barko's a charmer, man. Like his daddy. All the ladies love him."

He untied the pit. Barko ambled over, respecting Pansy's space. They sniffed each other. Pansy growled, but her heart wasn't in it, just testing. Barko stood his ground. They circled each other, sniffing again. Finally, Pansy lay down. Barko licked her face, lay down beside her.

"What did I *tell* you, man!"

"She gets in heat, I'll bring her back."

"Shake on it, partner," the demento insisted. He hadn't asked for any such reassurances about his bogus bonds.

I opened the door. Pansy jumped into the back seat. I climbed in, started her up. Leaned out the window.

"Elroy, this other scheme of yours . . . ? What are you going to pull?"

"All I been through, man, I'm gonna write a book."

50

The trick with moving phony paper, it has to look legitimate and smell crooked. Suckers think stuff's been stolen, they *know* it's for real. Stop at any traffic light in the right part of town—somebody'll come up to your car with a camcorder or a VCR, still in the brand-new carton, all shrink-wrapped in clear plastic. The professionals, they know how much deadweight to put inside to get an exact match. When the sucker gets it home, he learns the truth. Bearer bonds, it's a little trickier. Same idea, bigger suckers.

I docked the Plymouth behind Mama's, right under the neat row of Chinese characters warning the locals the territory belonged to Max the Silent. Nobody ever parked there for long.

Snapped Pansy's lead on and approached the back door. The thugs let me in, giving Pansy a lot of room, watching her in wonder and admiration. She was too well trained to make a try for any of the food, but she slobbered her usual three quarts in anticipation.

Mama came back from her post, smiling when she saw Pansy. She won a setup bet with her cooks once, wagering on who could tell what country the dog came from. After she'd asked me first.

"Puppy hungry, Burke?"

"Sure is, Mama. She may have met her future husband today . . . gave her an appetite."

I brought her down to the basement as Mama was firing instructions at the cooks. One of them came downstairs lugging a steel vat by the handles, steam fogging the air around him.

I no sooner had "Speak!" out of my mouth than Pansy plunged her snout deep into the vat, making noises they'd censor out of the horror movies.

Upstairs, I sipped my hot and sour soup while Mama fingered through the portfolio of bonds, a pair of white gloves on her hands.

"This real company, Burke?"

"Sure thing, Mama. Trades on the AMEX. The bonds are issued on its international division."

"This division . . . ?"

"Yeah, it issues bonds, some of them in bearer form." Real bearer bonds are as good as cash. Untraceable. No registration. You hold them, you own them. Like diamonds, only they don't have to be appraised.

"Some people, maybe they pay . . . ten percent, yes?"

"Sure."

"This take time, right? Send overseas, far away. Many people wash their hands in the same bowl, the water get cloudy."

"I understand. The manufacturer, he needs a third."

"One hundred thousand."

"A little more, I think, one-third."

"One hundred thousand. Everyone must be paid."

"Okay."

"For you?"

"Whatever you say, Mama."

She smiled her approval of my manners, ladled more soup into my bowl.

A shadow fell across the table. Max. He shouldered in next to me, bowing to Mama at the same time. She opened her mouth to yell something at the waiters, but one of them was there with a bowl for Max before she got a word out. She said something to the waiter anyway. "Smartass" sounds the same in Cantonese.

It was like old times, for a while. Yonkers had added a new feature to the evening program—some of the races were carded for an extra distance past the traditional mile . . . from a sixteenth to a quarter. I explained my foolproof, surefire, can't-miss handicapping system—the longer the race, the better the chance for the fillies against the colts. Class tells in the long run, and the female side of any species is built for endurance. They listened the way they always do: Max fascinated, Mama bored to narcolepsy. Mama isn't a gambler—her idea of a sporting event is a fixed fight.

Max had the racing form in his pocket and we went over it together. Mama politely excused herself, nodding toward the front door. In Mama's business, customers didn't use the front door. But every once in a while some ignorant yuppie would ignore the filthy tables, the food-splattered walls, the flyspecked menus, and the rest of the unappetizing ambiance and actually order food. It was Mama's job to make sure they never came back—people like that interfered with business. A health inspector once visited the kitchen, tried to shake Mama down. A small gratuity was expected. Otherwise, he said, they'd have to close the place down for a while until it was brought up to snuff. Maybe even publish a notice in the paper that the Board of Health had found violations. Mama gave him a blank look. When the Health Code Violation notice was printed in the paper, she pasted it in the window. The health inspector never came back.

I scanned the form the way I always do, looking for the intangibles, that combination telling me a horse was ready to break out, overcome its past. Everything important but the breeding, that's overrated. I'd like to own a trotter someday. They don't cost that much, and I've scored heavy enough to pull it off more than once. But you can't own a horse if you've got a felony record, so that lets me out. I could open a day-care center, though.

Finally, I settled on a six-year-old mare. She was shipping in from the Meadowlands, a mile track with a long stretch. She always ran from off the pace, so conventional wisdom says she'd come up short trans-ferring to Yonkers, a half-mile oval with a real short way home. But I figured the extra eighth of a mile in the fifth race would give her all the space she'd need. Morning line was 6–1. I put a pair of fifties on the counter, pointed to Max. He matched it. I got up to call Maurice. Max can do a lot of things, but he can't telephone a bookie.

Max didn't let me pass, blocking the booth, his hands working, asking me to explain things again.

I went through it again—the Patience card is always in my deck. Caught his eyes, made the sign for "okay?" His face was expressionless, body posture relaxed. I shoved lightly against him. Good luck. Finally, he held up an open palm like a traffic cop: Stop.

I hunched my shoulders, opened my hands: Why?

He pointed at my watch—almost four in the afternoon, shook his head. Not time yet? I looked over to Mama at her register, couldn't catch her eye.

The hell with it. I lit a smoke. Max took out a deck of cards, shifted out of the booth, and sat down across from me. Dealt out a hand of gin. First card up from the pack was the ace of spades. No knock, results doubled. I made a gesture like writing something on paper. Max pulled the last score sheet from his pocket, pushed it over to me. He was into me for more money than I could steal in a lifetime. We'd been playing for years and years—the fool was going to hang in until he got even or pass the weight on to his daughter when he retired.

I got lost in the game. Like I was back inside, where killing time was an achievement. Max reached for a card. Mama came up behind him, tapped him hard on the shoulder. He turned to look at her. She shook her head side to side, emphatically. Max ignored her advice the way he used to ignore the Prof when we all jailed together. Tossed me the four of hearts. Gin.

I totaled up the score. The Mongolian was down another two grand and it was only . . . damn! Six-thirty.

The front door swung open. Immaculata—Lily and Storm close behind. They walked to the booth. Mac kissed Max, bowed her thanks. Max slid out of the booth, his job done.

51

Immaculata slid in next to me, Lily and Storm took the facing bench.

"What is this?" I asked Lily. "A surprise party?"

"We couldn't wait to get you on the phone. Mac called Mama, told Max to have you wait. We had to talk to you. Now."

"Okay. What?"

The dark-haired woman leaned forward, all the juice gone from her voice. "There's been another murder. Luke was in a foster home, in Gramercy Park. They left him alone for just a few minutes. He was watching television with another baby, three years old. When the foster mother came back inside, the baby was dead. Face all blue. She thought the baby had choked, called the paramedics."

"The call came in to our hospital," Storm interrupted. "We ran over there, to make sure . . ."

"Where's Luke?"

Lily ignored my question. "The paramedics said the child hadn't choked on anything . . . marks on his throat, like he'd been strangled. Luke said he was watching the TV, didn't see anything. He was just watching the cartoons."

"You think the same people . . . ?"

"Only a ghost could've gotten into that room, Burke. They're on the ninth floor."

"There's fire escapes. Balconies. There's always a way in. I know a guy went up twelve stories with a ladder he made out of dental floss. Who knew he was there?"

"I don't know. It doesn't matter. Wolfe wants Luke."

"What d'you mean, she *wants* him? The kid can't be ten years old."

"Nine," Lily said. "If his birth certificate is the truth."

"Where is he now?"

Lily's eyes hard on mine. "Safe," she said.

"He's with us," Mac said. "At the temple." She meant the top floor of one of Mama's warehouses. Where she lived with Max.

"And you think Wolfe's crazy?"

"Not crazy," Storm put in. "Just wrong."

I turned to face Immaculata. "So you left him alone with Flower?"

Her eyes dropped. Wouldn't meet mine.

"You don't think Wolfe's wrong," I said to Lily, voice gentle and flat. If anyone was nuts, it was this crew.

"Luke needs to be in a hospital," Lily said, not giving an inch.

"We don't have joints for criminally insane babies."

"I know."

"What do you all want?"

Storm tapped her fingers on the counter, looking at her sisters, waiting. They'd talked this over before they came. "We want you to . . . negotiate. With Wolfe."

"Negotiate what?"

"For some time. We need time. If Wolfe takes him now, she's going to charge him."

"He's too young to be charged with a crime."

"No, he's not, Burke. Wolfe says anyone over seven can be charged."

"Yeah, as a juvenile delinquent, or something. But they can't . . ."

I stopped talking as the ugly fear banged on the door of my consciousness. I was younger than Luke when they locked me up for the first time. That's what they did to ungrateful orphans who ran away from beatings. And pitch-black closets. And basements that smelled of human rot.

"You talked to him . . . ?"

"He doesn't know anything," Lily said. "He'd pass a lie detector."

"You know what he is," I said, daring her to deny it.

"Yes, we know. But we don't know *why*. He wasn't born like this."

"So you want to make a deal. For treatment or something."

"That's a job for a lawyer. We can get him a lawyer. We have to know why. That's for you."

"I'm not a psychiatrist."

"We know what you are."

I started thinking like what I was. "Did the foster parents see you take the kid out of there?"

"I was there first," Storm said. "I called Lily. She came over with some more people. We talked to the foster parents while the others took Luke out. They didn't see a thing. Don't know where he is."

"Wolfe . . . ?"

"Doesn't believe it for a second," Lily said. "She said she's got the kid on the books as missing. APB running for him. Said if he doesn't turn up by tomorrow, she'll get a search warrant. For SAFE. For Storm's house. For wherever."

"It's like that, huh?"

"Just like that."

I lit a cigarette, buying time. The woman warriors watched me, waiting. "Remember that time Wolfe had this case . . . girl about twenty-five . . . she'd been molested when she was eleven, long time ago? So she charged the guy, even though the statute of limitations was long gone? Remember, Lily? You testified that the girl had been in a psychiatric coma . . . couldn't even remember what had happened to her until she'd been in therapy for something else."

Lily nodded, waiting for the punch line.

"It went all the way up to the appellate courts, but they let the indictment stand. Said this freak, it was no different than if he hit her in the head with a tire iron and she just woke up years later. The girl couldn't remember because of something *he* did, so he wasn't off the hook."

"I remember. We all do. It changed the law."

"Yeah. Well, Wolfe likes that kind of stuff. Making people pay."

We sealed the bargain without another word.

52

I pulled the Plymouth into the warehouse. It looked deserted, like always. Max closed the garage doors behind us. Metal stairs to the next floor, narrow landing. Max's temple to the right, living quarters to the left.

"I don't think you really understand . . ." Luke's voice.

He was sitting in a straight chair, facing the door. Talking to a young Chinese. Flower crawled around on the floor, gurgling happily.

The young Chinese stood up as we entered, bowing to Max. He was wearing a baggy bright-white T-shirt that came to mid-thigh over black parachute pants, billowing wide at the knees and tied at the ankles around white leather high-tops. His glossy black hair was sleeked straight back, glistening under the gel.

Max pointed two fingers straight down, moved them apart, drawing a circle as they met again.

The young man nodded. Bowed to Immaculata and left, ignoring me.

I didn't know his name but I knew his game. The loose T-shirt covered a pistol, the soft shoes wouldn't make a sound. And he'd have people all around the building.

"Hello, Burke," the boy said.

"Hello, Luke."

"Am I going to live here?"
"For a while, okay?"
"Okay."

53

The basement is full of tunnels. We stepped through, under the building next door, the one occupied by a team of Chinese architects. I hooked the alligator clips to the telephone junction box, connected the field phone. Listened for a minute: it was after hours, but Orientals aren't clock-watchers.

All clear. I dialed Wolfe's private line. No answer. Then I tried her home number. The one Lily had given me. It was picked up on the third ring.

"Hello." Man's voice, neutral.

"Could I speak to Ms. Wolfe, please?"

"Who is this?" The voice shifting down a gear, harder.

"A friend."

"You got a name, friend?"

"Ms. Wolfe will recognize my voice. I'm working on something for her."

"Hold on."

Muffled noise in the background. A dog yapped.

"This is Wolfe."

"It's me," I said, soft-voiced, going on quickly before she could say my name. "I apologize for calling you at home—it's kind of an emergency. Is this phone okay?"

"My housekeeper is especially good at sweeping. What do you want?"

"To talk to you. Face to face. About what you're looking for."

Sound of Wolfe muffling the phone, murmurs of talk.

"Tell me where you are—I'll come to you."

"That wouldn't work. I'll meet you. Wherever you say."

"When?"

"Now. As long as it takes me to get there—I'm in Westchester, just north of the city."

"You know where I live?"

"No."

More muffled conversation at her end.

"I'll give you an address. There's no number on the door. Just tap on it. Lightly. And don't go around to the side of the house . . . the dog's there."

"Okay."

"You're coming alone?"

"Yes."

"I'll be waiting," she said. And gave me the directions.

54

The Plymouth's exhaust bubbled softly as I made the turn into Forest Hills Gardens, the ritziest section of Queens, not far from the courthouse. I entered the neighborhood from Queens Boulevard after I exited the Grand Central. As if I'd come over the Whitestone Bridge from Westchester, in case she had people watching.

Beautiful homes, set way back from the narrow, winding streets. Brick, stone, exotic wood . . . they looked like little castles. I wondered how Wolfe could crack this kind of real estate on her DA's salary—maybe she had a rich husband.

The house was the whole corner lot of the street, surrounded by a man's-height stone wall, electronic sensors set at irregular intervals along the top. The gate to the driveway was standing open. Three-car garage at the end, just around a curve. Its door was closed, the driveway clogged with cars, mostly econoboxes except for Rocco's Firebird and a red Buick Reatta two-seater. Wolfe's Audi was nowhere in sight.

I closed the Plymouth's door just as spotlights snapped to attention all around the house. A patch of darkness to the side. Behind a flat-black grid, a dog's eyes blazed.

I tapped on the front door, like I'd been told, watching my reflection in the one-way bronze-glass panel. Lola opened the door, wearing an electric-blue shantung silk dress, party makeup still on her face.

"Come on," she said, walking away so I'd follow, "she's out back."

Hardwood floors, polished. Almost no furnishings. The living room had a vaguely Japanese tone to it, but I didn't get a chance to stop and look, feeling the presence of someone behind me.

The backyard was huge. A giant cherry tree stood in one corner, its branches blocking the sky. A hammock in the open space, brick barbecue, a padded weight lifter's bench. Bird feeders were suspended from the tree limbs that ran parallel to the ground.

I walked onto the fieldstone patio. Wolfe was seated at a butcher-block table, an overflowing ashtray at her elbow. The woman who'd been behind me walked around to my side, guiding me to the table without touching me.

"This is Deidra," Wolfe said. A big woman, more curvy than hefty, with short-cropped dark hair and a winsome face. Black Irish, Italian, Jewish—couldn't tell, it was all there. "She works with us too. You've met the others." Waving her hand around, eyes not leaving my face.

I sat down. A thick shadow moved in against Wolfe's hip. "Sit, Bruiser," she said, sweetness in her voice.

"Beautiful place you have here," I said, lighting a smoke, waiting for the others to step back, give us room to talk privately.

"I like it," she said, even-voiced. "Nice days, I can walk to work."

"You like birds?" I asked, looking around.

"They're really Bruiser's birds. He was raised with them. In the backyard, when he was just a tiny puppy, he used to lie in the sun. And the birds would come. They got used to him. I even have a picture somewhere of a sparrow perched on Bruiser's head. When a cat comes into the yard, his birds scream for him. And out he comes."

"That must be a pain in the neck."

"No, he gets in and out by himself. Dog door."

"If it's big enough for him, it's big enough for a person."

"No, it really isn't. We tried. Even Lola couldn't get through it."

The tall woman flashed a smile in the darkness.

"So this is a cat-free zone?"

"It sure is. One day I came out after this awful racket and there was this Siamese lying in the yard. In two pieces. The owner was my neighbor, claims he's a real animal lover. He came over screaming and yelling, said the cat was just following its natural instincts, hunting birds."

"What'd you tell him?"

"Bruiser was just following his natural instincts too. Protecting his territory. And my Bruiser doesn't invade other people's property like his cat."

"What'd he do?"

"Sued me in Small Claims Court." Wolfe chuckled. "The judge told him his cat was a trespasser and Bruiser had used self-help."

"Friend of yours?"

"No judge is a friend of mine," a chill lacing her speech, making sure I got it.

"Mine either."

"I know. We have a mated pair of cardinals living here. Blue jays, robins, doves. Even a stupid woodpecker who tries the cherry tree every now and then."

"Nice and peaceful."

"Yes."

She was going to wait. And I didn't know what she was waiting for. "I wanted to talk to you," I said.

"Talk."

"Alone."

"Not a chance, Mr. Burke. I'm not ungrateful for occasional help you've provided to City-Wide, but I'm not playing myself out of position."

"Neither am I. What if . . . just for the sake of argument . . . I wanted to discuss something with you . . . something that maybe I wouldn't want to admit I said if it ever went near a courthouse? I could say it to you, and then it's your word against mine. But if I said it to everyone, then I'm up against it."

"You don't trust me?" Hint of a smile.

"Sure, I trust you. It's how much that I'm wrestling with."

Wolfe lit another cigarette, patting her dog. At home, at peace. The redhead, Amanda, walked over, her hands full of papers like she was still in the office. Rocco and Floyd were doing something around the barbecue, arguing, it sounded like.

"Take your time," Wolfe said.

Fuck it. "I'm here to negotiate," I told her.

"Negotiate what?"

"Let's say . . . hypothetically . . . that you were looking for a missing kid. Maybe you *thought* you knew where the kid was, okay? Maybe you thought he was with friends. Your friends."

Wolfe's face was upturned, fingers absently stroking her cheek. A fire blazed to one side: Rocco finally got the barbecue going. The flames caught the white wings in Wolfe's dark hair. She didn't say anything, waiting.

"Your *true* friends," I told her. "Sometimes, even the closest of friends, even brothers and sisters, they can disagree. Before, you told me to take my time. That's easy to say, hard to do. Time. Hard to do. The State took my time from me. More than once. You know about that. It did me some good. Not the kind of good they meant. It scared me, but not so bad that I'd kiss ass to stay out. I had time—the time they made for me. I learned some things. Things about myself. Things about the way things work. You understand what I'm telling you?"

"No."

"Yes, you do. Some things *need* time. This . . . thing . . . between you and your sisters, it needs time."

"How much time?" Quick, no playing around, right to the center of it. Just Wolfe now—her people nearby but distanced.

"Couple of weeks."

"No way."

"The kid is safe."

"It's not him I care about. He's a killer. I should've dropped him the first time."

"He's nine years old."

"Everyone is, once."

"Everybody that gets to be ten. He's not a kid . . . that's what *you're* thinking. And you're right. Half right, anyway. He's not a kid, he's not a man either. Something else."

Wesley. "You're still a man," I told him, listening as he described a murder-mutilation. A message to his enemies. "I'm a bomb," the monster said.

And that's the way he went out.

"How do you know?" Wolfe asked, leaning toward me.

"I know. I paid the tuition, passed the course."

She flashed a quick grin at me, throaty, husky-soft voice. *"Dónde está el dinero?"*

The way I answered her question years ago. When she challenged me to say something in Spanish.

"There's no money in this. It would take me too long to tell you why. Even if you think I'm on a scam, you know your sisters aren't."

"Truth, justice, and the American way?"

"Truth, justice, and revenge."

"You said enough to get locked up already, pal." Rocco. Leaning forward, intruding.

Wolfe gave him a look. Patted her dog some more.

"You ever notice Bruiser's eyes?" I asked her. "They look straight ahead. The birds he guards, they look out each side. You know why?"

"Bruiser's a predator. The birds are prey."

"Not *his* prey, though."

She dragged deep on her cigarette. "Two weeks," she said. "Then he gets brought in."

I nodded.

"That's your word?" she asked.

I bowed confirmation.

55

I crossed over the Kosciuszko Bridge, heading south for Brooklyn. Slag yards underneath to my right, yawning black, spot-fires spurting. Suicides, they never jump off this bridge—water tells a better lie about what's waiting. Past them, way off in the distance, Manhattan neon told its own lies.

Two weeks.

Luke and Burke. Lurk.

I'd told Wolfe I knew. Didn't tell her how I'd learned.

1971. Lowell, Massachusetts, a struggling mill town. Sitting in a mostly empty downtown parking lot in the front seat of a dull brown Ford, stolen a couple of hours earlier. License plates looked good—they were two halves of two different plates, welded together with the seam at the back. Beer cans on the dashboard, radio turned down low. Two guys taking a break from their construction job. Me and Whitey, waiting. Watching.

Every Friday, a young woman walked past that parking lot. It was a joy to watch her. Pretty-proud, long brown hair bouncing on her shoulders, matching the swing in her hips. Not a traffic-stopper, but a juicy fine thing just the same.

We'd been watching her every Friday for a month. Watching her carry a leather bag over one shoulder. Her outfit changed each time, but the leather bag stayed the same.

She'd walk back the same way. Past us. With the leather bag heavier then. Her boss made the payroll in cash every Friday afternoon. The brunette made the bank run. Flouncing along, walking the way girls walk, one hand swinging with her rhythm, the other patting the bag at her hip. Taking her time, enjoying the sunshine and the stares.

We'd checked the traffic patterns, the escape routes. Had a garage all rented about a half mile away. One quick swoop and we'd make our own withdrawal. Hole up, listening to the sirens. Nighttime, we'd go down the back stairs, separate at the bus station.

Saturday, Whitey would be in Boston. I'd be in Chicago.

The brunette had on an egg-yolk-yellow dress that stopped at mid-thigh.

"Beautiful, huh?" Whitey whispered. He didn't mean the girl.

The radio said something about Attica. I turned it up. Riot at the prison, guards taken hostage, the whole joint out of control. State troopers had the place surrounded.

Whitey had done time before I was born. He cupped a cigarette, hiding the flame out of habit. Spoke softly out of the side of his mouth.

"They gonna kill all those niggers."

"How d'you know it's blacks?" I asked him.

"When the Man comes down on them, they'll *all* be niggers," Whitey said. "Dead niggers."

Blood-bought wisdom from an old man I'd never see again. We took the omen, aborted the snatch.

You stay in the sun long enough, you get a tan. I know why Ted Bundy went *pro se*, represented himself at his murder trial in Florida. You go *pro se*, you get whatever a lawyer would get. Like discovery motions. The prosecution wanted to introduce the crime-scene photos, show the jury the savage slasher's wake. Bundy got his copies too. So he could go back to his quiet, private cell and jerk off to his own personal splatter films. He told the TV cameras that pornography made him kill all those women, lying as smoothly as the lawyer he never got to be. Dancing until they stopped the music.

The Prof schooled me too. In prison and out. We're in the lobby of a fancy hotel. I'm dressed in a nice suit. The Prof is applying the final touches to my high-gloss shoes.

"Watch close, youngblood." Nodding at an average man. All in gray. Dull, anonymous. The uniformed bellman reached for the gray man's suitcase. The gray man snatched it away, keeping it in his left hand while he signed the register with his right.

A few minutes later the bellman came over to us, whispered something to the Prof. Cash flashed an exchange. A few blocks away, the little man ran it down.

"Man don't want to pay, what's it say?"

"That he's cheap."

"The bellhop walked him to the room. Opened the door for him, okay? Didn't carry the bag. And the man still throws him a dime, right on time. Take another look, read the book."

"I don't get it."

"The man ain't cheap, he's into somethin' deep. That bag's full of swag, son."

I read books too. Especially when I was inside. A plant's growth is controlled by the size of its pot. A goldfish won't grow to full size in an aquarium. But we lock children in cages and call it reform school.

I know some things. You don't turn off your headlights when dawn breaks, everyone will know you've been out driving that night.

56

I slept until past noon. Pansy trailed after me as I got dressed, begging with her eyes.

"You want to go see your boyfriend?" I asked her. "Barko?"

She made a little noise. I thought we'd established a new level of human-dog communication until she started drooling while I was eating breakfast. I scooped a couple of pints of honey-vanilla ice cream into her bowl. Watched her slop it all over the walls and floor in a frenzy. Then she curled up and went to sleep.

57

I found Storm in her office at the hospital. She saw me coming, said something into the telephone, hung up.

"We have ten days," I told her.

"And then?"

"Then he comes in."

"You think that's enough time?"

"I don't know—it's not up to me. I did what you asked."

"Not all of it." Lily, walking through the back door, her face sweaty, hair mussed, like she'd been exercising.

I lit a smoke. Lily was so worked up she forgot to frown at me. "Keeping him hidden won't do any good, Burke. Nothing will change in ten days."

"What do you want, Lily. Spell it out."

"He could go someplace else. Far away. Disappear."

"Until he does it again."

"No! Until he gets better."

"You know what that would take . . . ?"

"I don't care. I could take him. He couldn't do anything to me . . . he's too little."

"He'd try, Lily. When he got the signal, he'd try."

"We could use the time," Storm put in. Her parents must have picked her name because she was always so calm. "Luke will need a defense when he comes in, Lily. He needs to see a psychiatrist, maybe a couple of them."

"He wouldn't go to jail," I added.

We left it like that. Nothing settled.

58

I felt it as soon as I hit the street—an inversion in the atmosphere. Heavy air, ozone-clogged. Muggy, with a bone-chill core. Like in prison, just before the race wars came. You felt it in the corridors, on the tiers. In the blocks, on the yard. Skin color the flag, any target an opportunity. The Man would feel it too, but the joint wouldn't get locked down until they had a high enough body count.

I walked in the opposite direction from where I'd left the Plymouth, heading for the subway. Maybe it was just the neighborhood. Something going down, nothing to do with me.

Early afternoon, subway traffic was light. I scanned the car, pretending to read the posters. All the services of the city: AIDS counseling, abortions. Cures for acne, hemorrhoids, and hernias. Food stamps, Lotto, 970 numbers, party lines. Another promised you could *Ruin a Pickpocket's Day* if you followed its advice: avoid crowds.

When I came up for air at Fifty-ninth Street, it felt the same. Not the neighborhood, then.

I turned into a little gourmet supermarket, wandered the aisles, watching. A woman in a cashmere sweater-dress with a gold chain for a belt searched out a can of politically correct tuna. A guy in a dark blue suit over a striped shirt, port-wine tie with matching suspenders made the same two turns I did. I stepped to one side and he rolled past, his eyes linked to the gold chain.

Back outside. Streets thick with stragglers from lunchtime, shoppers. Crowds have a rhythm. You move through them the way you match your breathing to the sleeper next to you. Find the pattern and merge. I entered the stream, blending.

Lexington Avenue. I flowed with the clot, ignoring the traffic lights. A man on the sidewalk, younger than me, squatting on a piece of cardboard, a huge glass bottle like they use in water coolers next to him, some coins and a bill visible at the bottom. Sign propped up next to the bottle, something about Homeless. Humans passed him by. I did too. Took a couple of quick steps past. Whirled, like I'd changed my mind, reaching into my pocket for some change.

A dark-skinned black man in a black suit backed into a doorway just as my eyes came up. A fat white man was coming out and they bumped. The black man saw me watching and took off, running in the opposite direction. I ran to the street, saw a cab parked at the curb. Jumped onto the trunk, falconing from the high ground. Saw the black suit disappear into the front seat of a black sedan. Lexington Avenue is one-way, they had to go right past me. I stayed where I was. Every car that passed me by stared at the man standing on the cab. Except the sedan, a Chevy Caprice, one of those two-ton jobs with the rear fenders extending halfway down the tires. When it rolled by my post, the driver was staring straight ahead. And the passenger seat was empty.

59

A cab pulled to the curb, its hood popped open just a crack, latched in place to cool the engine. I jumped in, told the driver to head downtown. The driver didn't speak much English—I had the same problem with the No Smoking sign. Rolling downtown along Broadway, I started sorting it out.

Just before we hit Herald Square a bike messenger sliced in from one of the side streets as the cab in front of us was changing lanes. They T-boned and the messenger went down. Traffic stopped . . . for the red light. The bike was a twisted piece of metal tubing—the messenger had blood running down his calf, just below the bicycle pants. The cabdriver got out, started inspecting his hack for damage. The messenger unwrapped a heavy length of chain from the bike, started limping toward the cab. The driver jumped back inside, took off just as the chain smashed through his back window.

People watched as the bashed-in cab jumped the light, squeaking across the intersection to the blare of horns. The messenger stood in the street, swinging his chain. I heard sirens behind us.

The light turned green and we took off.

I caught a subway at Eighteenth Street, picked up my car, checked it over. Nobody had been playing with it. I drove carefully to Mama's, watching for heavy Chevys.

60

Ten days. I cut it shorter with Lily, leaving myself a margin. There's always an edge—sometimes it's not sharp.

I went through Mama's kitchen, took my booth in the back. She was at her register. I caught her eye, held my fist to my ear, telling her I had to make some calls.

First to SAFE. They called Immaculata to the phone.

"It's me. Is Max around?"

"Yes."

"Ask him to take a look around. Outside."

"For what?"

"Watchers."

"I understand."

Another quarter in the slot. Like Atlantic City, except nobody called me "sir."

Jacques came on the line.

"You know my voice?"

"Not so many white men call here, mahn."

"You have people watching me?"

"No, mahn. For sure. You have been a friend."

"That past tense?"

A cloud passed over the sun in his voice. "We were watching you, mahn, you would not know to ask."

"Any chance of Clarence free-lancing?"

"No chance. No chance at all. You have enemies, my friend?"

"I don't know yet. Maybe I'm just spooked."

"That is a racist slur, mahn?"

"Lighten up . . . I mean, look, a crew's been following me, I think. I'll know for sure later—there's not that many places they could watch."

"Our people?"

"I didn't talk to them, just saw them."

"We just *look* alike, mahn."

"Who does your material, Jacques? Listen up: I got a crew on me, maybe it has something to do with you, understand?"

"Let us know, mahn. Everybody knows, West Indians, we pay our debts."

One more call. I couldn't make it from the restaurant. I told one of the cooks I'd be right back. He said something in Chinese.

61

Found a pay phone near the OTB on the Bowery. Dialed Albany, listened to the operator tell me the toll for the first three minutes, forked over the coins. Good thing the State gives commissioners private lines— I'd use up the money I had on deposit just getting past the secretary.

He grabbed it on the first ring.

"What's wrong now?" Resigned good humor, a faint bluegrass flavor to his speech.

"Trouble on 7-Up, Doc. Microwave Marvin's not coming out of his house—the fool thinks he's got hostages in there with him."

"Who is this?"

"Your old typist, Doc. Please don't say my name on the phone."

"Good to hear from you, hoss. You must be on the bricks, talking like this."

"Yeah. For now, anyway. I need you to see someone, Doc. Give me an opinion."

"I don't make house calls anymore."

"This'd be outside. I need you to do your trick with the girasol."

"I've been hearing stuff about you, over the years. Never could be sure, jailhouse gossip and all that. What do you want me to look at?"

"A baby killer."

"Forget it. *That's* what I heard about you. You want information, go to the library."

"Not a freak who kills babies, Doc. A baby killer, you understand?"

"You mean . . . a killer baby?"

"Yeah. That's exactly what I mean."

"I'll be in the city in a couple of weeks. Some stupidass budget meeting. Give me a call at . . ."

"There's no time, Doc. None at all."

"Look . . ."

"Sophie would want you to do this, Doc."

"You calling in the marker?"

"If that's the only way."

"I'll be on the early train tomorrow, son."

62

I let myself back into Mama's joint. It was like I'd never left. It's always like that. I came home from jail one time—walked in, sat down in my booth. Mama came and sat down across from me, serving her soup. Maybe that's why she doesn't age—in her spot, she controls time.

I called around. Left word for the Prof, dropping seeds on the ground. He'd turn up. Michelle used to do that kind of thing for me, fronting between our world and theirs. She'd be back. I knew my sister—missing, not lost.

Then I called the Mole. To make a reservation.

When Mama made no move to come over, I got up, went to the register. Luke was sitting next to her on a padded stool. You couldn't see him until you got close.

"Hello, Burke," he said, his frail, strangler's fingers grasping an abacus.

"Hello, Luke. Mama's teaching you how to work that thing?"

"Yes. It's fun."

"Very smart boy, Burke," Mama said. "Teach him how to use beads, never could teach you."

"I was never good with math."

"Math is money," Mama said. Like God is Love.

"I've got to talk with you."

"Okay. You want soup?"

"Sure."

She patted Luke's fair hair, voice softening. "You go in kitchen, baby. Tell cooks bring some soup to Mama."

"I don't speak Chinese," the little boy said. Being serious, not a wiseass.

"Speak like Max, okay?"

A smile brightened his face. "Sure!"

He trotted off. We took our seats.

"Baby not right," Mama said, tapping her temple with one manicured nail.

"Why do you say?"

"This morning, Mac bring him by to stay with me. Very good boy, sit quiet, read a book, okay? But later, talk funny. Baby talk, babble-babble. His name Susie, he says. I say, that a girl's name. He say, I'm a little girl . . . pretty little girl. He *sound* like a little girl, Burke. Ask me to play with him. I just hold him. Then he says, why you holding me, Mama? Luke, boy's voice. I ask him, what about little girl? He look at me like I crazy. Just been sitting, reading his book, he say to me."

"Yeah."

"Not surprise?"

"No."

"Baby need a doctor."

"I know, Mama. I found him one. Tomorrow, okay?"

She bowed agreement.

Luke marched in with a tureen of soup as the register phone rang. Mama got up to answer it.

"Here's the soup, Burke."

"Thank you." I helped myself. The kid sat across from me, self-possessed.

"Luke, tomorrow I'm going to visit an old friend of mine. A couple of old friends, actually. You want to come along?"

"I guess . . ."

"We can do something you'd like to do first, okay? What would you like to do?"

His little face concentrated. Then he rubbed his head, like it hurt. "I'd like to go to the zoo," he said. "I always wanted to go."

63

We found a bench in Grand Central, a half hour before the Albany train was due. Doc had been the prison shrink back when I was Upstate on my second bit. The better class of cons, hijackers, thieves, the professionals, we all liked him. You couldn't gorilla him out of medication and he wouldn't write you a phony rehab statement for the Parole Board like the wet-brain we had in one of the federal pens, but he was stand-up all the way. I remember once, a young white dude, he climbed onto the tier railing, started screaming he was going to take the dive, check out of the hotel for good. Some of the cons, they shouted at him, go ahead and jump, motherfucker, don't be talking about it, do it. Cheered him on. Some of us just watched. The guards too. Doc shoved his way through the crowd on the ground floor, talking softly, urgently up to the guy, telling him it could be fixed, whatever was wrong. But the youngster took off, and he couldn't fly. The *sound* when he hit the floor . . . first the *whump!* of his body, then the crack of his skull. One-two. A piece of his brain jumped around on the concrete, still full of electricity, looking for answers.

Doc ran T-groups for the rapists. I was typing reports in his office once, scamming with both fingers, hunting and pecking a go-home for a guy who'd paid me the usual twenty crates of smokes. Doc came in, face all red. He's a medium-sized man, husky, big chest, thick wrists. Hair cropped short, wears glasses.

"You give the skinners some new insights today, Doc?"

"The group is done, Burke."

"How come?"

"Because I plain hate the slimy motherfuckers, hoss. They ain't sick, they're mean. They didn't teach me that part in medical school."

I liked him from then on. Once saw him go right into a cell with a con who'd ripped the toilet loose from the wall, he was that far out of his mind. And Doc talked him quiet. Saw him stop the screws from whaling on some poor bastard who'd just *stopped*—wouldn't move, gone catatonic. Now Doc runs the whole show for the State, manages all the joints for the criminally insane.

Sophie did her time in the psycho ward. She didn't start out there, but they told her what a ticket cost and she bought one. Bit off one of her own nipples and spit it out the cell bars. Doc ran a bunch of brain scans on her, figured her for some kind of seizure disorder. Started her on the medication, and Sophie was coming back to the world. But she terrorized the joint—when she went off, she didn't feel pain. But she sure handed it out. Doc found out she'd had a daughter. Kid would be about fourteen, wherever she was. Asked me to find her. Bring her to the joint, let her mother see her.

Took me almost a month, but I found the kid. On her knees in an alley, waiting for the next trick, not even bothering to get up while her pimp negotiated price with me. I paid the pimp what he was due, brought the kid to Lily. After a while, I took her up to see Sophie, like Doc wanted.

At first, Sophie didn't seem to know her. Then her eyes snapped open. She lunged at me, screaming. Doc had the hypo ready.

"It was worth a try," he said, later.

The little girl's okay now. Maybe she'll see her mother again. On Visiting Day.

Some of the little girls don't make it. Louisa looked up at me from her hospital bed. Sixteen, she was. Huge eyes in what was left of her face. The lost child had turned one too many car tricks. Bad skin and weak bones, held together with scabs and scores. Dying now, and she knew it.

"Anything I can do?" I asked her. "Anything you want?"

She turned her skeleton's face to me, no-soul eyes on the medical chart clipped to her bed. Where her death sentence was spelled out. AIDS. "I'd like my father to fuck me. Just one more time."

She died before she could say his name.

64

The train came in, only about ten minutes late. I took Luke's hand. If he bolted in that place, I'd never catch him. I wished Michelle was with us.

Doc had a dark blue Lands' End canvas bag slung over one shoulder, nothing else. He wasn't planning to stay. We shook hands.

"Doc, this is my friend Luke. Luke, this is Doc."

The boy stuck out his hand, clasped his left hand over Doc's right as they shook. The way I'd done.

The Bronx Zoo is nice and quiet during the weekday. Luke loved it all: the bears, the monorail that ran through a replica of an Asian forest, the jungle cats. I filled Doc in while the kid happily took a camel ride.

"Luke's video-phobic, went rigid when he saw a camera. Don't know much about his parents—a black-market adoption. He killed his baby brother, stabbed him to death. His eyes roll up sometimes. He loses time. In a foster home, he strangled a baby. Doesn't know anything about it. Or the stabbing, either. Genius IQ. Yesterday, he was a baby girl for a while. Doesn't remember that either. The DA knows, wants him to come in. We've only got a little time."

"Who's the DA? Maybe I can talk to him."

"Wolfe. From City-Wide."

"Forget it. Her crew accounts for half the rapist population in my joints."

"I know. I'm not looking for a play from her."

"What do you need me for? You know what's wrong with the kid as well as I do."

"I told you, Doc. The girasol."

Luke climbed off the camel, beaming. We took him to the reptile house. "Think he'll like the chameleons?" Doc asked.

"He doesn't know," I said.

"Don't be so sure," Doc said, watching the boy.

65

The Plymouth poked its way through Hunts Point, heading for the Mole's junkyard.

"Remember Elroy?" I asked Doc.

"Sure. Who could forget him? A rich fantasy life don't make you crazy, but Elroy flirted with it pretty good."

"He's writing a book."

"Why not, hoss? Probably make him rich."

Luke sat between us on the front seat, his hands on the padded dashboard. "You like dogs?" I asked him.

"Some dogs," he said, wary.

"These are wonderful dogs," I promised him. "You'll see."

I stopped the Plymouth at the gate. Waited while Terry came to open it. Pulled inside. The pack swirled around the car. Simba leaped lightly onto the hood, peering in at us through the windshield.

"Is he a wolf?" Luke asked.

"I don't know what he is. But he's the best at it."

Terry came around to the window. He'd been pulled loose from a kiddie pimp in Times Square by Michelle. A war-zone adoption, and Terry was her child. Hers and the Mole's.

"The Mole says to take you back in the shuttle," he said, pointing to an old Jeep, cut down so it had a flatbed rear. We climbed out. Followed Terry through the pack, climbed aboard.

He drove expertly, negotiating the minefield like it was a post-apocalypse gymkhana. Luke's eyes widened—this was wilder than the safari ride at the zoo. We pulled up in a clearing next to the Mole's bunker. The resident lunatic was nowhere in sight. I looked a question at Terry. "Mole won't be around unless you need him, okay?" he answered. "You can work downstairs."

66

Luke's eyes swept the area. The dog pack had reassembled, sitting patiently. Abandoned cars, interwoven with huge pieces of machinery, had rusted into a permanent necklace, blocking any view of the outside. Behind the necklace, a chain link fence topped with razor wire. Dots of firelight on the surrounding flatlands, sounds of diesels chugging past, a siren cut through, faded. The tip of the world. Junkyard or graveyard. The boy took it all in, observing and calm. Interested, not curious.

I started toward the bunker. "Come on, Luke. Let's go downstairs, so we can talk."

The boy stiffened. His little face went rigid, skull showing under the soft skin.

"Basement?" he said, like he didn't have enough air. "Basement?"

"Oh shit," Doc said, moving back to give the boy room.

Terry stepped forward. "It's *not* a basement, pal. Who said that? We don't have basements here. It's safe here, Luke. Burke's going to the cave. A *real* cave, like in the jungle. It's where we go when there's trouble. They can never find you there."

"Cave?"

"Sure. It's fun. We have all kinds of neat stuff there. Want me to show you?"

"I . . . don't know."

"Well, you don't *have* to go. You don't have to do anything you don't want to do. Not here. This is *my* house, see? And you're *my* friend."

"Friend?"

"Sure, my friend. Like I said. I protect my friends, and they protect me. We protect each other. If bad people come around here, we know how to fix them. Fix them real good, I promise."

"Fix them?"

"Sure," Terry said, kneeling next to the boy, not touching him. "Simba!" he called.

The tawny monster bounded into the clearing, ears tipped forward, bushy tail curling up over his back. Terry made a circle gesture with his hand, and the beast whirled in his tracks, facing me and Doc, standing between Terry and Luke.

"Who's in charge here?" he asked Luke. "Me or Burke?"

"Burke is the man," Luke said, more life in his voice now, reasonable.

"And I'm the kid, right?"

Luke nodded.

"Simba, watch!" Terry snapped.

A low warning growl from the beast. He backed up until his tail was brushing Terry, magnificent head swiveling on a narrow arc. Me to Doc, Doc to me.

I took a tentative step forward. Simba lunged at me, blood-ugly snarl from deep inside him. I stepped back. The other dogs made pack-noises behind me—I didn't turn around.

"Simba's *my* dog. Mine and the Mole's. He loves us. Nobody hurts us here. Nobody."

"Would he hurt Burke?"

"He'd kill him," Terry said, matter-of-fact, patting the dog on his shoulder. "Or anybody else."

Luke's little hand reached out, touched the dog. Simba watched us.

I knew better than to say anything.

67

"Come on, Simba," Terry said. He walked to the bunker, Luke right next to him. All three of them disappeared inside.

I walked over to where they'd been standing. Sat on one of the cut-down oil drums the Mole uses for outdoor furniture. Doc took a seat next to me. I lit a smoke.

"Got another one of those?"

"I thought you quit."

"This is one of those times, hoss."

I handed over my pack, cracked a wooden match for him.

"We almost blew it, partner."

"I know."

"Damn! How'd that kid . . . Terry . . . how'd he know what to say?"

"It's what his mother said to him—when she brought him here. His real mother, not the bitch who birthed him. He was a sex rental when he was younger. They can smell it on each other."

"Yeah. They're brothers . . ."

I dragged deep on my cigarette, watching the dog pack. "You got any doubts?" I asked him.

"No. Neither do you. So what am I doing here?"

"Diagnosis."

"Bullshit. You do diagnosis as well as I do. Probably better. Never met anyone who could spot a freak like you—you got a built-in detector. And I can't treat him in one session."

"There's a piece missing, between diagnosis and treatment. We know what he is—we don't know why."

"You don't mean why, hoss . . . you mean who."

"Yeah. That's your piece."

"And then . . ."

"That's mine."

68

Simba came out of the bunker first, Luke right behind him. Then Terry.

"Burke, it's great down there!" Luke greeted me.

"Yeah? What'd you see?"

"A laser. A real laser! It cuts right through steel. And an earthquake machine . . . wow!"

I didn't ask him whether he was talking about the Mole's seismograph or the panel of buttons that would launch big pieces of the junkyard like NASA.

"You ready to go to work now, kid? In the cave?"

"Sure! Can Simba come too?"

I caught Terry's eye. He stepped in next to Luke. "Simba can't come, pal. He's got to go on patrol. Make sure everything's safe. But I'll come with you," his eyes daring me to refuse.

"Okay," Luke said.

Simba trotted off. I led the way downstairs. I sat down on a stool next to the Mole's workbench. Doc pulled up the ottoman to the old leather chair, made himself comfortable. Luke took the armchair, Terry standing next to him, his hand on the smaller boy's shoulder.

Underground. Diffused, natural-sunlight quartz lighting. The industrial ionizer gave the air a fresh, just-after-the-rain smell. Faint hum of machinery. A panel of LEDs blinked a message only Terry and the Mole could understand. Luke gripped the arms of the chair.

Doc started talking, low, soft tones. Just about anything, engaging, drawing Luke along. The kid grew less and less guarded . . . flashing, showing his brilliance, giggling happily when he solved math problems in his head. "You know what this is?" Doc asked, taking a vitreous stone out of his pocket. It was attached to a thin platinum chain.

"A gem?"

"It's a girasol, Luke. A fire opal. Look closely, see the fire, see all the colors?"

The girasol moved in a gentle arc, back and forth. A liquid light show, soft, infinity-depthed. Fire in a teardrop.

The boy's eyes tracked the gem, like he knew what was coming. I breathed through my nose, shallow, measured breaths. Luke slumped in his chair, eyelids fluttering. Doc talked him to it, no pressure, telling the boy how sleepy he was getting.

"Sleepy . . ." Luke agreed, baby-voiced.

"Can I talk to the others?" Doc asked. "Can you let them come out for a minute?"

Luke's eyes rolled straight up into his head, only the whites showing. He blinked rapidly. "Baby, baby, baby." A toddler's voice, maybe two years old. Happy-babble. "Baby, baby, baby."

"What's the baby's name?" Doc.

"Baby. Baby Doll. Doll Baby. Sweet Baby." The boy's features softened, bloblike, drool in one corner of his mouth.

"Hello, Doll Baby. My name is Doc. Want to be friends?"

"Baby, baby, baby . . ."

"Yes, you're a good baby. A handsome little boy . . ."

"She's a girl, stupid." My eyes flicked up to Terry, but he hadn't spoken—standing there, mouth wide open, the color leached from his face.

"What's your name?" Doc asked Luke.

"Toby. Don't you recognize me? What's wrong with you?" Smartass kid's voice, maybe eleven, twelve years old.

"Hello, Toby."

"Yeah, hello. What do you want?"

"I want to talk to you . . . to talk to the others."

"One at a time, pal. That's the way it works. It's my time now."

"Do you come out often?"

"Whenever he's getting tricked. Luke's school-smart, but he don't know people. Not like me."

"And the baby?"

"That's Susie—she's a runaway. When they hurt us, she comes. Runaway. You can't hurt the baby—she doesn't feel things."

"Does that make you mad? When they hurt you?"

"I don't feel it. But when they do things, we remember. We remember. And . . ."

I was ready for it this time, saw the eye movement. The boy's face hardened, bone structure prominent, stretching the skin. "Blood," the skull said. It wasn't a human voice.

Doc didn't miss a beat. "Blood?" he asked.

"Baby blood. Clean new blood. Mine. I need it."

"Who are you?"

"Satan's Child. I am Satan's Child."

"What do you do?"

"I kill," the voice coming from Luke said.

"Who do you kill?"

"I kill babies. Little stupid babies."

"Why do you kill babies?"

"For their hearts. To eat their hearts."

"Why do . . . ?"

Luke launched himself at Doc, humming a baby tune, his eyes screaming. One little hand in a fist, the other pushing against Doc's chest, steadying the target. Stabbing motions, the blows so powerful Doc grunted in pain. I grabbed Luke from behind, pulling—his muscles coiled like steel snakes. I twisted his left hand behind his back. It took all my strength to bend it up toward his neck, right to the breaking point. He kept humming his baby tune, stabbing. Doc fell to the floor, Luke still on top. Terry yelled something. Luke went rigid in my hands, a piece of iron. I put him back in the easy chair. He lay like a board, spine not touching the chair back.

We watched. Luke was drenched in sweat, red and white splattering his face from inside. He went limp. More time passed. Luke squirmed, shrugged his shoulders. Rubbed his eyes like he just woke up.

"Hello, Luke," Doc said.

"Hi. It's a great cave, isn't it? Terry was showing me just before you came down."

"Yes, it's a great cave. How do you feel?"

"I feel good. Can we go to the zoo again someday?"

Doc didn't answer him, watching.

"Can we, Burke?"

"Sure," I told him. Hands in my pocket so he wouldn't see them shake.

69

Outside, in the air. Luke had gone off with Terry. Happy kid, fascinated with the secrets the older boy was going to show him. I handed Doc my pack of smokes without him asking.

"You ever see it before?" I asked him.

"Multiple Personality Disorder? Sure. I did a stint in a mental hospital while I was interning. You see it in women much more than men. Never saw a kid before, but it's supposed to always start in childhood . . . we're just not around to pick it up."

"You're sure?"

"The personalities have names. Different voices. The last one . . . you felt his strength?"

"Yeah. I could barely hold him."

"The big thing . . . he's amnesic. He loses time. You ask him what happened down there, he won't know. Push him hard enough, and he'll make it up . . . fill in the gaps."

"Lily says he does that. Fakes it."

"He's not faking, Burke. What he does, it's called confabulation. He can't account for the lost time, doesn't know what happened. But he knows *something* did. He's not ready to let anybody see his secret."

"Does he know we know?"

"No . . . I don't think so. Maybe some small part of him, some observer-personality. Sometimes, one of the personalities can listen in on what the others are doing. I don't know how distinct the splits are . . . there may be more of them inside."

A dog howled in the distance.

"He killed those babies," I said.

"Luke didn't . . . it was the other one. They're as separate and distinct as you and me."

"Tell it to the judge."

"I know."

"How'd he . . . ?"

"Get like that? Take a highly intelligent, sensitive child, subject him to intense, inescapable trauma . . . and he learns to dissociate. Escape inside his head. Splitting, it starts as. Some kids, it gets real. Child abuse, especially sexual abuse, that's the key predisposing factor."

"It's not genetic?"

"Not a chance. Two multiples could mate, and you wouldn't get another one from the union. Unless . . ."

I looked across at him, waiting.

"Unless they did the same things to him."

"You think . . . ?"

"I don't know what I think. This much you can take to the bank: you don't get a multiple personality without some severe, chronic trauma. Intense deprivation, torture . . . you know the game, how they play it. It'll take a while to sort it out. Lots of sessions. He's a good hypnotic subject . . . but he's got to feel safe before we can do anything."

"Is there a program?

"The way you treat multiples is with individual psychotherapy. Out-patient, generally. They save the closed facilities for the dangerous ones. When one of the personalities is homicidal. Or an arsonist, a rapist, whatever."

"You know a place?" I asked him.

"None that would take a kid."

70

I knew places that would take Luke. The same places that took me when I was a kid. They got different names for them, but they're all the same.

When I got my growth, I found other places. Places where Luke had already paid the price of admission. Places where they'd never look for him.

71

"You can never leave him alone," I told Immaculata. "Never, you understand?"

Luke was in the armchair across from us, the baby Flower balanced carefully on one small knee, a picture book opened flat on the other. Talking quietly to the baby, his spindly arm around her back, pointing at the pictures. He felt our eyes.

"I'm teaching her to read," he said. Luke's voice.

"That's very sweet, Luke," Immaculata said. "Could you read when you were so little?"

"Oh yes."

"And who taught you?"

"They did. They taught me . . ." Rapid eye blinks, bead of sweat on the bridge of his nose.

"You love the baby, Luke?" I asked, moving close to him like I wanted to talk, hands ready. "She's a beautiful baby, isn't she, Luke?" Saying his name, anchoring the peg in the slot.

"Everyone loves Flower," he said, himself.

"It's time for her nap," Immaculata said.

"I'll put her to bed."

Max stepped into the room. Bowed to Luke, then to me, then to Mac. He reached down, took the baby from Luke, his scarred hands armor plate around the delicate skin. Flower gurgled happily, safe.

"Go with Max, see if he needs help," Immaculata told Luke. "Make sure he's careful."

"I'll watch him," Luke said.

I lit a smoke. "You have it worked out?" I asked her.

"Yes. Teresa, the psychiatrist . . . do you know her?"

I shook my head no.

"Well, she says Luke has to have a routine, something he can trust. So she's going to see him every day, six days a week, one day off. Some days we'll take him to her office, some days she'll come to him. Mornings, I'll drop him off at Mama's—if somebody comes in there, there's a dozen places he can hide."

"After dark?"

"Luke will sleep here. With us. Flower's crib is in our room, between the window and the bed."

"He may try anyway . . . Max understands?"

Her sculptured face turned up to mine. "Better than I do," she said.

72

I went back to earning my living. Pulled the Plymouth into a spot on Central Park West, got out, sniffed the air. A large, frizzy-haired woman in an orange muumuu was trying to wedge her old Toyota into a spot between a white Honda Prelude and a beige Mercedes sedan using the park-by-Braille technique. She left them both worse for wear, stepped out, patted her hands together in satisfaction. I snapped the lead on Pansy. The woman noted the lack of a pooper-scooper in my hand, made a face like she smelled something bad. I stepped into the park.

Ten-thirty in the morning, most of the citizens already at work. A man and a woman came up the path, wearing matching shorts and jogging jerseys. Even had the same numbers on the back. Cute. Pansy sat next to me as I lit a cigarette. The woman grimaced disapproval as they pranced by.

A white stretch limo purred past, the back windows blacked out. "Very subtle, Carlos," I thought to myself, dragging on the cigarette, watching like I'd been taught. By now, I knew what was in the limo. One of the Prof's pack worked in the detailing shop where Carlos' driver brought the car in every week for sweetening. Cellular phone, color TV with VCR, fax machine, hand-rubbed teak bar with cut-crystal decanters, cashmere throw rugs on the blue leather seats, a pullout mirror so *el jefe*'s girlfriends could check their makeup before they hit the clubs. A hidden compartment in a hollowed-out door panel. Not for drugs: Carlos didn't touch the extra-strength dreamdust he peddled. No tiny rocks of crack for this boy—he dealt in weight. You want to cut it yourself, step on it, bake it, fry it, that's up to you.

It always worked the same way. The limo would glide to a stop— a man on a bike would pedal up alongside, a nylon gym bag slung over his left shoulder. The window would whisper down as the biker held the bag open. Something would drop in and off he'd go.

By now, we knew where the transfer-man went. Steaming along the bicycle path like he was leading the Tour de Chump, he'd leave the park and merge with the street traffic. A car would pull up alongside him. Sometimes a sedan, sometimes a wagon. Once it was a panel truck. A hand would reach out from the passenger side, pluck the bag from his shoulder.

Once we had it down just right, it would be our hand reaching for the cash.

The Prof was somewhere in the park, his pack scattered around.

Hard-souled homeboys, paying their tuition to the master, OJT on the highwire. One slip and it's Attica.

I patted Pansy's sleek head, sitting next to her on the grass, back to myself.

73

"What kind of dog is that?"

She was a chunky, freckle-faced woman, reddish-brown hair bursting in all directions from under the sweatband around her head, wearing a plain gray sweatshirt over blue bicycle pants, slate-colored running shoes. Little pug nose, china-blue eyes.

"A Neapolitan mastiff," I said.

"I never saw one before. Are they rare?"

"*She* is. The world's finest dog, aren't you, girl?" Pansy grinned happily, probably thinking of a marrow bone, how they cracked in her jaws before she got to the sweet center.

"What're you doing here?"

I looked hard into her innocent eyes, wondering how old she was.

"Exercising my dog—she needs room to run."

"You let that big dog off the leash?"

"Meaning I don't look like I run with her?"

"You're not dressed for it." She chuckled.

"I'm on my way to work."

"What do you do?" Hands on hips, tip of her tongue just poking past her lips.

I looked up at her, face flat. "What do *you* do?"

"I'm a hit-woman," smile slashing across her broad face. "Trying to kill this cellulite." Smacking the back of one thigh.

"I hope you don't overdo it."

"Why?"

"Women do that. You all have a mass psychosis about weight."

"If we do, it's men who gave it to us."

"Not guilty," I said, trying a smile.

"That's what they all say," she shot back, pulling her sweatshirt over her head, tying it around her waist. Her breasts flared under a white T-shirt as she arched her back.

I lit a cigarette. Her nose didn't wrinkle.

"Could I pat your dog?" she asked.

"Only if she likes you," I told her.

"How would I know?"

"If she likes you, she'll . . . Wow! Look at that," I said, marveling at how Pansy lay down in response to my hand signal.

"That means she likes me?"

"Sure."

She dropped to her knees on the grass, stroking Pansy expertly, talking to her.

"You have a dog?"

"I had a dog. Blackie. When I was a kid. I still miss him."

Pansy's slab of a tongue lolled from her wide mouth, enjoying the attention.

"Would you like to have dinner with me sometime?" she asked.

"Yes."

"I'm Belinda Roberts."

I held out my hand for her to shake, told her one of my names.

"I'll write down my number. Do you have a piece of paper?"

"I'll remember it," I told her.

She pulled my eyes with hers, seeking the truth. Finally nodded. "Okay," she said.

Got to her feet, tied the sweatshirt around her neck, jogged off. Very fine.

74

The white limo whispered by again. Empty now.

Done for the day, I got to my feet, unsnapped Pansy's lead, told her to heel. She took the point on my left side, shoulder against my thigh.

I cut through the trees to where I'd parked. A black man in a black suit sitting on a tree stump stood up as I approached, a dull silver automatic in his hand.

"Just stand still, mahn."

I stopped, Pansy next to me.

"I don't have any money," I said, letting fear snake its way into my voice to settle him down.

"This is no robbery, mahn. Just come along with me. Somebody wants to talk with you."

"Who?"

"Don't be stalling now, mahn. Just come along, take a nice ride."

"I'm not going anywhere, pal."

"Yes, you're coming, Mr. Burke. See, we know you. Don't be stupid, now."

"You won't hurt me?"

"No, mahn, we don't hurt you."

"What about my dog? . . . I can't leave her here."

"Just tie her to a tree, mahn. You be back very soon. Nobody take a big dog like that."

"But . . ."

"Last chance, mahn."

"Okay, okay," I said, reassuring him, reaching over to snap the leash on my dog, talking to her. Just as I was about to fasten the leash, I said, "Pansy, sit!," watching the gunman almost imperceptibly relax at the words just as Pansy launched herself without a sound, clamping her vise-grip jaws on his arm. I picked his gun off the grass, snapped "Out!"

at Pansy, and she backed off. The gunman was down, moaning, left hand gripping his right forearm, blood bubbling between his fingers.

"My arm! She crushed the bone, mahn! It's all water in there."

"Who wants me?" I asked him, bending close, patting his body, looking for another gun—came up empty. "You need a doctor, need one bad," I said. "Tell me and you can go."

Creamy dots on his dark-skinned face, pain in his eyes.

"You want the dog again?" I asked.

His eyes shot around the clearing. It was empty, nobody around. I felt ice in my spine—was Clarence in on this?

"Thana," he muttered.

"What?"

"Queen Esther Thana, mahn. The Mamaloi." His eyes sweeping the area again, looking for something.

"You know my name. Tell her to call me. On the phone, understand?"

He grunted something, sounded like yes. The gunman could walk himself into the Emergency Room. Where the triage nurse would ask him if he had Blue Cross.

I turned away, pocketed his gun, slapped my thigh for Pansy to come along.

Clarence was sitting on a bench near my car. "Better let me hold the gun, mahn," he said.

I palmed it to him.

"There was another one with him," Clarence said. "They have a car waiting for you. One block down," indicating with his eyes. "Better come with me."

He got up and started in the other direction. I walked next to him, Pansy right alongside.

"What happened to the other one?" I asked him.

The cobalt eyes were calm. "He's still there," Clarence said.

75

Clarence opened the back door of his Rover. I gave the signal and Pansy clambered inside. Clarence threw a smooth U-turn on CPW, heading back downtown.

"Where shall I drop you, mahn?"

"How come you were around today, Clarence?"

He shrugged his slim shoulders, face expressionless. "I'm just a soldier, mahn."

"Then take me to the general," I told him.

76

Clarence turned east on Fifty-seventh, working his way to the FDR, then south to the Brooklyn Bridge.

"That's some dog you got, mahn. Never saw something so big move so fast."

"She's the best," I said, reaching back to pat my pal.

"Pretty woman you got there too, mahn."

"Pretty woman?"

"Yes, mahn. In the park. Pretty woman. Nice big butt on her. Never trust a woman with one of those little-boy butts, it's a sure sign."

"Who told you that?"

"Everybody knows, mahn. Big butt, big heart."

I thought of my Blue Belle, gone now. The fire-scar on Flood's rump. Blossom walking away. Maybe it was true.

I rolled down my window, lit a smoke. "You saw the woman in the park?"

"Yes, mahn. Like I said. Good age on her too. Not like some of those flighty young girls. Just right for an old man like you."

"Yeah. You were there a long time, huh?"

"All the time, mahn. Ever since you call Jacques."

"How'd you pick me up?"

"Easy enough, mahn. Your car, the places you go, all like that."

"Where else?"

"The shelter-place. The one for kids. The restaurant. I'm a shadow, mahn. Thin and dark. Nobody sees."

"I appreciate what you did, Clarence."

"You have been our friend, mahn. Jacques said."

"Here's some friendly advice for you, Clarence. Don't go into that restaurant."

"I know, mahn."

"Who told you . . . Jacques?"

"Everybody knows, mahn."

77

Jacques was at his table in the basement. He didn't blink at Pansy. Pansy didn't blink back.

Clarence handed him the pistol I'd taken from the man in the park. Jacques released the clip, pulling it from the butt, worked the slide.

"Empty, mahn. Nothing in the chamber. Safety was on too."

I nodded. The gunman was what he said he was—not a shooter.

Jacques turned the gun over in his hands, put one polished thumbnail inside the chamber, sighted down the barrel. "Hasn't been cleaned in a year, mahn. A piece of junk. Iron Curtain stuff, not even military." Jacques's fine-boned nose curled into a faint sneer. "Whoever had this, mahn, he was not a professional."

"There was another one," Clarence told him.

Jacques raised his eyebrows, waiting for the rest.

"He had no gun, nothing. And he never saw me coming," Clarence said, a leather-covered sap in his hand, showing Jacques what had happened to the watcher.

"You talked to the man with the gun?"

"He said he just wanted to take me someplace. To see someone named Thana. Queen Thana."

Jacques's eyes didn't change but his cheeks went hollow.

"You know her?" I asked.

"Everybody knows *of* her, mahn. I have not met her. And I do not want to. Obeah. Very powerful obeah. A voodoo priestess. Her followers are all from the Islands. People say she can make a man do what she wants. That she can kill you with a thought. Reach across the sea, back across time."

"She's in business?"

"Not our business, mahn. Not for money. But she is no love goddess, that one. A warrior priestess. They say her soldiers are the dead come back to life."

"What does she want from me?"

"I do not know, mahn. But if she wants you, she will find you."

"You can reach out to her?"

"No, mahn. Not with the phone. But I know . . . some things. I can, maybe, get a message through."

"The bag . . . the juju bag," Clarence whispered.

"What?"

"That was hers, maybe. Swinging from that tree in the moonlight. Evil. She knows."

"Knows what?"

"I went back. Later, I went back. In the daylight. And the bag, it was gone."

I lit a smoke, hands steadying with the answer. She hadn't taken the bag, but her watchers knew who did.

"Tell her I'll come and talk to her," I told Jacques, and walked out of the basement.

78

In prison, I used to lift weights. Just to be doing something—I was never any good at it. Bench presses. Some days they put too much weight on the bar—I couldn't get it up off my chest.

I felt like that now. Put a cardiogram on my life, you'd get a readout: sharp spikes, deep valleys.

I drew a red dot on a piece of mirror. Drew it with some lipstick Belle had left behind. I'd been meaning to throw it out for a long time now, that lipstick. I went into a halfass lotus position, looking into the dot. Until it got bigger and bigger, deeper. I went down inside, clearing my mind.

There's always a pattern. Any crazy thing makes sense to somebody at the other end. I didn't know anything about smuggling until I went to prison. You can get whatever you want inside the walls if you can pay the freight. Guards smuggled in guns, but they never crossed the color line: you wanted a pistol, you asked a guard of your own race. Drugs they'd sell to anyone.

In prison, there's lead pipes just lying around. If you hold them just right, you can still feel them vibrate with the skulls they've crushed.

I pictured a lovely glass ball. As pure as a teardrop, on a polished black marble surface. Pictured it rising from the table, floating gently in the air, hovering. I was holding it up with my will.

I blinked my eyes and came out of it just before the glass ball splattered on the marble.

79

Meetings. Always bullshit meetings. Talk talk talk. And rules. Made by the rulers. In prison, what you want is to get through it. You can't stay by yourself—they won't let you. So you mob up. Get a crew. Someone to watch your back. On the Coast, they call it getting in the car. Going along for the ride. Or the drive-by. If a crew splits up, the other side picks them off one by one, so you stay together. You change sides, nobody trusts you. The first choice is the only one you get.

I wished I could explain it to Wolfe and Lily.

80

I stayed out of the loop for a while. Prairie dog careful—just barely peeking out of my hole in the ground, ready to spook if I saw a strange shadow. Wolfe's time limit pushed me back up to ground level.

Max opened the back door to SAFE, held it while I slipped inside. I don't know how he does that—he can't hear my knock. He pointed toward the back office, made a "be careful" gesture, and went back to the gym.

Lily was standing with her back to me, hands on hips, arguing about something with a calmly seated Storm. I tapped lightly on the doorjamb. Lily whirled, not missing a beat.

"What is it, Burke? We're busy here."

"I needed to talk with you," I said mildly.

"Your telephone's broken?"

"I didn't know who'd be listening."

"Who'd be . . ." Lily sneered.

"Wolfe," Storm cut in.

"She wouldn't . . ."

"Sure she would," Storm told her. "What's wrong with you, girl? You know how she is."

"I thought I knew."

"That's what she's saying to herself right about now," I replied, even-toned, "saying it about you. You're doing what you're doing to protect a kid . . . so's she. Just different kids."

"She doesn't know Luke," Lily said. "All she knows is crimes— that's all she cares about."

"Stop it, Lily," Storm said, lighting her one cigarette of the day. "The doctor says stress is bad for my baby."

Lily fought a giggle. "Sure."

I lit a smoke of my own. "I got an idea," I told her.

Storm silenced Lily with a look. I went on like I hadn't seen it.

"Wolfe doesn't know Luke, that's what you said, right? *That's* the idea. How about if they meet?"

"Sure. What's a kidnapping on top of everything else?"

"Not a kidnapping, Lily. I'll make a deal with her."

Storm tapped her fingers on the desk, thinking. Lily brushed some of her thick glossy hair away from her face, waiting.

"She won't break her word," I said.

"It's true," Storm added.

"She's clever, though." Lily came back, stubborn-sulky.

"And you're glad enough for that, most of the time," I told her. "What's happening, you're all convinced you're right. You know what Wolfe wants . . . what she really wants?"

"She wants the killing to stop," Storm said.

"And she wants someone to pay," Lily put in. "That's Wolfe— someone always has to pay."

I sat on a corner of the desk, where I could see both of them. "Once I was involved in this case. Guy killed his mother. Pointed a .357 magnum at her face, blew out the back of her head. The defense attorney put him on a polygraph. Asked him: Did you kill your mother? Answer:

No. And the machine said: No Deception Indicated—Truthful. That's when the lawyer called me in. Figured, bad as it looked, it must be that someone else had done it, understand?"

They both nodded. Storm interested, Lily suspicious.

"So I talked to the man, where they had him locked up. I'd seen guys like him before, when I was inside. Anyway, I went back to the lawyer, asked him to try the polygraph again, only this time ask *my* questions. So they asked him again: Did you kill your mother? No. Then: Did the gun kill your mother? Yes. Were you holding the gun when it killed your mother? Yes."

"What's your point?" Lily wanted to know. "That you have to ask the right questions?"

"What if the guy was telling the truth?" I fired back.

"Huh?"

"What if he was telling the truth? What if it was the gun who killed his mother? Not him, the gun."

"I understand what you're getting at, Burke," Storm said, "but I don't see how it helps us. The gun couldn't do the killing by itself."

"Neither could Luke."

Lily walked right up in my face, her chin tilted at an aggressive angle. "What?" she demanded.

"You know Wolfe, how she is about playing with the law. Remember the time she proved that rapist wasn't having 'flashbacks'? No 'Vietnam Vet syndrome'? Remember when she shredded that 'episodic dyscontrol' defense . . . when that guy shot his wife and said he had some kind of brain seizure that made him do it?"

"You're a real fan of hers, huh?"

"Oh, chill out, Lily," Storm said. "Burke, all the stuff you talked about, it was Wolfe fighting some sophisticated defense. That's what she does, she attacks . . . not defends."

"No, that's not what she does. Not all of it. *Victims* get defended, right?"

"Or avenged." Lily.

"Yeah, or avenged. Sometimes both. But how about this: Luke comes in, okay? The defense is this Multiple Personality Disorder. Insanity, okay? And Wolfe'll know the kid's crazy—no way he's faking—he'll stand up to any test. But you can't end up like Luke unless somebody does something to you. Something real ugly. For a long time."

"You think she'd want to go after Luke's parents? For child abuse?"

"Not for child abuse, Storm. For homicide. Like Luke was the gun, but they pulled the trigger."

Nobody said anything.

I lit another smoke, letting it percolate.

Storm made a noise. "The baby kicked," she said.

I bowed. "She agrees with me."

Lily smiled her Madonna's smile. "You really think she'd go for it?"

"She's *your* sister," I reminded her. "You tell me."

81

I went by the restaurant the next morning, to check my messages before I called Wolfe. Immaculata was at the register. A fear-jolt hit me—I never saw anybody but Mama there before.

"Where's Mama?" I asked her. "You taking over for her?"

"Downstairs. With Luke."

Something in her voice. I came close, leaned over to her. Her face was set in hard straight lines, white streaks under the golden skin, jaw tight, eyes moist.

"What?"

"He . . . tried last night. Max had to hold him. Flower . . . she woke up. He was . . . like demons in him. When he finally stopped, he just slept. This morning . . . like it was nothing. I brought him here."

"Do you want . . . ?"

"No! I'm just . . ."

"I know," I told her. Like trying to sleep in prison. With the cell doors unlocked.

82

I left her there. Called the DA's office. They told me Wolfe was on trial, in Long Island City, Part L-3. Bureau chiefs don't try cases. I put it together. Threw on my lawyer suit and headed out to Queens.

When I walked in the courtroom, Mary Beth was already on the stand. That's the way Wolfe trained them: no prelims, no dancing—come out throwing bombs, try and drop the other guy soon as you hear the bell. Lola was leading the little girl through her testimony, her body language suggesting she was pulling softly, coaxing the child out past her fear. Bringing the monster into the light. Lola's slim body was a gently weaving wand in front of the little girl, pacing back and forth on her high heels, blocking the defendant's view of the witness box.

Sheba sat next to Mary Beth, the little girl's hand on her head. The dog's eyes followed Lola.

"Just one more question, Mary Beth. You told us what he did, what he did to you. It went on a long time—how come you never told anyone?"

"He said . . . he told me he'd make something bad happen to Mommy. He said he'd made her get sick and die. He showed me . . . in the paper . . . where a little girl's mother got sick and died. He said he did that to her. Because the little girl told."

"No further questions," Lola said, sitting down as Mary Beth brushed tears off her cheeks.

The defendant's lawyer got to his feet. A fat, jowly man, his hair was plastered to his scalp with sweat, carefully combed up and over his head from one side to advertise his baldness.

"Your Honor, I again renew my objection to the presence of that animal while the witness testifies. The *Rulon* decision clearly holds that . . ."

The judge was a regal-looking woman, reddish-blonde hair cut stylishly short, square shoulders, almost a military bearing. I'd seen her before—she started out in Family Court, where they get closer to the truth. Hard to tell her age, but her eyes were old. "Counselor," she said, "the court is familiar with the *Rulon* case. That involved a witness who testified sitting on the lap of a social worker. Surely it is not your position that the dog is signaling to the witness?"

"No, Your Honor. But . . ."

"The court has already ruled, sir. You may have a continuing objection, and your exception to my ruling. Ask your questions."

Sheba watched the fat attorney like he was mutton in a three-piece suit.

The questioning wasn't much. The usual: Did she ever watch horror movies? Ever see a porno tape on the VCR in her mother's house? Have bad dreams? Anybody tell her what to say?

Mary Beth answered the questions. Sometimes the judge had to tell her to speak up a little bit, but she was getting through it. Patting Sheba, drawing comfort and strength.

The defense attorney asked, "Do you know it's a sin to tell a lie, Mary Beth?"—stepping aside dramatically so the jury would understand it was his client being lied about.

"I know it's a sin," the child said, calmly. "I'm not lying."

"She can't see me!" the defendant hissed suddenly, whispering for his lawyer's ear but loud enough for everyone to hear. "She can't see without her glasses."

Wolfe was on her feet and charging forward like they just rang the bell for the last round and she needed a KO to pull it out. "Was that an objection?" she snarled.

"Yes, that was an objection!" the defense attorney shouted, scrambling to clean up the mess the molester made. "My client is being denied his Sixth Amendment right to confrontation."

"He doesn't want confrontation, he wants terrorism. The law says he gets to see and hear the witness—it doesn't say anything about her having to stare at the likes of him."

"That's enough," the judge snapped. "Take the jury out."

The court officers hustled the jurors away as everyone sat in silence. One of Wolfe's people took Mary Beth and Sheba out a side door. The judge turned to the lawyers.

"That will be just about enough, counselors. You both know better than to make arguments like that in front of a jury. I don't want to hear a lot of rhetoric now. Mr. Simmons, have you any authority for the proposition that the Sixth Amendment requires a witness to wear corrective lenses?"

"Not specifically, Your Honor. But if she can't even *see* the witness, how can she identify him?"

"She already did that, counsel. On the prosecution's direct case, remember?"

"Yes, I remember. But she was wearing her glasses then."

"What's your point?"

"My client has rights."

"None that have been abridged by this court. Now . . . that won't be necessary, Ms. Wolfe . . . I have already ruled. Bring the jury back in."

"Your Honor, in light of your ruling, I have no choice but to ask for a mistrial."

"On what grounds, counselor?"

"Prejudice, Your Honor. The jury heard what my client said. A statement like that will poison their minds."

"Are you claiming the prosecution caused your client's outburst, Mr. Simmons?"

"Well, yes . . . I mean, if they hadn't . . ."

"Denied! Let's go."

Wolfe turned away from the bench to return to her seat. Caught my eye.

The defense attorney stood up again. "Your Honor, may I have a few minutes with my client before the jury comes back in?"

"No, counsel, you may not."

"Your Honor, I ask for this time because I believe it might promote a settlement of this matter."

"There is no settlement," Lola snapped out at him. "It's too damn late for that."

"I don't need your permission to plead to the indictment," the defense attorney shot back.

"Then do it. It's a B felony, and we're asking for the max."

"Your Honor, could we approach?"

The judge nodded. Wolfe and Lola came up on one side, the defense attorney on the other. Couldn't hear what they were saying. Finally, the defense attorney walked back to his table, began talking urgently to his client, waving his arms.

I felt it coming.

The defense attorney stood up one last time. "Your Honor, my client has authorized me to withdraw his plea of Not Guilty and to plead to the indictment as charged. My client is a very ill man. Besides that, he wishes to spare the young lady the trauma of cross-examination. I believe . . ."

"Counselor, save your presentation for the dispositional phase of these proceedings. If your client wants to change his plea, I will take his allocution."

They kept the jury out of the courtroom while the defendant admitted the whole thing. His lawyer promised extensive psychiatric testimony to *explain* the whole thing. Lola and Wolfe sat silently.

The judge discharged the jury, thanking them for their attention. I watched their faces—the defense attorney had read them right—if they had gotten their chance, his client was going down.

The defense attorney asked for bail to be continued. Lola pointed out the defendant was now a convicted felon, facing mandatory imprisonment, with great motivation to flee the jurisdiction.

The judge listened, asked the defense if there was any rebuttal. Listened again. Then she revoked the defendant's bail, slammed her gavel for emphasis, and walked off the bench.

The fat defense attorney turned to Wolfe and Lola. "You just put a very sick man in prison. I hope you're pleased with yourselves."

Wolfe and Lola looked at the lawyer, blank expressions on their faces. Then they slapped each other a loud high-five.

83

She stopped in the aisle next to where I was seated, like she'd forgotten something. Never looked down.

"I need to talk to you," I said, just past a whisper.

"You know the Sun Bear bar. On Continental, just off Queens Boulevard?"

"I can find it."

"Seven o'clock," she said, walking away.

84

I got away from the courthouse complex. Found a pay phone and went to work.

"My bread is upon the waters, mahn," Jacques said. "When a message comes back, I will reach out for you."

"Okay, thanks. Is Clarence around?"

"Yes, my friend. He is around *you*. Guard your health."

"Gardens," Mama answered the phone.

"It's me, Mama."

She waited, not saying anything. Hell, she's the one who taught me.

"Is the boy there?"

"Sure, boy here. Good boy, helps Mama."

"Doesn't he have an appointment? You understand . . . ?"

"Sure, understand. With the lady. Lady come here now."

"Every day?"

"Sure, every day."

"Okay, anybody call?"

"Your friend, say to meet him at car wash, tomorrow at seven."

She didn't say who called. Didn't need to.

"Thanks, Mama."

She hung up.

85

Plenty of time. I found a Korean joint in Jamaica, combination green-grocery and deli. I was eating a bagel and cream cheese, sipping a cold Ginseng-Up, watching the owner's daughter test pineapples for ripeness by pulling up on the stalks. If the stalk comes out, the pineapple's ready to eat. The cash register had two sliced lemon halves on either side on the drawer. The clerk ran his fingers across the lemon's surface as he counted bills. Big sign by the register. NO CHANGE. A stocky guy with one of those small-billed painter's caps turned backward on his head came in, mumbled something about change for the bus. The counter-clerk pointed at the sign, said something in Korean. The guy kept pressing, raising his voice, sounding drunk. I came up behind him, tapped him on the shoulder. He whirled on me, face snarled. "You got a problem?" I shook my head, smiled. "No," I told him, "I got change." I gave it to him. He swaggered out of the joint, sneering. A guy who knows the score—probably bets on pro wrestling. Before the clerk took the money for my bill, he slipped the revolver he'd been holding back under the counter.

86

The main branch of the Queens Public Library wasn't far away. I parked in the lot nearby, went inside. Used the InfoSearch computer to track down articles on Multiple Personality Disorder. There were a lot of them. Found a quiet place to myself. Killed some time.

The Sun Bear had little round marble tables scattered all around, long dark wood bar against one wall, blue smoke mirror behind. Wolfe was sitting alone, wearing a plum-colored sheath, black stockings, and matching heels with ankle straps. Her hair was tied up in a loose knot with a black ribbon around it. Man sitting one table away: sunglasses hooked over some gold chains resting on his chest, gold coin ring on his little finger. He shot back a cuff, checked his watch. More gold.

I walked up on Wolfe's left just as he approached from the right. Focused on his target, he didn't see me.

Wolfe dragged deeply on her cigarette, eyes straight ahead.

The man leaned over her table. "I wish *I* was that cigarette," he said, flashing a mouthful of caps, white against tan.

Wolfe took the cigarette out of her mouth. Looked at it carefully. "So do I," she said, looking right into his face. Dropped the cigarette to the barroom floor, ground it out with the tip of one shoe.

The man flushed red under his tan just as I pulled out a chair, sat down next to Wolfe.

He muttered something as he walked away.

Wolfe turned to me, smiled. "I think that man just called you a runt."

I ordered a ginger ale from the Japanese waitress. Wolfe took a beer.

"Nice job today," I said.

She shrugged. "The real work is always before the trial. You train to go the distance, sometimes it ends early."

"And sometimes, they add a few rounds at the end."

"What does that mean?"

"Two weeks . . . remember?"

"Sure."

"Things happen."

"Yes. Like babies getting killed."

"I know. I'm in the middle."

"No, you're not, Mr. Burke. You're nowhere in this at all. What's between Lily and me . . . well, that's a lot of things. But one thing it isn't—it isn't *you*, understand?"

"I didn't mean between you and Lily," I said. Mildly, to take the edge off her harsh tone. "I mean between two right things, okay?"

"There aren't *two* right things. There never are."

"You're sure?"

"Yes."

"Would you be willing to take a look—make sure it's always that way?"

"Take a look at what?"

"At some things I found . . ." Rushing ahead as her eyebrows went up. "I'd have to take you there."

"Just give me the address."

"I can't do that."

She lit another smoke, ghost of a smile curling around the filter in her mouth. "You want me to wear a blindfold?"

"No. I'd trust you."

Her eyes were a gray-green, set wide apart. "Let's do it with the blindfold," she said.

"I'll let you know. Soon."

87

I was at Lily's a little past nine. The programs were winding down for the evening—the place was jammed with mothers and fathers picking up their kids. That's what they call whoever comes for the kids—parents. Biology doesn't count down here.

Max spotted me. Put a finger to his lips, motioning for me to come with him. He led me to the one-way glass on the side wall of one of the treatment rooms. Inside, Immaculata, in the lotus position, dressed in a loose white cotton outfit. Facing her a couple of feet away, Luke. Her arms gently parted the air, like she was conducting an orchestra in slow motion. The kid followed along, copying every gesture. Max tapped my shoulder, pointed at his stomach. Inhaled deeply through his nose, expanding his stomach. He exhaled sharply, in a steady, powerful stream, his chest growing as the air poured out. Yoga breathing. He pointed back into the treatment room. Luke had a blissful look on his little face as Immaculata pressed both hands against her midsection, exhaling as Max had done. Luke was with her, locked in synch.

Lily was in her office, talking at her daughter Noelle, the dark-eyed limit-tester. Noelle's around fifteen, couple years older than Terry. Lily snapped something at the kid, who responded by cocking her head the exact same way her mother does.

I stepped inside, lighting a smoke. Mother and daughter both made a face. "Hi, Burke!" the kid said.

"Hello, Noelle. How's school?"

"It's summertime," she said, like I was brain-damaged.

"Okay. Listen, I need to talk to Lily for a minute."

"Where did you get that suit?" she asked, ignoring what I'd said.

"Orchard Street."

"What's it made of?" Stepping over to me, fingering the lapel.

"I don't know."

"It doesn't look like anything."

"It's not supposed to, Noelle."

"Oh, ugh!" She was wearing black leather high-top shoes, white anklets with little red hearts on the cuffs, black bicycle pants to her knees, a gauzy white skirt over the pants, cheerleader-length, a black silk tank top covered by a red bolero jacket. Two earrings in one ear, no makeup, her glossy black hair cut in a radical wedge, jaunty white beret on her head. I was her father, I'd start stockpiling weapons.

"Noelle . . ." Warning note from Lily.

"I'm going, Mother." She looked at me again. Turned to Lily: "Could I buy Burke a decent jacket . . . something nice, so he'd have a look?"

A smile blossomed on Lily's face. "Sure, you want to waste your money."

Noelle pivoted like a ballerina, held her hand out to me. "Give me some money, I'll get something for you."

Lily chuckled. "How much money?" I asked.

"Oh . . . three hundred dollars, okay?"

"No."

"You want me to buy junk?"

"Look, I'm perfectly happy with what I got, okay?"

"Oh, *pul-eeze*, Burke. Your gear is seriously heinous. How about two hundred?"

"For two hundred, do I get something *stuupid* dope hype fresh?"

"Oh, you're so down there," she giggled. "Okay, two hundred."

"How about one hundred? And how about you leave your mom and me alone?"

She held out her chubby child's hand again. I put a couple of fifties in it. "Thank you *so* much," she said, no sarcasm, just a trace of breathiness. Practicing, getting it right. Then she gave her mother a kiss and made a dignified exit.

88

"How's it going?" I asked Lily.

"He's coming along. It's not something you can do in a week."

"I know. Not in ten days, either."

Lily put her elbows on the desk, nestling her chin in the V of her fists. "What are you saying?"

"I got an idea. Or the beginning of one, anyway."

"Before you play around with any ideas, you should look at this stuff," indicating a handful of paper covered with typing.

I looked a question at her.

"Treatment reports," she said. "From Teresa."

89

I let Pansy out to her roof, made us each some supper while she took her pre-dump stroll. Then I sat down to read the reports. Had to hold the pages almost at arm's length to make out the words. I'd need reading glasses soon.

Hair fell into my eyes. I combed it back with my fingers. Seemed like they were sliding through easier than they used to these days.

The report was a war-zone dispatch—no overheated adjectives, no proposal writer's lies . . . cold truth. They were at the stage where they could call up the individual personalities, speak to them like they were different people in the room. I used the stuff I learned from the library like a Rosetta Stone, read it through.

Individualized Reactions to Psychotropics:

The core personality (Luke) was administered a single dose (1¼ mg) Valium, PO. Within 45 minutes, subject was almost comatose, language was fragmented, dream-state, startle-response almost nonexistent, pinprick produced no reaction.

At session #6, subject hooked to IV, simple glucose solution administered. No reaction. Hypnosis brought "Satan's Child" to surface. Subject was in a rage, restrained by flex-straps. In this state, 10 mg Valium administered IV. No reaction: subject remained agitated, angry. When "Satan's Child" personality departed, "Toby" emerged . . . and promptly fell asleep. IV immediately discontinued.

Conclusion: The varying personalities are physiologically as well as psychologically distinct. The violent personality accesses significantly greater adrenaline flow, exceeding even limbic rage, producing phenomenal strength disproportionate to age and physical structure.

The report went on. More about "core personality" and "fusion goals." But every word sang the same song.

Inside Luke, different children.

One a monster.

90

I nosed the Plymouth east on Houston Street, covering the distance from the West Village to the Lower East Side in minutes. Turned right on Ludlow, right again on Delancey, back the way I'd come.

The car wash is on the corner of Delancey and the Bowery, the supplies stored on the concrete island at the traffic light. I pulled over just past Chrystie Street, watching the action. Cars pulled up to the light, two black men detached themselves from the island, dipping their squeegees in a big white plastic bucket, swinging them briskly to throw off the excess water. They walked the line of cars, looking for customers. One tried persuasion—you could read his gestures from a block away. The other just went to work, ready to demand money when he finished. Some drivers turned on their windshield wipers, others waved their hands signaling "No!" Some just sat rigid behind the wheel, staring straight ahead.

I watched for a while. Cabdrivers never went for the windshield wash. Not truckers either. The washers were lucky to score one paying job every four, five lights. A bad time to work, early in the morning, dealing with commuters. Nobody was where they wanted to be.

Seven o'clock. I pushed off from the curb, watching for a gap in traffic. Rolled to a stop right at the light. The Prof was perched on an abandoned car seat, smoking a cigarette like he was on the deck of a cruise ship. He flicked the smoke aside, majestically got to his feet, moved to my car as one of the washers ceremoniously slapped a squeegee into his hand.

"Watch how it's done, son," the Prof sang out.

I hit the switch, sliding down the driver's window.

"Good morning, my man. Here's the plan: pay a buck and change your luck. Do something right and you see the light."

I handed him a bill. The Prof did the windshield in a half dozen expert swipes, bowed deeply, tossed the squeegee to one of the washers, and resumed his seat. I took off, straight ahead onto Kenmare, turned left at Crosby, and waited.

Halfway through my second smoke, the Prof slid into the passenger seat.

"Where to?" I asked.

"Head over to Allen, find a place to park."

91

I found a spot just off Hester, pulled in behind a red Acura Legend sedan. A man in his thirties crossed the street, oiled muscles gleaming under a cut-down T-shirt, baggy shorts, baseball cap and sunglasses, zinc ointment covered his nose. Surf's up, somewhere. A battered pale green Cougar pulled to the curb. Two kids got out: teenagers, a boy and a girl, dressed alike in black, sporting matching asymmetrical hair-cuts. They wobbled down the street together as the Cougar roared off. Home from a night at the clubs? A dark sedan stopped at the light, overflowing with Vietnamese. The guy riding shotgun swiveled his head to look at me—I could feel homicidal eyes behind the sunglasses, mea-suring. Up close, he'd stink of cordite.

"What's up?" I asked the Prof.

"Queen Thana, schoolboy. Word is, you've been dancing with the devil."

"What word?"

"The drums hum, bro'. Stay close to the ground, you can hear the sound."

"And . . . ?"

"And stay away, don't play, okay?"

"I'm not playing."

The little man's deep brown eyes turned to me. "I can't keep squaring your beefs, chief. You wanted to go play gunfighter games out in Hillbilly Harlem, I tried to make you see some sense, but I didn't press too hard, right?"

I nodded.

"This ain't the same, lame. The Queen is mean, Jack. She got people who *want* to die, that's no lie."

"I'm not in anything with them—I don't even know who they are."

"Don't be slick with the man who taught you the trick, schoolboy. Got to be, you holding something they want."

I lit a smoke, thinking it through.

"You talked to them," I said.

"We rapped across the gap, exchanged some ideas, like the UN."

"They lean on you?"

"That's not the way they do—I thought you knew. Just asked me to talk to you."

"Come on, Prof."

"You took something of theirs. They say, maybe you didn't know whose it was, okay? They want it back. Said to bring it with you when you come."

"Come where?"

"Man said they'll tell the dealer. Jacques. But you got to have it with you, understand?"

"Yeah." Thinking of Wolfe. How to get it back.

"I'll call, every day. Once in the morning, once at night. You get it, leave word. I'll set up the meet. Better if it comes from us."

"I'll try."

"Try *hard*, homeboy.

92

It was still early. I rolled by Central Park, telling myself I was scanning Carlos. Practicing my lies. But the woman who said her name was Belinda didn't come by.

93

The white dragon was still on guard in the window. Always a dragon there—white for clear, blue for cops, red for danger. I drove around the back. The guys in the kitchen looked me over like they'd never seen me before.

I found my booth, waited. Mama wasn't at her register. No waiter came by.

A copy of the *Daily News* was in my booth. Five kids murdered so far this week. Separate incidents. Gunned down—cross-fire killings. The city's loaded with homicidal punks, and not a marksman among them.

If you wrote a book about it, the critics would say it was full of gratuitous violence.

Letter to the editor from some cop, arguing with a citizen who complained the police don't ticket off-duty cars parked near the precinct house. The cop said he put his life on the line every day—he was entitled to park on the house.

That was true, they should give cabdrivers free rent.

I turned to the race results.

94

"You not want soup?" Mama materialized at my elbow.

"I was waiting for you."

"Cook not come out?"

"Nobody came out."

"Cooks nervous—strangers in the basement."

"Luke?"

"Luke not a stranger. Woman . . . Teresa . . . come every day."

"I know."

"Alone with the boy. Every day," she said, eyes narrowing. Mama doesn't trust citizens.

"I'll go talk with her."

"Not now. She come up here, finished. Talk then, okay?"

"Okay. Could I have some soup, then?"

Mama smiled with a corner of her mouth, spewed out a torrent of Chinese with the other. One of the waiters came through the back door. Bowed, nodded, went away.

"You bet horse?" Mama asked, pointing at the open newspaper.

"Maybe. If I see something I like."

The waiter came back with the soup. Also some hard noodles and a plate of dim sum floating in clear sauce with tiny flecks of green. Mama watched me eat, taking only token sips herself, tapping her long fingernails on the cheap Formica tabletop. I waited—she wouldn't say anything she didn't want to.

The waiter came back. Said something to Mama. She nodded.

"Woman coming up," she said to me.

I stood up to greet her. Silver-streaked blonde straight hair parted in the middle, hanging down almost to her shoulders. Brown eyes, nose slightly off-center, small nostrils, tiny jaw at the bottom of an oval face. Dressed in a camel's-hair blazer over a silk turtleneck, wide dark blue skirt, sensible bone pumps.

"Hello, I'm Dr. . . . ah, Teresa. You must be Burke—Lily described you."

"But I'm even better-looking than she said, right?"

"No." She laughed gently. "You're not."

I made a sweeping gesture and she sat down across from Mama, who showed no sign of moving. I slid in next to her.

"What can you tell me?"

"In a way, it's good news. Luke is very young to have gone full multiple. We can get to fusion a lot easier if the behavior isn't calcified over time—if the membrane between the personalities doesn't harden. For a child, there's no real investment in any of the alternates. So when the situation changes . . . Are you following me?"

"The safer he is, the easier it is for him to come together."

"Yes." She smiled. "That's a good way to put it."

"How long?"

"I don't know. There's no schedule for these things. But I don't feel it will be that much longer."

"What did Lily tell you about his . . . situation?"

"Luke is a patient, I'm a physician." Meaning she knew the whole story.

I lit a smoke as the waiter came to clear away the plates. Noticed Mama didn't offer Teresa anything.

"Lily tell you how I fit in?"

Teresa let her gaze trail across Mama's face. "There are . . . confidentiality issues. If Mrs. Wong would . . ."

"Mama is my family," I told her. "I have no secrets from her."

Mama smiled—at the truth and at the lie.

Teresa watched my face. I dialed sincerity right up into my eyes. Waited.

She took a breath. "Lily said you were her friend. That you specialized in some sort of currency transfers . . . she wasn't specific. And she said you could be trusted."

"She tell you I was in the middle of a goddamned war between her and one of her sisters?"

"Yes. Wolfe."

"Yeah, Wolfe. And this Wolfe has a pack, understand? I'm about out of time. What I need is to have you talk to her. Let her see where things are. Back her off a bit."

"I'm on shaky ground with that," she said. "I can't reveal information about a patient."

"She doesn't have to know your name—she'll play square."

"You think if she believes Luke is close to recovery, she'll give him more time."

I dragged deep on the cigarette. Mama's face was bland, like she didn't understand English.

"Wolfe's gonna give *somebody* some time, Doc. Somebody has to pay. I know that's not your department, but that's the game. I'm no psychologist, but I know Luke wasn't born like he is, right?"

"Yes."

"Somebody did something to him. Something bad. You go far enough, you'll find out, yes?"

"Probably. Not for sure."

"That's what I need you to tell Wolfe. Just like that."

"I don't understand what good that will do."

"Wolfe's a hunter. That's what she does. Sometimes she does it by trading, you understand? Gang rape, four punks involved, okay? The evidence is weak . . . dark in that alley, hard to make a stand-up ID, like that . . . but they nail one of them—say with a DNA match. The rest are gonna walk. Rape's a B felony here: twenty-five max on top. So she offers the one freak she has cold maybe four-to-twelve . . . and he rolls over on the others, nails them down."

"Yes, I know. Plea bargaining."

"No, you don't know . . . not the way Wolfe plays it. When she deals, it's a bargain for the victim, not the rapist. She'll take any case to trial, go the limit. She makes a deal, it's gotta be a good one."

"So . . ."

"So whatever Luke did, he was just the messenger. The freaks who turned him out, Wolfe'd take them in exchange, see?"

"Yes. All right, tell her to call . . ."

"That's not the way it's done. I'll bring her here. You'll talk to her here."

"Why not just . . . ?"

"I think I know Wolfe, how she'll act. But if I'm wrong, if she won't play, then I'll take her away . . . she won't find this place, she won't know your name."

I ground out my cigarette, waiting for her answer.

She got up to leave. Turned to speak to me. "I am treating a patient.

A seriously disturbed patient who also happens to be a child. If someone shows up in my office . . . wherever that is . . . and I believe it to be in my client's interests to discuss the matter, I would do that."

"Thanks."

She offered her hand. I shook it. "Goodbye, Mrs. Wong," she said to Mama.

Mama inclined her head a fraction of an inch.

Teresa went out the back, one of Mama's waiters just behind her.

95

I took the Manhattan Bridge to the BQE, heading for Queens. Shoved a cassette into my tape player. Judy Henske. Making a comeback now, playing clubs on the Coast. She wasn't back in the studio yet—the bootleg tape cost me fifty bucks. Fucking thieves. It was like she'd never been away—still had all the chops—wailing, growling, cooing at the crowd, owning the audience. Shining her torch. "Duncan and Brady," her own take on "StagoLee." Perfect. The Plymouth hit one of those lunar craters they call potholes here—I just caught the tail end of some Primo Bitch piece I hadn't heard before.

> *I've had just about enough of your love*
> *It's time to take it on the road*
> *It started out with a hug, darlin'*
> *But now it's a stranglehold*

> *You say you've been saving for our future*
> *You say you got some Master Plan*
> *Well, you can keep your Social Security, sonny*
> *What I need now is a man*

I listened to the end-tape hiss, thinking about the waiter in Mama's joint, the one following Teresa. Sword or shield?

96

I found a pay phone on Queens Boulevard. They put her through.

"This is Wolfe."

"It's me. Could you spare a few minutes to talk to me about something?"

"You don't want to come here?"

"No."

"Remember where we last had lunch?"

"Sure."

"One-fifteen, more or less, okay?"

"Okay. Remember what I brought you—last time we ate there?"

"Sure."

"Can you bring it with you?"

"Why?"

"I'll explain."

"I'll see."

97

They were in the same place, Wolfe and Lola. I sat down, ordered another chef's salad. It wasn't much—the restaurant's produce buyer had gotten to the market after the Koreans that day.

"You bring it?" I asked her.

"Tell me why you want it."

"Okay with you, I talk like this . . . ?" Eyes on Lola.

"Yes. In fact, it's the only way."

"You looked in the bag, right?"

She nodded, not saying anything.

"And you took it apart real careful, one pin at a time, analyzed what you found inside?"

Nodded again.

"No baby?"

"Chicken parts," Lola said. Caught a warning look from Wolfe.

"I need it back. You probably tagged it, so you'll have to put something else in its place in the evidence locker."

Wolfe pushed her salad aside, lit a smoke. Raised her eyebrows to ask why.

"The people who it belongs to . . . they want it back. You opened it, you know what it is. These aren't people I can play with. It was evidence of the homicide, I wouldn't say anything."

Wolfe pulled on her smoke, thinking. Lola scanned the room over my shoulder.

"You get the divers yet?" I asked her.

"Couple, three days," she said.

"What I asked for . . . ?"

"Your turn to pay the check," she said.

98

Lola opened the trunk of her Reatta. I transferred the package to the Plymouth.

"Is she married?" I asked, nodding my head toward Wolfe, sitting in the front seat.

Lola held her finger to her lips in a "ssssh" gesture.

99

Back in my office, I took a look. Carefully unwrapped the layers of plastic, bracing myself for the smell. It didn't come.

The juju bag looked like it hadn't been touched. Somehow smaller than when I'd first seen it, not as menacing lying on my desk.

Pansy poked her nose over the desktop, trying to see what I was doing. I told her to go to her place. She ignored me. Snarled—a higher pitch than I'd heard before.

I still didn't want to touch it.

100

There's places even zombies won't go. I walked to the station at Chambers Street, slipped into the underground. Dropped a token into the slot. The Exit door was propped open—most of the citizens just walked through without paying. Social protest, like the yuppies who throw Israeli shekels into the Exact Change baskets on the highway. Sure.

It didn't look like rain, but I carried a little red umbrella—the kind you can compress to baton size. A real piece of junk—so cheap that one of the ribs had worked itself loose—one pull and it would come right out in my hand. The tip was real sharp.

At West Fourth, I changed to the F train. Got a seat next to an old man who looked like he snorted interferon—pinch-faced, thinning hair nicely parted at the back to reveal dime-sized dandruff flakes. He opened a copy of the *Times*, spreading it across my face. His hands were liver-spotted, nails long and yellowing, curving at the tips. He smelled like his life.

The train picked up speed, rocking on the rusty tracks, overloaded with human cargo, paradise for the rubbers and the gropers. And the boys who carried box cutters to slice wallets free of clothing. If the air conditioning was on, it never had a chance.

The old man slammed a sharp elbow into my chest, shoving for more room, making high-pitched grunting noises, rattling his newspaper, flakes flying off his skull like greasy snow.

A good-sized Puerto Rican woman got on at Thirty-fourth, a plastic shopping bag from a drugstore chain in one hand, using it as a purse. She was wearing a white uniform of some kind, white flats with thick soles, white stockings. Coming from work. She worked her way over to a pole in the subway car, leaned against it gratefully.

I saw my chance.

Caught her eye, rose to my feet, my back to the rest of the humans, bowing slightly, gesturing with my hand like an usher showing a customer to her seat. There was maybe eighteen inches of seat showing— she dropped into it just as the vicious old man slid over to close the gap. She pancaked him like he was Play-Doh—the *Times* went flying, a thin shriek came out of his mouth. After that, they fought in silence.

My money was on the right horse. The old man finally extricated himself, stumbled off to another part of the subway car, reeking hate.

The Surrogate Ninja Body Slam—it doesn't always work, but when it does, it's a thing of beauty.

101

I got off the train at Rockefeller Center, stepped out and walked back along Sixth to Forty-second. It wouldn't be dark for hours, but clots of teenagers were already on patrol. "Driving the Deuce," they call it, cruising Times Square, eyes lusting into the windows full of *things*:

electronic gear, overdose jewelry, flashy clothes, battery-powered body parts. Down here, the only culture is Cargo Cult.

I had more pieces to put together before I brought Wolfe to meet Luke. The library had signs all around—the Campaign to Combat Illiteracy.

They should have asked me to be a consultant. I learned to read, really read, in prison. The Prof told me you could steal more money with a briefcase than with a pistol. I know that's true—but I never seem to get it right.

When I came back outside, it was just getting dark. I called Bonita at the place she works—told her I'd come by later, take her home.

102

Almost four in the morning when I stepped out of Bonita's building. Lighter, not happier. She'd made sweet little come-noises in her bed, following the script.

I lit a cigarette to scan the street, feeling the night shift. I'm not usually a target, but predators work the same way lonely losers do in singles bars—the closer it gets to quitting time, the more desperate they are to make a connection.

Almost to my car when a van prowled up on my right. I stepped behind the fender of a parked car, reaching inside my jacket when I saw what the van was tracking . . . a woman in a red dress slit up one side, walking unsteadily, like she was drunk. A street snatch is high-risk—maybe the van held a pack of gambling beasts, out to gang-rape Lady Luck. Or maybe I spent too much time on the dark side, manipulated by memories.

"Linda! Wait for me!" I yelled, loud enough to make her turn around.

The van took off.

103

Still wasn't tired when I got back to the office. I gave Pansy a couple of pints of chocolate chip ice cream I'd picked up at an all-night deli, smoked a cigarette, read through Michelle's letters again.

I flicked the channels on the black&white set, ignoring Pansy's annoyance when I couldn't find any pro wrestling. Finally settled for *Mayberry, R.F.D.* Fell asleep wishing Andy Griffith had been the Sheriff last time I'd stuck up a liquor store.

104

In the morning, I thought it through again. Stepping back, watching the edges. I had the bag. Wolfe had agreed to the meeting. It didn't feel dangerous to me. I could square it all up, get out, go back to taking off Carlos.

Time to roll, right? Get on with it.

Something holding me back.

Maybe I wasn't scared enough, yet.

105

At Mama's, waiting for Teresa. After my soup, Luke brought out a deck of cards, asked me if I wanted to play.

"What do you know how to play, kid?"

"Gin. Max taught me."

We played a few hands. Played a few more before I realized the little bastard was no amateur.

"How many cards left outside your hand?" I asked him.

"Twenty-six," he said, guilelessly.

"Where are they?"

"You have ten, there's one up, so there's fifteen in the deck."

"What are the cards, Luke?"

"If I tell you, then you'll know what's in my hand, kind of."

"Yeah. Like you kind of know what's in mine, right?"

"Right!" He smiled brightly.

"So you always beat Max?"

"No. Sometimes, it doesn't matter what you know. Some of it's just luck."

"Un-huh. You like it better when it's not luck?"

"Yes. Mama's going to teach me another game. Blackjack."

Mama loomed over my shoulder, putting her finger to her lips, smiling indulgently at her prize pupil. "Luke, remember what Mama tell you . . . blackjack a secret, yes?"

"I don't like secrets," the boy said, his voice dropping a register, eyes flickering.

"It's okay, Luke," I said, shooting a warning look at Mama. "There's no secrets here. Nobody's going to give you secrets. Mama was only playing."

"Playing?"

"Yeah. Like joking. Understand?"

His eyes flickered again. "Can I have some duck, Mama?"

Mama only serves duck about once a week—says it's a real pain to prepare properly.

"Sure, baby. Maybe some prawns too?"

"Yes!"

"Good baby," Mama said, reaching over to muss his hair.

106

While Teresa was downstairs with Luke, Max came in. Sat across from me, watching.

The phone rang in the back. Mama came to the table. "For you," she said. "Sunny man."

"It's me," I said, picking up the receiver.

"It is me too, mahn. With some news for you. I spoke to those people. Tomorrow night, you know Corona?"

"Yes."

"On Astoria Boulevard, city side of Ninety-fourth, a few blocks down, you will see an old drive-in. Hamburger joint, abandoned now. Drive there, midnight. They will meet you, take you to her."

"Okay."

"You have her property, mahn?"

"Yes."

"Sure. You understand."

"Can I bring a friend?"

"You are, mahn. Clarence will meet you there too."

"Clarence is afraid of those people."

"Everyone is, mahn."

107

I explained it all to Max. Slowly. Usually, he gets things as sharp as anyone who hears, but he was playing it dumb. Like he does when he doesn't like what I'm saying. He kept trying to deal himself in. I kept shaking my head.

Mama came back, sat down with us, a paper bag in her hands. "Bonds all gone," she said.

"That was damn fast—you score ten points?"

"Not all. Three hundred for us."

"Elroy gets a hundred, Mama. But it's still a giant hit."

Mama bowed. Put the money on the table, shuffled it like a casino dealer, spun it into piles. Three stacks, a hundred grand in each. Brushed one to the side, Elroy's money. I counted off five grand, handed it to Max. He gets ten points for deliveries. That's what he does, deliveries. Guaranteed. I made the signs for Elroy. Max's thin lips curled—he clapped his first two fingers hard against his thumb, like jaws snapping. I knew what he meant: yak yak yak. He pointed at me, made the sign of driving a car. He'd have to borrow mine to make the delivery. I nodded okay. Then he made the sign of dialing a phone—also my responsibility to tell the maniac Max was on his way. Okay again.

I fanned out the five grand I'd set aside for Max, looking hard at Mama. She knew the rules—she was just as responsible for the money getting back to Elroy as I was. Besides, she probably clouted the bonds for three-fifty or even four hundred and we both knew it.

Finally, she nodded. "Oh yes, pay fair share, okay?" Handed over five grand of her own.

I took twenty for myself, pushed the rest over to Mama. "For the bank, okay?"

"Okay."

She leafed through her money, still keeping the stacks separate. Counted off a bunch of bills, handed them to Max, making the sign of rocking a baby. "For Flower, yes?" she said, looking at Max, talking to me.

Max bowed his thanks.

Mama smiled. "Fair share, yes?" And counted off some of my money, handed it to Max.

He gravely bowed to me as well.

Mama counted off still more money, looking at me. "For Luke, yes? To pay the woman downstairs."

"Lily's taking care of that, Mama."

Her eyes went agate. "Our house, our family, *we* pay."

Max dropped his eyes from the challenge, handed over his entire stack of money. Mama took some, handed the rest back. Looted my pile again.

Finally, she smiled. Got up and left.

108

Max wasn't going to lose two in a row, renewing his demands to come along to my meeting. I made the sign for Lily. For Storm, Immaculata, Wolfe. It took a long time. I pounded my fists together, conflict. Pulled them apart. Separation. Then I pointed at Max. Tapped my heart. Locked two hands together. We wouldn't be separated, he and I, okay? His time would come.

Finally, he nodded.

I went into the back to call Elroy.

"It's me," I said by way of greeting.

"Hey, Burke! Is Pansy in heat? I mean, Barko ain't been himself, man. Don't want to pull his load, nothing. He needs his woman, buddy. Give my boy a break."

"Look, fool. I called you about something else. Everything's all set, okay? You'll get what's coming to you real late tonight . . . maybe two in the morning, okay?"

"Yeah, yeah . . . You gonna bring Pansy?"

"I'm not coming. I'm sending my brother . . . and don't say his name on the phone."

"Oh, the Chinaman who don't talk? You sending him? I heard he does deliveries . . ."

Fucking moron.

"Just calm down, all right? He'll be driving my car. And keep those damn dogs out of his way."

"Sure, sure. But when you gonna . . . ?"

I hung up on him.

109

Eleven-thirty. I made a slow circuit of the empty drive-in at the wheel of the Plymouth. Nothing. Max and I lit cigarettes, smoking in silence. He'd reopened the argument on the way out to Queens, and we'd reached a compromise.

I was wearing a dark suit, white shirt, black tie. Unarmed—not even a knife. Max was dressed in his thin-soled black shoes, baggy white pants, a white T-shirt. A better target if that's what they wanted. He's never weaponless.

The immaculate green Rover pulled in a few minutes later. Clarence killed his lights, got out of the car, lounged against a fender, his body not quite making contact with the metal.

I popped the trunk. Max and I got out, walked around to the back. I took the package in my arms. We walked over to Clarence.

"Clarence, this is my brother, Max the Silent."

Max bowed.

Clarence extended his hand, slim and delicate. Max took it in his bone-crusher of a paw, shook.

"Let's put this in your trunk," I said to Clarence.

His eyes were distressed, but he said nothing. Unlocked the trunk, didn't look as we put the bag inside.

"I heard of you," Clarence said to Max.

Max bowed again.

"He really doesn't talk?" Clarence asked me.

"Not with his mouth," I told him.

A black Chevy Caprice rolled into the lot, followed closely by its twin. A tall, slim black man got out of the passenger seat of the lead car, walked toward us. He was dressed exactly as I was except his tie was string-thin. And he had a tiny red ribbon in his lapel.

"Mr. Burke?" he asked.

"That's me."

"You will come with us, please?"

"Yes."

"And your friends, they will come too?"

"Only one friend," I said, nodding at Clarence. "My brother will be leaving."

"Certainly."

Max closed the gap between him and the messenger, gliding without a sound. He stared at the man's face, eyes slitted, memorizing. He bowed slightly. Moved over to the cars, walking around them front to back, taking it in.

"Would you ask your people to get out of their cars?" I asked politely.

"Certainly," he said again. Walked over to the driver's window of one car, then another. They lined up in the darkness, all dressed alike. Max stared deep into the face of each one, bowed his thanks. Squeezed my shoulder, climbed into the Plymouth, and took off.

"Will you come with us now?" the man asked.

"Yes, I'm ready."

"Very well," he said, gesturing toward the lead car.

"Hold up, mahn," Clarence said, his voice barely under control. "I'm not leaving my ride out here for some thief to steal. I'll just drive right behind you, okay?"

The messenger smiled. "Yes, you and your friend can follow me. You have nothing to fear."

"Do you want your . . . ?" I asked.

"No. You must present the offering to Queen Thana yourself, sir."

I shrugged. Went with Clarence to his car.

110

Clarence followed the Caprice's taillights to Ninety-fourth Street, made a left toward the airport.

"The other one's right behind us," he said.

"Makes sense."

"I don't like this, mahn."

"It's okay. They could have wasted us right in the parking lot, they wanted to. They're not going to do anything."

"You sure, mahn?"

"Yeah."

"So why was the monster-man there? The Silent One. I heard scary things about him."

"In case I turn out to be wrong."

"So what's he gonna do *then*, mahn—be too late for us."

"It's never too late to get even."

111

The Caprice swept east on Ditmars, turned right on Northern Boulevard, back toward the city.

"You have your pistol?" I asked Clarence.

"Always," he said, whipping it loose.

"Leave it in the car, Clarence. And anything else you got."

"You crazier than they are, mahn. I'm not going in no voodoo house without . . ."

"Yeah, you are. They're going to search you anyway, what's the point? It's too late now—we trust them or we don't."

"I *don't*, mahn."

"Then stay in the car."

"Look . . ."

"You look, Clarence. This is my play, my way."

He glared through the windshield. Finally, he slipped the pistol under the front seat. Pulled out a couple of spare clips, his straight razor, the leather-covered sap.

"That's all I got, mahn."

We turned left into a short block. A drug supermarket: dealers sitting in parked cars, working the traffic crawl. Cars with Connecticut plates, Jersey plates. Flames licked from a 55-gallon oil drum, winos warming their hands. A man staggered out of the doorway of an abandoned building—why pay rent when you're running a crack house? If citizens lived on that block, they were indoors.

Daylight wouldn't be any better.

A three-story wood frame house stood squarely between two others. A centerpiece, white with black trim. The surrounding houses were standing open to the night, in the process of being rebuilt. The Caprice pulled into a driveway, drove around to the back. We followed, the trail car behind us.

We stepped out. I looked around as Clarence opened the trunk. High wood fence, the planks nailed solidly together. Chicken coop in one corner, a small black-and-white goat tethered. A two-car garage, doors closed.

I took the package in my arms again. Car doors slammed. The others got out. The messenger came over to us.

"Will you follow me, please?"

112

The back door opened into what had probably been a kitchen once. We followed the messenger through an entranceway into a long rectangular room. Neatly dressed men and women crowded the place. Sober clothing, spots of color on the women—a small red feather in a hat, a white scarf. The front door had a steel gate behind it.

"This way," the man said.

Down the stairs, to a basement. Under the ground, under the surface. In the blackness, I wished for Sheba. Sharp, clean smell, like cloves cooking, everything whitewashed.

At the bottom of the stairs, against the far wall, a woman. Sitting in a huge chair of dark, oiled wood, the back fanning into a seashell shape behind her. She was wrapped in red silk, loose around her shoulders, falling into a natural V at her breasts. Long dark hair, coffee-with-cream skin, dark red lips.

The messenger stepped ahead, motioning us to stay where we were. Bowed to the woman, said something in a rapid-fire language I didn't know. Sounded like some kind of French.

"Speak their tongue," the woman said, her voice darkly rich, gold-laced loam.

"We have done as you commanded," the man said in reply.

"Come forward," the woman said.

I approached, Clarence just behind me on my right. I bowed, folding my upper body protectively over the package.

"They have no weapons," the woman said.

Sounds in the darkness: a pistol taken off full cock, a sword being sheathed.

"What is your name?" she asked.

"Burke."

"You have brought us our offering?"

"Yes," I said. "That and an apology."

"Your friend, he is the one who hurt one of our people? In Central Park?"

"No."

"Yes, he is the one. You would lie for a friend?"

"I would die for one," I said quietly, cursing myself, clutching the juju bag.

"Your friend is young. He did not know what he was doing?"

"He only thought I was to be attacked."

"Yes. Give what you have brought to us."

The messenger stepped forward. I handed him the bag. He placed it reverently on a dark slab of polished wood. At a nod from the Queen, he unwrapped it carefully, gently removing the plastic. Held the bag up for her to see.

"It is as it was," she said. "You will return it to the sacred place."

He bowed.

"Come closer," the woman said.

Clarence and I started toward her. "Just you," she said. "Let your friend stay—I have not asked his name."

She was younger than I first thought—hard to tell exactly. Even in the flame from the candles, I could see she was exquisite. One eye darker than the other, a black dot high on one cheekbone. Seated before me, knees together under the red silk, one hand on each arm of the dark wood chair, she looked into my eyes as if she were looking down. A long distance.

"Why did you take our offering?"

"I was looking for a missing baby. I came across your offering, but I didn't know what it was. I thought it might be evidence. Something that would help me find the baby."

"What did you *think* it was?"

"Witchcraft."

"You do not fear witches?"

"Yes, I fear them."

"You have known them, then?"

"One of them." Strega. Flame-haired and fire-hearted. At peace now. And so gone from me.

Her chin tilted, studying me. "Yes, you have. But not one of us."

"No."

"The juju is an offering. When one of us dies, his spirit will be doomed unless we make a loa so it can return to earth. That is what you took."

"I am sorry. Had I known . . ."

"Yes. Are you afraid now?"

"Yes, I am afraid now."

"What kind of man admits he is afraid standing before a woman?"

"A man who has seen things."

"Tell me about the baby, the missing baby."

"A grandmother was told her grandchild had disappeared. The baby was too young to run away. Her daughter had been with a man. A bad man, the baby's father. She believed something had happened to her grandson. Her people asked me to look for the child."

"What have you found?"

"The baby is dead."

"How do you know this?"

"The mother told me. The father killed him. Beat him to death. I was looking for the body."

"So she who loved the baby could help his spirit rise?"

"Yes. Not the mother."

"I know. You are a hunter. The young one too. It is the father you seek now?"

"The authorities are looking for him."

"Yes. Have you found the body?"

"Not yet. The father, his name is Emerson, he lived at the Welfare hotel by the airport. When he left, the night of the death, he had the baby's body with him. When he came back, he did not. I think the baby's in the water, right by the airport."

"He killed the child the same night you took our offering?"

"No. A week or so before."

"So when you saw the offering, you thought . . ."

"Yes. I thought the baby was in there. Parts of the baby."

The woman closed her eyes, brought hands to her temples. It was so quiet in the basement I could hear the candles flicker.

I could feel Clarence behind me, waves pulsing in the room.

Her eyes opened.

"Describe the man," she said.

I reached in my pocket, handed her the razor-cropped picture we'd taken from the hotel room.

She took one quick look. I heard a snake's hiss—didn't look around to see where it came from.

"Please go upstairs. Outside. Smoke some of your cigarettes. I must talk with my people. Then we will talk again."

I bowed.

113

I kicked a wooden match into life in the night air, dragged deep on my cigarette.

"Why'd you tell her you was scared, mahn?" Clarence asked.

"It was the truth. Still is."

"You really think she knew we had no weapons?"

"Yeah."

"How would she know that, mahn?"

I shrugged. "Maybe that's what she wants to tell us."

We waited, listening to the crime sounds from the street.

114

The messenger came into the yard. "Will you come back with us?" he asked me.

I nodded. We started for the basement. The messenger held up his hand. "Just you, please."

I looked at Clarence. "Wait in the car," I told him.

He scanned my face carefully, nodded.

They took me right before her this time.

"You have returned our offering to us. In exchange, I will answer your questions."

"I have no questions."

"All men have questions," she said, her voice so low and dark I had to strain for the words. "Do you think I am some foolish fortune-teller, some thief with a crystal ball? I am the third daughter of a third sister. That is the mystical number, three. People of confused religion say Father, Son, and Holy Ghost. That is idolatry. Before religion, there was Earth, Wind, and Fire. Always three. Primitive man did not understand that sex makes babies—if it were not for sex, there would be no man. Sex is the drive force, and it is controlled by women. There are three ways into the female body, but only one will make children. A man would have no preference. That is why a woman's sex is a triangle. Three again. The true root of all communication with the spirits. Only a queen may know all the truth. A man may know only what he is told. People first mated like animals, never face to face. This changed only when women grew tired of bending over. When there is famine, women are not fertile. Their bodies know the spirits—their bodies are the link to the earth. Do you understand this?"

"Yes."

"Do you believe it?" Something else in her voice, testing.

"Yes." Thinking of Blossom, lying on her bed, listening to her chuckle. "No wonder men are so stupid—their brains are all in such a small place."

"You are Wednesday's child, born to sadness. Yes?"

"Yes."

"Many children are born without a father—only the most damned are born without a mother. You know this?"

"Yes."

"Why did you look for this baby?"

"It was a job."

"No."

"I can't explain it, then."

"I know. Listen to me, child of sorrow: the baby is in the water, as you believed. I know this. The man you seek, he worshiped with us. Pretended to worship. The night of the child's death, he came to us. The baby's body in his arms. He said the child had choked to death in his crib. He asked us for a sacrifice. To save the baby's spirit. He thought what you thought . . . what you are afraid to say . . . that our offerings contain the bodies . . . that the baby would be cut up, placed inside the bag. When we told him how we would make the sacrifice, he walked away from us. We thought it was grief then. Now we know the truth— he feared the baby's spirit would walk."

"I understand."

"Do you? Do you understand that you are a baby's spirit? Spirit walking? Go now. You will search for the evil—I see that in you. When the time comes, return to me. I will show you the path."

115

No cars followed us from the house. Rain misted around the Rover, overmatching the puny wipers.

"Where shall I take you, mahn?"

"Anywhere over the bridge."

"You don't want me to see where you live, then?"

"Better you don't know, right? You were planning to drop in one day, have a visit?"

"Maybe I do that, mahn. Bring you some Island beer, sit around, talk some . . . would that be so bad, now?"

"That's not what I'm saying, Clarence."

"Yes, I know," he said. But his eyes were hurt.

116

I let Pansy out to her roof, ignoring her attitude because I came home without a treat.

I never have to ask myself why something scares me. So much does. A child doesn't fear death—doesn't understand what it is. A child fears pain. Immediate pain. The terror is to remember.

The freaks count on it.

117

I walked all the way to Chinatown the next morning. Stopped at a bakery for a bag of small hard poppy-seed rolls. Chewed them slowly, one at a time. To settle my stomach. Stopped again at a greengrocer, got a handful of fresh parsley and cold bottle of pineapple juice. Sipped it slowly, crossing the still-wet streets, watching.

By the time I got near Mama's, I was munching the parsley, cleaning out my mouth.

The Plymouth was parked in the alley, the rear end too close to the wall. Max could catch flies in the air without hurting them, but he couldn't drive worth a damn.

I knocked on the back door, thinking about Luke in the basement. How basements used to frighten him.

About last night.

One of Mama's crew let me in, nodded his head toward the dining area.

Max was in my booth, the Prof across from him. The little man was rapping away, waving his hands like it was sign language.

I sat down next to Max. One of the waiters brought me a glass of water, went away.

"How'd it go, bro'?" the Prof greeted me.

"Okay. It was okay. I gave them their property. We're all square." I didn't bother to ask him how he knew about the meeting.

I looked over at Max. Spread my hands in a "what?" gesture. He nodded. Rapid-fire universal gestures, the kind you can use anywhere in the world: thumb rubbed against first two fingers, finger pointing straight ahead, same finger making small circles next to his temple. Then he made the sign for "okay." He gave the money to the crazy man, no problems.

The Prof wasn't satisfied yet. "Come on, homeboy. What was the scene with the Queen? What'd she say—how'd it play?"

I ran it all down to him, gesturing for Max. After all these years, I could do it pretty fast. If Max doesn't get something, he lets me know.

"You know what I was thinking, Prof? How I wasn't scared . . . you understand? I'm in a basement in Corona, some kind of voodoo temple. They decide to do something to me, I'm gone. Nobody'd even hear a shot on that block. Nobody'd care. But I'm calm. From the beginning. Like nothing's gonna happen to me."

"Her game's not pain, bro'."

"Yeah. You believe . . . ? I mean . . . you understand what she told me?"

"All preachers the same, Burke. They say what makes the people pay."

"You think it's a hustle?"

"*You* think there's one answer, babe? The Catholics are right about what they sell, then all the Jews are goin' to hell. The Muslims be the only ones who know the way, it's the Buddhists who're gonna pay. Live righteous, the Man knows, whoever he is, get it? Ain't no pie in the sky when you die. Here and now, on the ground . . . what's true is what you *do*."

"You think it's all different names for the same thing?"

"Afterwards? Here's the truth . . . you won't know until you go."

I saw Wesley. In a fiery pit, the stare from his dead eyes chilling the air, the Devil backing into a corner, afraid.

118

I drove to the South Bronx by myself. Muddy Waters for a soundtrack. A live performance from the fifties, taped in Chicago. The Master, still fresh from the Delta then, getting it down right. Shouting about catching the first train smoking. Nobody in the audience thought he was planning to buy a ticket.

The last cut on the tape. "Bad Luck Child."

Terry let me inside, his small face animated with news.

"I got a letter from Mom. She's learning modern dance. She said she'd show me when she comes back."

"Yeah? She tell you to mind the Mole?"

"Sort of. She said to watch out for him. To go with him, when he goes outside but . . ."

"But not when he goes with me, right?"

"Yes. But . . ."

"It's okay, Terry. I'm not taking the Mole anywhere. I just need to ask him some stuff."

119

The Mole was peering intently into a glass beaker the size of a mason jar, surgical gloves on his hands. I looked over his shoulder. A jet-black spider in a triangular web, a fat bulbous teardrop, glistening. The Mole slowly rotated the jar. On the spider's underside, a bright red hourglass. Black widow.

He took a pair of metal tweezers from his shirt pocket, plucked a piece of white spongy material from his workbench. The white stuff was maybe half the size of the nail on my little finger, a monofilament line strung through it. He took the screen off the top of the beaker, grabbed the line, held the white lump delicately poised over the rim, dangled it gently, slowly letting it descend.

I could feel Terry's kid-breath on my cheek as he pressed forward to get a look. The web trembled as the white lump caught. The spider's legs pawed, reading the vibrations.

Time passed. The spider worked its way toward the lump, confident. The Mole delicately feathered the line—the white lump struggled in the web. Suddenly, the spider shot forward, burying its fangs into the lump, forelegs grasping to immobilize its victim.

After a while, the spider released its grip. It began to exude webbing from its vent, starting to wrap the victim so it could later feast in peace. The Mole pulled up the line. The spider clung fast, refusing to surrender its prize. When the lump neared the top, Terry handed the Mole a can of compressed air with a long needle-nozzle. The Mole hit the button and the spider was blown free, falling harmlessly back to the floor of the beaker.

The Mole dropped the white lump into a petri dish, holding the line taut while Terry clipped it close with a pair of scissors. The Mole capped the petri dish, put it inside a small refrigerator, the last addition to a small, neat row already on the shelf.

"What do you want with black widow venom, Mole?" I asked him.

"Don't know yet."

"Yeah, okay. Can I ask you something?"

"What?"

"You know tinted glass . . . like they use in limos, so people can't see in?"

The Mole fiddled with some dials on what looked like a transformer they use for electric trains, ignoring my stupid questions. Waiting.

"Well, could you make it so it was reversed? So anyone could see in, but nobody inside could see out? Just the back, not the windshield?"

"Yes," he said. Meaning: sure, stupid.

"Could you do it, like . . . now?"

"Your car?"

"No. I need a car with . . ."

"Cold plates," the kid piped up. Michelle would have slapped him.

"Yeah. Just for maybe twenty-four hours. Less."

"With a barrier?"

"Yeah. Like, maybe, a gypsy cab or . . ."

"We have one, Mole. The old Dodge. Back in the . . ."

The Mole gave him a look. Terry stared right back. Finally, the Mole nodded. The kid ran upstairs.

120

I watched the Mole carefully measure the windows on the old Dodge, watched him cut the dark film with an X-acto knife, press it into place with a rubber block. Terry used a socket wrench to put on the new plates, changed the oil and filter, checked the battery, fan belt. Ran some kind of gauge on the ignition.

"The tires are okay, Burke. But don't go too fast with it."

"It's not for a bank job, kid."

"Oh, I know." Wise little bastard.

When they were done, I walked around the car. From the outside, it looked like a gypsy cab, better condition than most, in fact. I climbed in the back seat. Sat down, closed the door.

Blackout. The Mole had even treated the Plexiglas barrier between the front and back seats with the same material. A blindfold with wheels.

"Perfect, Mole!" I told him.

He nodded, unsurprised. "Prisoner?" he asked.

"No. A volunteer. But they can't know where they're going."

He nodded again. Shambled off. I wasn't even finished with my cigarette when he came back with one of those gooseneck Tensor lamps. When he was done screwing it onto the shelf behind the back seat, you could light up the interior even with the windows closed. Terry removed the door handles and window cranks from the back seat, covering the holes with metal discs.

The Mole got a hose and a battery-powered vacuum. We cleaned it inside and out.

"Thanks, Mole."

He nodded again.

Terry jumped up and down, excited now. "Mole, can I . . . ? You said when Burke came again . . ."

The Mole shrugged. Nodded again. The kid took off. The Mole held up his hand in a "wait!" gesture to me.

Terry came running back, a fat dirt-colored puppy in his arms.

"Burke! Look, isn't she beautiful!" Setting the puppy on the ground.

I knelt down, rolled the pup over, rubbed her belly. "She sure is, Terry. Where'd you get her?"

"She's *Simba's* . . . Simba's and Elsa's. She was born right here—the pick of the litter," he said proudly.

"Which one is Elsa?"

"The one who looks like a bull mastiff. When she went into heat, Simba wouldn't let any of the others near her . . . Mole explained it to me."

"Oh yeah?"

"Yes. Do you like her?"

"Sure. She looks like a real tiger. What's her name?"

"She doesn't have one yet. She's for Luke, okay? Okay, Burke? Please? Mole said I could ask you."

"Terry . . ."

"Burke, he *needs* a puppy, he does. She won't be any trouble . . . she's real smart and all."

I lit a smoke, buying time. The Mole looked away like he was busy with something. No help.

"Terry, Luke's . . . sick now. He won't always be sick, but . . . he could hurt the puppy, kid. He wouldn't know what he was doing, but . . ."

Terry's eyes were his mother's then, Michelle's legacy blazing at me, never backing up. "He wouldn't! I know him too, Burke. I talked to him. He wouldn't."

"Look, maybe . . ."

"He needs a puppy *now*, Burke. To make him feel safe. I . . . promised him."

"You got a blanket for her?" I surrendered.

121

The gypsy cab pulled a little to the left when I tapped the brakes, but otherwise it stumbled along well enough. I looped over the Triboro, caught the FDR south. It was down to two lanes . . . some construction project . . . and the yutz in the Lincoln in front of me decided to take his half out of the middle, blocking and guarding so I couldn't get past.

The puppy yawned, half sleeping in her blanket on the front seat. I admired the slick way Terry had hijacked me into delivering her—the Mole was teaching him science, but Michelle had given him art.

Horns blared behind me. I extended my arms in a "what can I do?" gesture and let them blast away.

No cassette player in this heap. I found the all-news station, listened to the body count that passes for electronic journalism in this town. Ninety-one degrees, humidity eighty-eight percent. Some ballplayer was demanding a few more million bucks a year to do whatever he did. Gas prices going up—politicians demand a complete investigation. Body of a baby found in Bowery Bay, just off La Guardia Airport. City-Wide Special Victims Task Force Chief Wolfe says indictments will be sought against those responsible once autopsy is completed.

I lit a smoke, thinking about spirits.

122

Just past eleven. The guy who opened the back door to Mama's nodded at me, ignoring the bundle in my arms. He glanced over my shoulder, pointed at the gypsy cab, said something I couldn't understand, pointed to me. I nodded. He made a "wait here" gesture, came out with a small pot and a brush. Painted some Chinese characters on the trunk of the cab—looked like whitewash, nice calligraphy. He bowed—okay now. You park in Max the Silent's spot and they don't know your car, the neighborhood recycling program goes right into action.

I showed Mama the puppy. She patted its body, clucking at the plumpness. Opened its mouth, raised its tail.

"Good puppy, Burke. Strong."

"Yeah. It's for Luke. A gift."

"Okay. Puppy hungry?"

"Probably. Let's let the kid feed her, okay?"

"In basement. With the woman."

"We'll wait."

123

No lunchtime customers yet—one of Mama's thugs in place at the door, across from the register. Mama was scratching behind the puppy's ears with one hand, the other waving in front of the dog's nose. The pup's eyes were locked on Mama's waving hand.

"Train dog this way," she said. "Rub hand in liver, dog follow everywhere."

Something to that. Something Blossom told me about pheromones, the copper-estrogen smell still sharp in my nostrils whenever I thought of her.

"Hi, Burke!" Luke bounded into the front room, Teresa trailing in his wake.

"Hello, Luke. How's it going?"

But the kid wasn't looking at me anymore, his face rapt with the wonder of the puppy.

"What a puppy! He's yours, Burke?"

"No. The puppy is yours. A gift from your friend Terry. And it's a girl, not a boy."

"Can I . . . ?"

Mama handed him the pup. Luke sat on the floor, cuddling the dog, pushing his face into the animal's snout, giggling when the pup licked his face.

"She *likes* me. What's her name?"

"She's your pup, kid. So you name her, okay?"

"Okay," the child said, his face all concentration, patting his dog. "Prince," he said. "Prince. Prince the Puppy. My good old puppy."

He was rocking back and forth on the floor, holding the puppy, face wet with tears. "Don't take Prince!" he screamed, rolling over, trying to shield the pup with his body. Teresa started toward him. The front door opened, three men in business suits. Mama barked something at the waiter standing across from the register. He leaped up, his body between the customers and us, chesting them out the door into the street, door closing behind him. Two more of her men ran from the kitchen, the first one pulling an automatic from under his white coat. Teresa had the boy in her arms. The kid was sweat-drenched, mouth open, no sound, veins popping on his neck.

Luke went rigid. Teresa crooned, stroking him like he had the puppy. The boy's eyes closed. A shudder shook him. The puppy stood next to him on its stubby legs, guarding.

Luke's eyes opened. His fine hair was matted to his scalp, blood in one palm from his nails.

"It's okay, Luke," Teresa said to him. "A bad dream, that's all. You're safe. The puppy's safe."

"My puppy . . ."

"Ssssh, child. It's all over now."

"They killed his puppy." Toby's little wiseguy voice coming out of Luke's body. "They hung it upside down. They cut it open. The man with the hood, he cut out the heart and he ate it. He said he'd cut out Luke's heart too. If he ever told. Luke swore he never would. Luke's a little fucking pussy."

I dropped to my knees, my hand on the back of Luke's head, the way you support a baby who can't hold his head up yet. "Tell what, Toby?"

"Baby baby baby," the child babbled. A murderer's mantra. I watched his eyes. The shift came. "Baby," the voice hissed. "Bad baby. Killed my puppy. Baby wouldn't play like they wanted. I am . . ."

He launched himself off the floor, scrambling for one of the table settings. Where they had knives. I took him down, smothering his rage with my body, smelling his blood.

He went rigid again. Then I felt him soften beneath me, let him loose. He shook himself, sweat droplets flying. Teresa was talking to him. One of Mama's waiters swept the restaurant with the barrel of his pistol, looking for the evil with a blind eye.

124

Luke sat on Mama's lap, sipping from a glass of ice water. One of the waiters put a Closed for Repairs sign in the window—no customers today. The puppy plodded around on the tabletop, investigating all the smells.

"Luke, listen to Mama," the dragon lady said, soft-voiced. "Nobody hurt puppy. *Nobody*, understand? You take puppy with you. Everyplace you go, people watch you. Safe, okay?"

"Sure, Mama," the kid said, watching the puppy lick up a mixture of tuna flakes and rice from a saucer.

I stepped away from the table, spoke to Teresa in a corner.

"Dissociation. Trauma-memories. He was reliving, reexperiencing."

"Did he have a puppy . . . before?"

"I don't know. Now's not the time to ask him. He comes back more quickly now . . . we're getting closer."

"Is it safe to leave the puppy with him?"

"You saw for yourself. It's babies he thinks are the enemy . . . a part of him, but he doesn't see that yet."

"Remember what we talked about . . . ? I want to bring that woman tomorrow. To talk to you. Not here, but a place close by. One of Mama's people will take you there, okay?"

She nodded.

I went to the pay phone in the back.

"This is SAFE. How can I help you?"

"You buy my clothes yet?" I asked Noelle.

"Oh, Burke! Not clothes, just a jacket. You didn't give me enough money for . . ."

"Never mind. Is your mother around?"

"No. She went somewhere with Storm."

"Okay. You know Wolfe's number?"

"Sure. She's so stylish. She's going to take me to the . . ."

"Noelle, listen to me. Give her a call. Tell her to go to a good phone and call me. Understand?"

"Sure. Want me to do it now?"

"Yes."

"Okay. When you come over I . . ."

"Now, Noelle."

"Well, *fine!*"

She hung up.

125

"**W**here's Luke?" I asked Mama after Teresa left.

"Nap," she said, nodding her head toward the kitchen.

The phone rang. I walked back to answer it. Caught a glimpse of Luke, curled up on a dark green futon just outside the kitchen door, the puppy asleep against his chest. Baby's breath soft between them.

"Hello," I answered the ring.

"What's up?" Lily's voice.

"I'm trying to arrange a meet. Let her see what's really going down."

"What if . . . ?"

"There's no 'what if' here anymore. It's what we have to do, now. It's time."

"When is it? I'm coming too."

"No, you're not. Let me do this, get it done."

"I . . ."

"I'll call you."

Luke was up from his nap, playing with the puppy on the floor, Mama watching over the rim of her newspaper.

"I love her," the kid said, looking at me.

"Seems like she loves you too."

"Yes. She does. I can tell. Burke, will you help me with something?"

"Sure."

"I need a name for her. A *good* name, just for her."

"I don't know, Luke . . . I mean . . . a name, that's a special thing."

"Yes, I know. And it has to be a *real* name, Burke, you understand?"

"Sure. But . . ."

"Remember our names? Luke and Burke?"

"Yes. Lurk."

"That's right. Together we're more than just the two of us. Friends. That's what I want . . ." His forehead furrowed, thinking so hard his body trembled. I lit a smoke, wary of his eyes, but he was okay, still Luke.

"Do you know his father's name?"

"Sure," I said. Thinking how I'd never know mine. "His dad's name is Simba."

"I know Simba—I met him. What's his mother's?"

"Elsa."

"Simba and Elsa . . . Elsa and Simba . . . I know, Burke! Her name is *Simsa!* Do you like it?"

"Yeah. It's perfect."

"Simsa," the boy called. The puppy wagged its tail happily.

127

Wolfe called just past three.

"Can we do it tomorrow?" I asked her.

"What time?"

"I'll pick you up around ten . . . ?"

"Okay. At the diner."

"I'll have a black Dodge. Gypsy cab. I'll be at the curb at ten."

"See you."

"Yeah. By the way, congratulations. Autopsy done yet?"

"See you tomorrow," she said. And hung up.

128

I drove over to Max's around eight the next morning. Went upstairs. He was arguing with Immaculata about something—I couldn't tell what.

"You ready?" I asked Immaculata.

"Everybody's ready. You can drop us off at SAFE, okay?"

"Sure."

Max and his woman got in the front seat with the baby, me and Luke and the puppy took the back.

"Wow, Burke! It's dark in here—I can't see outside."

"It's okay, Luke," I told him, switching on the Tensor light. "We're safe here. With Max up front and Simsa back here, nobody would dare bother us."

"Don't forget Immaculata," he corrected me gravely. "She's tough too."

"Yeah, you're right. You know you're going to see Teresa over at Max's house today?"

"It's Immaculata's house too."

"Okay, okay, kid. I got it. What are you . . . studying to be a feminist?"

"What's a feminist?"

"Ask Lily, okay?"

"Okay. Are you mad at me?"

"Hell no. I'm not mad at anyone. Just embarrassed that a kid's smarter than me sometimes."

"Oh, you're very smart. Lily said so."

"Lily said I was smart?"

"Tricky, is what she said."

"Oh."

"It's okay, Burke. You're my friend. Like my big brother."

"More than you know, kid."

Couldn't hear anything from the front seat. I wouldn't anyway—Max and Immaculata can battle to a fever pitch without making a sound.

"How was Simsa's first night?"

"Oh, it was *good*. Mac told me I could wrap an alarm clock in a towel and the puppy would feel like it was his mother's heartbeat . . . but she slept with me instead. My heart beat for her."

129

The cab slid to a stop. Luke scrambled out, holding his pup, eager to show everyone. Mac put a hand on the boy's shoulder, made some gesture at Max, stamped her foot. Max pointed at me, shrugged his wide shoulders. Mac stepped in close to me.

"He says you don't want Lily to be at the meeting with Wolfe."

"That's right. You guys are battling each other—I got no time for it. You asked me to persuade Wolfe to jump back—I'm trying to do that—what'd you want to get in the way for?"

"Oh, go away," she snapped. "Go someplace with your pal. Come on, Luke," turning away from me.

On the way to Queens, I tried to explain things to Max. He kept his eyes on the road, pretended he couldn't pick up my gestures.

130

We were waiting at the curb by the diner a good twenty minutes in front. I picked Wolfe up in the side mirror, stepped out and opened the back door like a chauffeur, climbed in after her. Max took off smoothly, heading for the highway. If she had people following us, they'd have an easy time until we hit Chinatown.

Wolfe threw a quick glance at the blackout windows. Her mouth twitched. "Very clever," she said.

"Better than a blindfold, huh?"

"Sure."

"Want a drink? This thing isn't air-conditioned," I said, offering her an unopened bottle of cold spring water I'd bought from the deli across from the diner.

"Thank you." She unscrewed the bottle cap, took a long pull.

"I appreciate you doing this."

She took another sip. "The baby's been positively identified."

"How'd you do that? He was in the water a long time."

"The coroner said it was Battered Child Syndrome—just about every bone was fractured, some of the old ones had healed. Derrick had been X-rayed before—the last time there was a child abuse complaint. The pictures were a perfect match."

"You know for sure what killed him?"

"He was beaten to death. Hard to tell exactly what finally did it—

lungs punctured, blood in the spinal column . . . maybe all of that and more. Doesn't matter now, it's a homicide, not an accident."

"Who's gonna be indicted for it?"

She looked at me like I'd have to step up in class to be stupid. "Both of them—the mother's already made statements. Lots of statements. Sometimes she says the kid fell down the stairs, sometimes he choked on his bottle. Doesn't matter . . . the coroner said the baby was killed over a long period of time. She had to know."

"She did know."

"Yes. She'll come up with some kind of defense—they've always got new ones. She's going down for this, just like he is, once we pick him up. He won't go far. He's a Welfare vulture, living off dead-souled women. We'll find him."

"Find him? I thought he was locked up on another charge."

She looked at me squarely, faint traces of disbelief in her face. "He made bail—they never set high bail for beating up a woman."

I offered her a smoke. She shook her head, rummaged in her purse, came out with one of her own. I lit it for her.

"This won't take long today," I promised.

The cab rolled along. Felt like we were still on the highway.

"How did you know . . . about the water?" she finally asked me.

"I figured it out," I told her. Meaning: the mother hadn't told me.

She dragged on her smoke, pale eyes focused on something not inside the cab. "You started this . . . investigation, it was a job, yes?"

"Yeah."

"To find the baby?"

"Yeah."

"So the job's over . . . ?"

"Un-huh."

"And you're not looking for Emerson?"

"I didn't even know he was out. How come all the questions?"

"You know now. The way most people would look at this, we'd need her testimony to convict him, understand?"

I nodded.

"We don't. What we need, we need his testimony to convict *her*. The only way they both get dropped for this is for them to point the finger at each other. Try them separately."

"Okay."

"Yes, okay. That means, we want to find this Emerson. If he turns up in the water himself . . . if he just disappears, it might get her off the hook."

"Why tell me?"

"You have different . . . reputations, Mr. Burke. Depending on who's talking."

"My record speaks for itself."

"Very funny. We've got records too. Like the visitors' logs from the jail."

"So?"

"So you visited a man named Kenneth Silver three times over the past couple of months."

"He's an old friend."

"He's an assassin. For a white supremacist gang. The way the prisons are today, he may be more dangerous inside than out."

"You don't understand the way things are in there. It's not politics, it's survival. I've known him since I was a kid. We went different ways, he got caught in a cross, but I'm not gonna turn my back on him when he's down."

"Is that loyalty . . . or peer pressure?"

"You put a lot of guys in there, but you don't know how it works. Inside the walls, what you call peer pressure, it's as sharp as a knife sometimes . . . You understand what I'm saying?"

"Better than you think. Like I said, about Emerson . . ."

"You think I'm some kind of vigilante?"

"No. I think you're some kind of mercenary. And I think you do what you're paid to do."

"Nobody hired me to do Emerson. I'm not looking for him."

She ground out her cigarette. "I'm sure you're not, you say so. But if you happen to run across him in your travels, give us a call, okay?"

"Okay."

131

The cab's rhythm changed. In the city now. Harsh, hypertense traffic sounds. We'd have picked up our outriders by now. If Max spotted a car too interested in us, he'd flash his high beams—maneuver so he was first off at a light. The driver of the car trailing us would never see it coming, wouldn't even have time to wonder why a pack of Chinese teenagers dressed in bright silk baseball jackets would be trying to clean his windshield. Never hear the ice picks puncture his tires.

Wolfe never glanced at her watch. Didn't make comments like she would if she was trying to give a tape recorder some clues. She'd know— no matter where we held the meeting, she wouldn't find Luke there again.

The cab was down to a crawl now, swivel-hipping its way past the potholes. One final turn, and it came to a stop. I heard Max shut off the engine.

I took a black silk scarf out of my pocket, held it out to Wolfe.

"Okay to put this on now? Just for a minute, until we get into the room?"

She took it from me, adjusted the thick band over her eyes, tied it over her long hair. Held out her hand to me. I helped her from the back seat.

We were in the first-floor garage to Max's warehouse.

132

Max shut the garage doors, walked past us, started up the stairs.

"There's no railing," I said to Wolfe. She put her hand lightly on Max's back, mine went to her waist. Even in the high heels, she handled the climb like it was level ground.

At the landing, we walked past Max's dojo to a room at the end. Luke was talking to Teresa, being himself, explaining something, a deck of cards in his hand.

I nodded to Teresa, took off the blindfold as Max floated down the hall like smoke. He'd wait at the top of the stairs. Nobody'd bother us.

"Hello, Luke," Wolfe said.

He nodded at her gravely. "You want to talk to me again?"

"No. Just to listen, all right? You're safe here—with your friends. I haven't come to take you."

"Okay."

Wolfe sat down on a straight chair, smoothed her skirt, crossed her legs.

"You can smoke here," Luke said.

She flashed a smile, reached in her purse. I looked over her shoulder. No gun, no tape recorder. Caught Teresa's eye, nodded.

I cracked a wooden match, lit Wolfe's cigarette.

"How have you been doing, Luke?" she asked.

"Okay."

"Don't be afraid. Your friend is here."

"Who?"

"Him," she said, nodding her head in my direction.

"Who's he?" the kid said, face cleaned of deception, innocent. Mama was teaching him more than cards.

Wolfe's smile was brighter this time. "His name is Burke."

"Hello," the boy said, extending his hand for me to shake.

I sat down in a chair next to Wolfe, moved her ashtray so we could both use it.

"Are you ready to work now, Luke?" Teresa asked.

"Yes," he said, sitting in a child-size armchair, looking straight at her.

Teresa didn't use a girasol, didn't use anything at all. The library articles told me about this—how the multiples get used to reaching a trance state in therapy—the splits are born from autohypnosis anyway. "Relax," is all Teresa said, and the boy's eyes started rapid-fire blinking. Then closed.

"Can I talk to Toby?" Teresa asked.

"What is it now?" Toby's voice, pitched like Luke's but with a sharp, sarcastic undertone.

"How are the others doing?" Teresa.

"How should we be doing? I mean, nobody's hurting the baby, but Luke, you know him, he's still scared. But he's better. We don't get out so much anymore."

"What did they do to the baby?"

"They don't do *nothing* to the baby. What's wrong with you? It's Luke they do it to."

"The baby, she doesn't feel things?"

"The baby runs away. I told you all this. The baby runs away. Susie."

"Do you like babies?"

"I don't care about them."

"Does Luke like babies?"

"Yeah. Luke's a sucker. He likes everyone. He even liked them. When they'd scare him, the baby would come out. To take the pain."

"Did you ever come out when they scared him?"

"Do I look crazy to you, lady? I did . . . once . . . to talk to them . . . and . . . they hurt me."

"How did they hurt you, Toby?"

"It wasn't me . . . when they started, Luke came back. When they hurt him, the baby came. The runaway."

"What did they do to Luke?"

"They scared him. They tied him up. All with hoods. Black hoods. They put things in him. Burned. He screamed. They told him to be good, be a good baby. He screamed and screamed until the baby came out. Then he was good."

"What did Luke do when he was good?"

"Suck."

"Suck what?"

"Suck . . . them."

"Men?"

"Not just men. Women too. And another boy, once. Then they put things in him. He was bleeding."

"Did he fight them?"

"No. He was scared. Luke had a puppy, Prince. They killed the puppy. Cut his heart out. One of them ate the heart. It was just a little thing, so small."

"The puppy?"

"The *heart*. You listening to me or what?"

"I'm listening to you, Toby. How many people were there?"

"Lots of them. All in hoods—they never took off the hoods. They had candles. Candles and smoke. And stuff on the wall too. They always said Satan. Like in church. And a table. A big table. That's what they put Luke on, the table. It had stuff on it, carved. I saw the knife."

"Did they cut Luke with the knife?"

"No. They put something in him. With wires. When Luke screamed, they'd make it burn so bad inside him. They did it. Every time. They said he had to be a good baby. Good baby. When the baby came to run away, then the baby saw the cameras. Then we could all go."

"Go?"

"Like . . . pass out, you know? Go away. It hurt when we came back . . . tried to go away, far away. We didn't want to come back."

"When did the other one come?"

"What other one, sister? There's only Luke and the baby Susie. And me."

"Toby, you're smart, yes? You see things Luke doesn't?"

"Yeah, Luke ain't that smart. He *thinks* he is . . . but he don't know some things."

"Do you know who killed the puppy, Toby?"

"Yeah. Those hoods, they didn't fool me. Voices. I know their voices."

"Whose voices?"

"Dad. And Mom too, she was there. Dad killed the puppy. Mommy, she was the one who said to be a good baby. Good baby. They had a baby, you know. A little baby. A boy baby. Like us. They wanted a girl baby—I heard them say. It would be good if they had a girl too. Better product. A little girl. Baby Susie. Luke thought, if he was a girl, they'd be nice to him. But I know them. Luke's stupid."

"Why is he stupid?"

" 'Cause he don't remember the way I do. He thinks it all started when he was older . . . if he was a baby, they wouldn't hurt him. Luke was jealous."

"What did he want?"

"He wanted them to love him," the voice sneered.

"Tell me about the baby?"

"We *made* the baby. Me and Luke. What they did to Luke . . . it's what they do to make babies, so we made a baby. Luke wanted her so they'd love him. Not hurt him. But I knew . . . I wanted the baby to run away. Take the pain. So we made the baby. But the baby . . . the other baby, they knew that was the *real* baby."

"Toby . . ."

"Baby." The voice had no age. I held my hands rigid, had to let the monster come out, let Wolfe see it.

"Who . . . ?" Teresa asked.

"Baby!" The voice was a snarl. Luke's eyes were slitted, muscles jumping in his little face. "I want the heart," he said. "Baby baby baby," a crooning child's voice. "*I* am Satan's child. *Me!* I am the one . . ." He launched himself at Teresa, the right fist frenzy-stabbing, low grunts from somewhere in him. I took him down, wrapping my arms around his spasming body, saying his name over and over.

It felt like forever. Then he went rigid against me. I rolled over on my back, the boy against my chest. Let go my hold.

Luke sat on my chest, giggled. "What are you doing, Burke?" he asked. "You're always playing."

133

The air reeked with Luke's scent. Bloody fear. He didn't seem to know, his back to the women in the room.

"We've got company," I told him.

He looked over his shoulder, not getting off me.

"Hi, Teresa!" he said. He looked at Wolfe. "Hello."

"Where've you been, Luke?" Teresa asked him.

"Playing with Bur . . . my friend," the boy answered. "I was showing him some card tricks." Eyes on my face now, begging me to be his co-conspirator, not to rat him out.

"Yeah," I said. "The kid's a real gambler."

"It's not gambling, playing with you." Luke laughed, getting to his feet, extending his little hand to me to pull me off the floor.

"I got to talk to these ladies, Luke, okay? How about if you go next door, play with Simsa?"

"Can I show her to Teresa first?"

"Okay, go get her. But just for a minute, all right?"

"Yes!" He took off like a shot.

134

He came running back in, the puppy in his arms. "Look!" he said, thrusting the dog almost in Teresa's face. She patted the dog dutifully.

"Can I hold her?" Wolfe asked him.

Luke turned slowly, cradling his pup, watchful. "You be careful," he said, walking to her.

Wolfe took the pup on her lap, patting the dog's large head, stroking its ears. She lifted the pup right into her face. The puppy licked her. She licked it back. "Oh, ugh!" Luke laughed. "You licked her!"

"Well, she licked me first. Probably smells my dog on me. Do you smell Bruiser, Simsa? You smell my big boy?"

The puppy yapped like she was answering.

"You're a real beauty, aren't you? A lovely dog. Look at those paws . . . you're gonna be a *big* girl, yes? A big, tough girl," nuzzling the pup.

"You have a dog?" Luke asked, stepping close.

"Yes, I have a Rottweiler. You know what that is?"

"No."

"Want to see a picture?" she asked, playing the kid like a fighting fish—setting the hook before she jerked the line.

"Sure!"

She handed Simsa back to Luke, took a bunch of photos out of her purse. Handed them to the boy. He put Simsa on the floor, stood next to Wolfe, leafed through the pictures.

"Is that him?"

"Yes. That's Bruiser. When he was a pup."

I looked over her shoulder. Wolfe holding a fat black puppy, one hand under its rump, the other around its chest. The little beast's paws draped over her arm, tiny tip of his tongue showing. Wolfe was wearing an old flannel shirt, her hair loose and free. Looked like a college girl.

Another photo: Wolfe all dressed up, wearing a black leather coat and heels. Bruiser at her side, his head at the top of her thigh.

Another: Bruiser bursting through the open gate at her house in full cry, ears flapping, mouth a snarl.

"He got real big, didn't he?"

"Yes, he did, Luke. He's my true friend. Bruiser will always protect me . . . like Simsa will you."

"He was a puppy?" Luke setting a hook of his own.

"All dogs are puppies, once. He was a wonderful pup. Just like Simsa."

"I love Simsa. Do you love your Bruiser?"

"Yes. I love my true friends. And I would do anything for them."

"Anything?" The kid tugged at the line.

"Yes. Anything."

"Is he your friend?" Pointing at me.

"We are . . . professional friends, do you understand?"

"No."

"Well, it means we are on the same side. So we're friends. We don't do things together, the way some friends do. But we're close . . . in a way."

"If he's your friend, what's his name?"

"Burke." Wolfe smiled. "He's the one who brought me here. To see you."

"You don't like me," the boy accused, remembering.

"That's not true, Luke. I didn't like you so much when I first met you. But that was my mistake. I see that now. Now I really like you."

"Is that true?"

"Look in my eyes, Luke. Come here. Look in my eyes. See for yourself."

The boy studied her. "You like my puppy. Burke is your friend. And . . . you *do* like me."

"Yes."

"Am I going to be your friend?"

"Yes, we're going to be friends."

"Then you could love me . . . like you love your friends?"

"Yes, sort of like that."

"Okay," Luke said, wandering over to me, done with his testing.

Wolfe reached for a cigarette. "Burke has matches," Luke volunteered, watching me under his long lashes. I handed the little box to Luke. He went back over to Wolfe, lit one for her.

She leaned forward, cupping her hands around his.

"Thank you, Luke."

"You're welcome. I have lots of friends. They love me. Like you said. Burke is my friend." A sly grin flashed across his poker face. "Do you love Burke?"

Wolfe dragged on her smoke. "Uh . . . sure!"

"Are you going to get married?"

"I don't think so, Luke. People who love each other don't always get married. You understand?"

"Sure." Moving close to her, looking at the photos in her hand. "What's this one?" he asked.

I looked to see what he was holding. Picture of a racehorse, a winner's circle photo of a trotter, still hooked to its sulky, a groom holding the bridle, the driver in blue-and-white silks holding the reins, smiling. Small print at the bottom: Jasper County Fair, Illinois. July 4, 1990, Second Race, 3 y.o. ECS Trot, First Filly Elimination winner: The Flame. Owner: The Syndicate, Inc. Time: 2:07.1, single heat.

"Is that your horse?" the boy asked.

"She sure is. Isn't she beautiful?"

"Yes! Could I go see her someday?"

"Yes. But now, go take Simsa in the other room. So I can talk with your friends, okay?"

"Okay," he said, gathering up his puppy.

He started out of the room. Hesitated, watching me. Gave Wolfe a quick kiss on the cheek and walked out. Hiding behind cute.

135

"**D**id you understand what you saw?" Teresa asked Wolfe.

"I think so," she said, voice flat, not playing a role for the kid anymore.

"He's much better now."

"Better?"

"Oh yes. Did you see the way he asked Burke to help him? When he lost time? He knows he does it now. Knows we know too. I can't talk to the baby, Susie. And Luke, when he's on the spot, he's just himself. He's not ready to talk about what he knows."

"On the spot?"

"When one of the personalities takes center stage, so to speak. The others stand off in the darkness. Watching. Luke uses Toby to tell us . . . tell us what happened to him. We get closer every day."

"And what happened was . . . Luke was tortured? Sodomized? And they filmed it?"

"Yes. He's got an incredible IQ. When the pain got too much, he split off. It's all a nest of twisted snakes in his mind. It was his parents who did this to him. His mother and his father. They kept telling him to be good. *Good!* To hold still for the torture so they could film it. Luke became the baby, Susie. He knew . . . that rational part of him knew . . . they wanted a baby girl. He didn't understand that they wanted a girl to make more torture films."

"There's a market for both," I said. "Boys and girls, so long as it's kids."

Wolfe nodded, her pale eyes on Teresa.

"Toby's the street-wise one. All he knew was that the baby didn't feel the pain. He could go away. Be safe. But children have so much love, it's incredible. Their love doesn't die of natural causes—you have to kill it. No matter what parents do to them, they try to find an excuse for it. So Luke, he blamed the baby. His baby brother. In Luke's mind, the torture didn't start until his baby brother came. It all merged, overwhelmed him. The Satanic rituals, cutting out the puppy's heart. He needed strength. Power. And he had so much rage. The nightmares intruded. He wasn't safe even when he slept. And so the other personality came. The Satan-monster."

"He killed those babies?"

"The other one did. Satan's Child, he calls it sometimes. Sometimes, he just says Satan. All that blood, the chanting, the pain . . . it was a tidal wave in his mind."

"His . . . parents. They're devil-worshipers? The puppy was a sacrifice?"

My turn. "They're not devil worshipers," I said to Wolfe. "They're terrorists. All child molesters are, you know that. Fear's always stronger than force—it stays with you even when you're alone. Even when you try to sleep, night terrors come. It's happening all over now. They frighten the child into silence, make the kid believe they have magical powers. Life and death. That's why they killed the puppy. It wasn't some bullshit sacrifice to Satan, it was them proving to the kid that they held all the cards. Telling him they could do anything they want. Anytime they want. Those maggots're no more Satanists than you are. There's real ones—I mean, people who fucking worship the devil, okay? Some true believers, some charlatans. Just like Christians. Or Jews, or Muslims, or whatever. Sodomizing kids, making kiddie-porn films, it's got nothing to do with religion. Any religion. A priest molests an altar boy, you call it *Catholic* child abuse?"

"Okay. I get it."

"No, you don't get it. Not the whole thing. This Satanic child abuse thing, it's just a criminal conspiracy. Set up so they can't lose. The kid buys into the insanity, he grows up to become one of them. Recruits others. Puts on the hood himself, works the cameras, chops up the bodies if they make any. And if you guys find out, if the kid tells you the truth, he fucking *sounds* nuts, right? You want to take a victim before a jury, have him tell about some devil-worshiping cult? That's for

Geraldo, not the real world." I bit the inside of my cheek, tasting acid. "It's all a hustle—like kids committing suicide because they heard subliminal messages on heavy-metal music. Some lawyer's idea, right? Next thing you know, some fuck's gonna shoot up a bank, say he read the Bible backward, got a new message."

"It's true," Teresa put in. "Almost like they know what they're doing. You can deliberately introduce dissociation. Splitting. All it takes is inescapable pressure. Stylized sadism. One shock to the psyche after another. Even in a concentration camp, the prisoner knows he's not alone. There's a reason for him to be there . . . even if it's an evil reason. But a child like Luke—he was all by himself until he split off."

Wolfe lit another smoke, using a lighter from her purse. "We've had cases like this before. Not the multiple-personality thing. Not even with cameras. But kids being sexually abused by a group. Devil-signs, black hoods. We don't even mention it to the jury . . . just try it like what it is. Rape. The defense wants to bring it up, that's their problem. They can't even cross-examine the victim on it without telling the jury they knew about it. And where would they know except from their slimy clients?"

"Luke didn't kill those babies," I told her. "Those people, his parents and the others, they did it. Sure as if they'd held the knife."

"They'd never go down for homicide on the facts we have," she said. "But it doesn't matter. We've got no death penalty in this state. And they're looking at forever-to-life for what we *can* prove." She turned to Teresa. "Is he going to be able to testify?"

"We're working on bringing his personalities back together. Fusing them so there's no splits. The core, Luke, is very strong. Maybe someday. But . . . if he's pressured too much, too early . . . he could go back over."

Wolfe's eyes glowed in the white room, shining like Strega's had when she told me her truth. "There'll be something else, somewhere. The films . . . could Luke maybe tell you *where* it happened? Not on the stand . . . just tell *you?*"

"Yes, I think so. He's a brilliant child. All the memory is there. Just . . . fragmented."

Wolfe ground out her cigarette. "Okay." Turning to me. "Let's go."

"We have to wait here a little bit, okay? Until the driver comes back."

She settled back into her chair. Teresa said goodbye, said she was going to talk to Luke. She'd tell Max it was time to take off.

I lit a smoke of my own. "That racehorse, it said on the photo it was owned by something called the Syndicate. Is that just the corporate name you use?"

"The Flame isn't just mine. We all bought her together."

"Who?"

"My . . . sisters. We're like a family, all together. We thought it would be fun."

"Your sisters?"

"She means us," Lily said, stepping into the room, Immaculata right behind her.

136

It was like someone hit the Mute button on the TV. They all looked at each other, frozen in place, too much playing over their faces for me to read it.

Lily muttered something in Italian, grabbed Wolfe in a fierce hug, tears flying as Wolfe squeezed her back, Immaculata shouldering in between them, their so differently beautiful faces pushed against one another, makeup melting as they merged.

I stood away from them, an outsider, feeling the void inside me like a brick in my chest. Turned my face to the window. A filthy city wall returned my blank stare, undeceived.

137

It took them a while, the warrior women rebonding, speaking in tribal-talk. I wasn't in the room for them.

Finally, Teresa came back in. Pulled Lily aside, said something to her.

Lily caught my eye, held a clenched fist at her waist. Thanks. Immaculata bowed. Teresa stepped out with them.

"Ready to take me back?" Wolfe asked.

I wrapped the blindfold around her eyes, guided her carefully down the stairs, into the back of the cab.

Max had it rolling as soon as I slammed the door.

138

My watch said it was three-thirty. Wolfe sat to my left, her back against the door, turning so she was almost facing me. She lit a cigarette.

"Are you going to look for them?"

"Who?"

She waved her hand at me, trailing smoke, elegantly impatient. "Luke's parents."

"No."

"No?"

"That's what I said. It's not my job."

"You mean nobody's paying you?"

"Yeah, that's what I mean."

"Who paid you for Bonnie Browne?"

"I wasn't paid for her—I was paid to find a photograph." Paid by Strega, forever ago.

"And her husband?" The freak in the clown suit. The cops found him at the bottom of the stairs, his neck broken.

"The way I heard it, it was an accident."

"You don't trust me."

"With what?"

"I just don't want us to get in each other's way with this."

"There is no 'this,' okay? You want something, spell it out."

She ground out her smoke, opened her purse, took out a mirror, balanced it on her knees as she ran a comb through her hair. Put on fresh lipstick. A bit of it smeared as the cab hit a bump. She dabbed at it with a piece of tissue. Crossed her legs, looked back over at me.

"Vigilante. That's real popular now. People lose confidence in law enforcement, they start using self-help. But you . . . it's like your profession. What you get paid for."

"That's not me," I told her. Thinking: Who's a citizen in all this? Lily, Storm, Immaculata . . . even Wolfe, they were all over the line. I lived on the other side, they crossed over when they needed to . . . what was the difference?

"I think it is," she said. "You're known to half a dozen law enforcement agencies, and they all say the same thing. There's not enough to charge you with anything, but there's homicides going back to the last time you were in prison. And they all have one thing in common."

"Dead people do."

"It was always about children, that's the thread."

"It doesn't tie to me, whatever it is. If I went around snuffing baby-rapers, I'd be on overtime—the city's full of them."

"What're you saying?"

"You really want to know? A vigilante, he straps down, goes hunting. It's not personal. Me, you leave me alone, that's the end of it. I'm not a hunter. The newspapers, they got this vigilante thing all screwed up. A woman gets grabbed in an alley, pulls out a knife and stabs the guy trying to rape her, the press says she's a vigilante. She's not. Just someone defending herself."

"And that's what you do?"

"I don't *do* anything. I have my own people. That's what I have. All I have."

She leaned forward, pale eyes not merging with the darkness in the back of the cab—a light of their own. "I'm trying to tell you something, you want to listen," she said. "Lily doesn't have what you want—the CWA reports, the pedigree on the parents, last known address, associates, DMV, IRS. All that. She doesn't have it. I do."

"So?"

"Usually, we'd share. My crew and Lily's. But . . . the way things started out with Luke, we didn't . . ."

"She shared with you now."

"I know. But Lily's no investigator. I mean . . . she investigates inside children's heads, you understand? My people, we work outside. Like you."

"Your people worked like me, I'd never get hired."

"You're saying you're better at it than we are?"

"I'm saying . . . you can't use your kind of stuff with freaks. Especially when they run in packs. You can't use undercovers—they have an acid test. Like a day-care center where they're doing the kids. You suspect it, right? So you get somebody hired. Know what they do? They leave your guy alone in a back room with a kid. Wait to see what happens. Your guy doesn't start groping the kid, they know he's not one of them. Simple, right? You can have undercovers shoot up, snort some coke, help out in a heist, even turn a trick, that's what it takes. But you haven't got anybody who'd fuck a kid just for a credential."

Thinking about what the Queen called me. When I hunted, it wasn't for evidence.

"Proof isn't what we need here," she said. "There's enough proof. They get brought in, I can get them indicted."

I lit a cigarette, catching it for the first time. "You've been looking for them all along, haven't you?"

She nodded.

"And come up empty?"

Another nod.

"So you want me to take a shot?"

Her generous mouth wrinkled at one corner. "Was that a pun?"

She was quiet for a while. I felt the grid beneath the tires on the Fifty-ninth Street Bridge. Max was going straight up Queens Boulevard to the courthouse.

"You think people really worship the devil?" Wolfe asked.

"Sure. It's the perfect religion—you fuck up, you go to heaven."

Her rich laugh filled the cab.

139

The rolling blindfold slowed to a stop. Max rapped twice on the barrier to let us know we'd arrived. Wolfe gathered her purse. The back door opened on my side. Her hand touched my forearm.

"Don't take this the wrong way, okay? All this . . . the way you are . . . did you ever see a psychiatrist?"

"Yeah. One of them owed a guy I know some money once."

Her smile came. "Don't take this the wrong way either," she whispered. Kissed me softly on the cheek.

She didn't look back.

140

Max drove us to the junkyard. The Mole wasn't around. Terry gave me back my Plymouth. I told him Luke loved the puppy, told him her new name.

Max didn't communicate all the way back. Inside himself. I dropped him off at the warehouse. He stood there in the shadows, holding me with his eyes. Finally, he gestured like he was shuffling a pack of cards. Dealt them out around an imaginary table. Pointed at himself, face set in concrete lines.

I nodded.

He bowed, sealing the pact.

141

Still early, but I went back to the office. I could make a call, see if the Central Park lady wanted to have dinner. Or take a drive, pick up Bonita, bend her over the convertible couch in her living room, try and get lost in it. Come and go.

Thought about getting lost in it. What I'd lose if I did.

I kicked back, lit a cigarette. Watched the smoke drift toward the ceiling. Why had Wolfe mentioned Silver to me? The Prof had sent me to him, a long time ago. When we were all inside.

"Listen and learn, schoolboy," he said. "Silver knows the play, the old way, see? He's a quality thief—good gunfighter too, way I heard it."

"A hit-man?"

"No, fool. I said gunfighter, not gunman."

SACRIFICE

"What's the difference?"

"A gunfighter, the other guy has one too."

We were talking quietly on the yard, Silver telling me a secret in his hard-sad voice. "I don't mess with the sissies in here. They're like bitches on the street, get you into a knife fight in a minute. My wife's picture's in my house—I jack off to it every night, looking at her. These other guys, they do it to girls in the skin magazines. Those ain't real people—they don't know those girls. Me, I'm making love to my wife. To Helene. Those other guys, they're just playing with themselves."

Like I was with Bonita.

Silver did his time, counting the days. Never made trouble for anyone. Someone went in his cell, stole his wife's picture. Anyone could have done it, prison's like that. If it hadn't turned out to be a black guy, Silver might have turned out different himself.

The Prof tried to ease it down. Told Silver it was just a picture—his wife would send him another one. Told the thief, Horace his name was, a rapist, told Horace he was risking a shank in the back for nothing. Even volunteered to handle the transfer himself.

Horace had a better way, he thought. Got himself an African name, joined some crew.

I filled out the pass for Horace to report to the psychiatrist. Silver was waiting for him in the corridor. He was only going to cut him, but Horace had a blade too.

Silver got cut. Horace got dead.

Blood on the institutional green concrete walls, drying to an abstract painting only a convict could interpret.

When Horace's crew came after Silver, he went the only place he could.

A white supremacist, Wolfe called him. An assassin. He was doing better than me. Even locked up, he had his love.

142

Things went back to the way they'd been. A few days later, Lily gave me a thick envelope. From Wolfe. Whatever she had was in there. Wasn't much, and her people would already have worked it to death.

I was in a Manhattan courtroom. One of the motion parts. They were supposed to bring Silver over from the jail, some kind of bullshit bail application. A farce—they wouldn't cut him loose.

A halfass defense attorney was in front of the bench, babbling something about the Constitution. Roland was his name, a certified dummy. He'd been an ADA once, a stone incompetent. Plenty of guilty men walking the streets because of his fuckups. Now he was working the defense side, sending innocent folks to jail. Balancing the scales of justice. In the dog-eat-dog world of the criminal court, Roland was a fire hydrant.

I caught Blumberg's eye, got to my feet, walked over to him.

"You're looking good, boychick. How's business?"

"The same."

"Silver said he wanted to talk to you—you couldn't visit him in the house?"

"This is the way he wanted it. I'll just stand next to you at the table. Won't take a minute, okay?"

"My bail application is complex, my boy. Don't distract the judge's attention."

"You couldn't wake that weasel up with a flame thrower."

Blumberg ignored me. The wily old bastard hasn't tried a case in a hundred years, just does arraignments and applications. He knew why Silver hired him.

They brought him up from the pens in cuffs, but the guards stepped back, let him stand next to Blumberg at the counsel table. I stood on the other side of him, wearing my suit, briefcase in my hand, role-playing.

Blumberg mumbled something, just clearing his throat before he let loose. One thing he was good for—he could talk nonstop for days. As soon as he got into full stride, Silver bowed his head, talked to me out of the side of his mouth.

"You do something for me?"

"What?"

"Helene. She needs some cash. She wants to move Upstate, be close to me on this bit."

"You gonna be hit long?"

"They're going to bitch me, Burke. I'm looking at the book—a quarter-to-forever."

Twenty-five-to-life. Silver was ten years older than me—he'd never come out.

"What does she need?"

"Twenty, thirty G's, like that. She's gonna buy a house, get a job. Live like a citizen."

"Can't . . . ?"

"The Brotherhood would get her the money, but I don't want her in this, understand? It's a life sentence once you join. *She* never joined, just me. I *got* the money, Burke. From when I was stealing. I'm not sure exactly how much is there but . . . I'll tell you where it is, you pick it up, get it to her."

"Who . . . ?"

"It's in a house. Basement of a house. In Gerritsen Beach. You know where it is?"

"Yeah."

"In the basement, farthest left-hand corner from the front of the house. Patched in with cement, wrapped in plastic, maybe a foot down."

"Can't she . . . ?"

"She can't do nothing. The house, I owned it once. Helene, she sold it. To get bail money for me one time. Years ago. Just forged my signature, sold it. I couldn't tell her—didn't have time. You understand? Some citizen owns it now—you gotta go in the basement."

"What if it's not there?"

"Then I played my last card. There's nobody else I can ask—didn't want to take a chance the feds have the jail miked."

"Tell me the address," I said.

He told me, gripping my arm so hard it hurt, looking down, trusting.

143

Gerritsen Beach is in Brooklyn, just past Sheepshead Bay. Sunday, we drove the Boulevard, Marine Park running swampy to our left, reed grass high, people walking their dogs, Bensonhurst Boys cruising in Mustangs and Camaros, checking out the teenage girls on the promenade, watching other circuit riders for cues. Eyes would meet at a stoplight. Just one word . . . *"What?!"* . . . and they'd be at it. In the trunks of their shiny cars, baseball bats. For a harder game than the one you play on grass.

We looked for the opening. Turned right, into a tight grid of narrow streets. Some converted cottages, some two-story newer construction, flat-faced. Followed Silver's directions. Dead-ended at a canal, went back one block, located the house. Guy working in the yard, building something. Couple of kids playing catch, wearing Little League uniforms. Houses jammed together, yards deep front to back but no space between them. Neighbors all over the place, windows open, men washing cars, women talking.

I looked over at the Prof.

"It's no go, bro'," the little man said.

I shook my head, giving in to the truth.

144

Helene lives in Ridgewood, Queens. Top-floor apartment, walk-up. She let me in when I said the name Silver gave me.

The living room was all cheap furniture, poison-neat, Silver's picture on the mantelpiece. I wondered if there was another one in the bedroom.

She was in her mid-forties, maybe. Hard to tell—no makeup around her wary eyes.

I gave her a paper bag. Inside was $31,450. Most of what I had left from the score with Elroy's phony paper.

I get up against it bad enough, I can always go in that basement.

145

Done, then. Loose ends all around, but they weren't mine.

Off cycle, somehow. Pansy wasn't in heat. Michelle wasn't ready to come home. Luke would need more work. Wolfe would find the freaks who built the bomb.

It would all happen without me.

I should have been glad to be out of it.

146

The next morning, I took Pansy, went back to the park. This time, I had an old army blanket with me, big sketch pad, charcoal pastels. I set myself up in a good spot, halfway up a rise, strong outcropping of rock to my right. Facing west, the sun behind me.

I propped up the sketch pad, swirled the charcoal over the paper a few times, my eyes sweeping the terrain. Pansy lay on her stomach, face between her paws, wrinkling her nose—the park didn't smell like her roof. Yet. I unzipped the gym bag I'd brought with me. Still-warm loaf of French bread inside, a bottle of water, slab of dark chocolate wrapped in white paper, pack of smokes. And a couple dozen of those little round cheese pieces they wrap in red string.

The white limo came into my field of vision, making the circuit. I could track it pretty well from where I was—no hurry.

I opened one of the cheese pieces, put it right in front of Pansy's snout. She ate it with her eyes, not moving. When there was a river of drool rolling down the slope in front of her, I said "Speak!" in a soft voice. She delicately snarfed it up, ripping a divot out of the grass.

"Good girl," I said, patting her. She snounted up against me, the sun sparkling baby rainbows over her dark fur.

A woman jogged by beneath us, hair flying loose behind her. Couldn't tell if it was Belinda—bad angle. Lots of bicycles, more runners. Mostly cabs on the road. Carlos wouldn't be back my way for a while.

I worked on my drawing, occasionally unwrapping another cheese for Pansy, looking around.

A woman's figure left the path, working her way up the rise toward me. Belinda.

"Hello, stranger," she called out, pulling Walkman earphones off her head. She put them around her neck, covered them with the towel from her waist. Bounced up and sat down. Dressed the same way she was last time, fine sheen of sweat on her face, blue eyes lively.

"What's up?" she asked, indicating my sketch pad.

"Interpretive art. A hobby of mine."

"Could I see?" Pushing close to me, perfume under the sweat. "What's it supposed to be?"

"Just . . . patterns. Light, shadow . . . like that."

"It's . . . I don't know what to say."

"That's okay. Neither do I."

Pansy watched her, not moving.

"Your dog . . . I never got her name."

"Betsy." It just came out that way—I went with it.

"That's a funny name for such a big dog."

"Oh, I think it suits her. Doesn't it, girl?" Making a gesture with my hand. Pansy put her head on my lap, still watching the woman.

"You remember me, Betsy?" she asked, reaching out to pat. I gave Pansy the signal—she took the pats. I felt her neck muscles under my hand. Steel cable.

I lit a cigarette. "You never did call me," she said, a teasing undertone in her voice, less than a challenge, more than an accident.

"Dinner, you said. I've been working nights."

"Oh." She arched her eyebrows, brushed some sweat from her pug nose—a gesture like you'd see in the ring.

"Nice day for a picnic, it looks like, you had some food." Clarence's voice, materializing from somewhere behind us.

"Yeah, it is," I told him. "Sit down, join us."

He folded himself onto the edge of the blanket, indifferent to the risk to his lime-green pants. "This is Belinda," I said to Clarence. "Belinda, meet John."

He extended his slim dark hand into her thick white one. They shook, smiling. I rummaged around in the gym bag, came out with the bread, broke off a piece, offered it to Belinda. She took it, bit off a nice-sized hunk with her small white teeth. Clarence took one too. I opened the water bottle. We each took a drink. Unwrapped some cheese. Clarence declined. Belinda took one. Pansy glared at her harder than ever. I unwrapped another half dozen pieces, pulled Pansy's head close to mine, whispered the word in her ear. She mashed the cheese like a compactor, licked her teeth to get the remnants.

We finished off the bread. I broke out the chocolate. This time Clarence went for it, Belinda passed.

Peaceful there, delicate as an underwater bubble, the four of us in that park.

"What is that thing, mahn?" Clarence asked, looking at my pad.

"It's art."

"It is, yes?" His black silk shirt rustled as he took it from my hands, examined it from different angles.

"Do you work with James?" Belinda asked Clarence.

"No, we are members of the same club."

"What club?"

"A health club, miss."

"Oh! I'm a member too. Which one do you go to?"

"You never would've heard of it, miss. Way out in Queens, by the train station."

She got to her feet, patted herself like she was checking something. Her calves flexed under the exercise pants, heavy, shapely things. I got up too.

"I'll call you," I said. "Soon."

"Do it," she said, low-voiced. Stood on her toes, gave me a quick kiss near my mouth. Made her way down the hill, turned onto the track, jogged off.

"You were right, Clarence," I said. "She is a pretty woman."

"She's a cop, mahn."

147

Winter sun on my back, throwing shadows. Burning cold.

"You sure?"

"I been out here a long time, mahn. Not just today. She jogs around the park, got that Walkman in her ear. Only thing, she don't just listen, she talks too. Two white men, just past the Fifty-ninth Street entrance, two more, just off Central Park West on Eighty-sixth. Dressed like she is. Ankle holsters, walkie-talkies too. The black guy with the ice-cream wagon . . . the one by the big pond? Same thing. She talks to them all. That's all, mahn. She don't talk to nobody else."

"Damn."

"Yeah. Thought you knew, mahn, the way you change my name and everything. And she don't know yours, you think, yes?"

"Just playing it safe—I didn't know."

"It's the truth, mahn. Sure thing. Somebody snatch that lady, he gonna get himself hurt."

"You think that's what she's doing . . . trolling for rapists?"

"Wrong hours, mahn. Wrong time. She stays off the bad trails too. It's you she's working, boss."

"Why?"

"Way I see it, the man in the white limo, he's made him a trade."

"White limo?"

"This is Clarence, mahn. Your friend. Your true friend. Give it up. Don't look back. You follow that big bouncing butt right into the penitentiary."

I lit a smoke, thinking about it. About not looking back. About how that comes natural to some people.

148

Clarence sat quietly next to me. Pansy swept the area with her eyes. Smarter than me, going in.

I packed my stuff in the gym bag, snapped on Pansy's lead, told her to stay while I folded the army blanket.

"Thanks, Clarence," I said, holding out my hand, goodbye.

"That's not why I came, mahn. Got a message from the Queen. One of her people called Jacques. Said to come see her. She has your answer. Come anytime, after dark."

"Anything else?"

"Word for word, mahn."

We walked through the park, heading west. A collie galloped by, off leash, a kid chasing it. Pansy ignored the other dog—she generally does.

"You know about this obeah thing, Clarence?"

"I know some, mahn. What my mother told me, from her mother, she said."

"Tell me."

"It comes from the old ways. From slavery, way I heard it. It's all about sacrifice, mahn. When you die, you wait. To cross over. The sacrifice, that lets you come back. In spirit. There are many spirits . . . they call them loas . . . a joker, a warrior, a lover."

"The bag . . . the one we found that night. That was a sacrifice?"

"Yes, mahn. The Queen, she is the Mamaloi, the priestess. There's two kinds obeah. The white and the red. The red, their god is the snake."

"What's the difference?"

"In white obeah, in that juju bag would be a chicken, maybe a goat . . . an animal."

"In the red . . . ?"

"The goat without horns, mahn," Clarence said, his hands clasped together. A quick shudder passed through his thin frame.

149

Belinda was a cop. In books, people are fascinated with mysteries. Can't let them slide. Books have plots—life has plotters. Maybe Belinda was the front end of a decoy operation, maybe Carlos had already rolled over for the Man and she was with the backup team. Or maybe it was me they were looking at—maybe she heard about me, wanted to free-lance a bit. Get a gold shield to pin on that fine chest.

I wondered if she'd ever had a dog named Blackie. If she'd really liked Pansy.

Clarence picked the lock on the privacy of my mind. "You gonna do it, mahn? Go there, see the Queen?"

I nodded.

150

Two more dead days. Then I went out to answer the call. Just before midnight, I crossed the Triboro, took the far right lane to Queens, exited at Ninety-fourth Street, just before La Guardia. Rolled south to Northern Boulevard, turned left to the voodoo house. The gate was open. I pulled the Plymouth inside, all the way around to the back. Two men in the yard, dressed in their black and white. I got out slowly so I wouldn't spook them. They looked through me, said nothing.

I walked to the back door. A bright red arrow was freshly painted on the side of the house, pointing to a set of stone steps. Down.

Another way to the basement. I followed the steps to the bottom. By then, I knew better than to knock. No doorknob. I pushed, it opened, and I was inside.

The underground room seemed bigger than the last time. She was where she was before, a faint shape in the gloomy shadows. I walked to her. Candles popped into life all around the room, thick and stubby as fists, fat-flamed. Red and white, lacing the dark in an alternating pattern like the pin heads on the juju bag. Cloth-sounds on either side of me as I moved. Deep dampness from the stone walls. The floor felt like packed earth beneath the soles of my boots.

"Do you believe now?" she asked, soft-voiced as I approached.

I sat before her. "The baby was in the water," I replied.

"Yes. And now you hunt again."

"Not for . . ."

"I know. Not for him. For the false gods. For what those like you call the devil."

"Yes."

"You do not ask how I know. Have you learned, then?"

"Yes."

"Where is your son tonight?"

"I have no son."

"Yes, hunter, you have a son. The young one who was with you when you last came. He is dark like us, but his heart is like yours. A son looks to his father for guidance. For the Way. Your way is to hunt. And he follows."

"No, it's just a job. He works for others."

"And to those others, you are a hired man, yes?"

"Yes."

"And so then is he. Like you. It is from you he learns, not from them. And he protects you, like a son."

"He's a professional—it's his job."

"No. His master gave him the message. From me. To you. And so you are here now. But the boy, he has been here since yesterday afternoon. Just across the street, in one of the rooms they rent."

"How . . . ?"

"He paid the lady extra so he could have a room with a window on the street. The bathroom is down the hall. In his room, in his suitcase, he has a rifle. One that comes in two pieces. It is our house, there. The lady is not one of us, but she knows what to do. It is your son."

"He won't do anything. I'll . . ."

"It is all right. He is safe. Ask me your questions now—we have work to do before the sun."

"The people I'm looking for . . ." I started, reaching in my pocket for the mug shots Wolfe had given me.

She held up her hand. "We do not know them. Not by their faces. But by their practice, they are known. They are not sorcerers, they have no magic. Poison is their weapon. Their poison, it makes the wolf who walks."

"No. They . . ."

"What Europeans call a werewolf, child of sadness. Before there was legend, before there was myth, there was truth. Their poison, it makes a beast. When the beast feeds, when it is satisfied, it is a man again. You have seen this."

Luke. Baby baby baby. Stabbing. Toby. A different child. The runaway. Running in his mind. Splitting off.

I nodded. So deeply it felt like a bow.

"The poison-masters leave a spoor. It is their track. The dead sheep tells us its killer by the marks on its body—a man kills differently than a wolf. The hunter knows."

"I know who. Not where."

"Take this," she said. Handing me a leather thong, long glossy feathers attached to it. Black and white. "Wrap the strap around your wrist, hold it like this." Her forearm straight out, fingers pointing to me.

Ki.

The feathers hung limp. The tips of our fingers touched.

"They know each other, the vampire and the werewolf. But know this too, hunter. They are not brothers."

Electricity in my fingers, in my wrist. The feathers fluttered in the candlelight but the flames held steady. I couldn't feel the breeze.

Her hand moved, covered mine. Untied the thong from my wrist. Leather and feathers disappeared somewhere behind her throne.

She closed her eyes, tilted her chin up. I could see the long muscles in her throat. Her eyes opened, held mine.

"Come here," she said.

I stood up. She made a gesture. I bent toward her. Her face was close enough to kiss. Her arms went around my neck. Something there, soft.

I stepped back. A tiny muslin bag bounced against my chest, thin silken strap around my neck.

"Wear it against your body until your hunt is done. Wear it inside their cave—it will protect you."

I bowed.

"Take your son. And go now."

151

I parked the Plymouth right in front of the building across the street. Got out, sat on the hood, lit a cigarette. The window shade in the front room flickered. The kid had a lot to learn. I waved my arm in a "come on down" gesture. Waited.

Clarence came out the front door, suitcase in one hand, his pistol in the other.

"It's okay," I told him, opening the trunk for the suitcase, lifting the panel next to the fuel cell so it would disappear even if some cop wanted to play Probable Cause on the way back.

He climbed in the front seat. "How'd you know, mahn?"

"Never mind. Where's your car?"

"My car?" he said, looking across at me like I was on lithium. "I wouldn't bring my ride to this place, mahn. Where would I park it? I took the bus."

152

I rode the BQE toward Brooklyn. The Plymouth's independent rear suspension absorbed the potholes in the middle lane, just a touch under the speed limit.

"You should've told me you were working backup, Clarence."

"I figure, I tell you, you have an attitude, mahn. Give it away."

"It's not professional, surprise your partner, okay? I didn't know it was you in that window, might've been the first thing I took out, I made it to the street. Specially if I saw that curtain move. What'd you figure . . . you were gonna lay down some cover for me, spray their house with the rifle?"

"Something like that." Paying attention, sullen.

"You had the high ground, that was good. Probably got a couple of extra clips for the piece too."

He nodded.

"That's not the way, kid. You'd never get out of there alive. That's cowboy shit. Kamikaze. You send a partner into a meeting, you want to get out, not get even, understand?"

"How would you do it, mahn?"

I reached in my jacket pocket, feeling the Queen's amulet against my chest. Handed him a palm-sized black plastic box, tiny toggle switch on the top.

"What's this, mahn?"

"Throw the switch, Clarence."

He flicked his finger. A tiny red LED light came on. He looked over at me.

"My car is parked in their backyard, okay? There's trouble, I take out this little box. Show it to them. Flick the switch. The light comes on, just like it did with you. I tell them my partner's close by . . . maybe circling in another car. The red light, that's his signal. I don't drive the car out of there in ten minutes, my partner's gonna push a switch of his own. In the trunk of my car, there's enough *plastique* to make the whole block disappear. And even if they got somebody crazy enough to try and drive the car away, they couldn't start it, even with the keys. They open the trunk, the whole thing goes up. Understand?"

"What if they search you, find the box right away?"

"I tell them the same thing, only it's gonna happen if I *don't* throw the switch, see?"

"It's a cold bluff, mahn."

"I had a partner on this, it wouldn't be."

He didn't say another word until I turned off Atlantic, heading for Jacques's joint.

"You gonna show me stuff like that, mahn?"

I looked over at him, at his fine-boned face, thinking about what the Queen told me.

"Yeah," I said.

153

I know how to be alone. How to get there by myself. Where I was raised, privacy was more precious than diamonds. In the orphanage, nothing was your own, even your clothes—gifts they could take away. They made sure you knew it. Most of us only learned to hate each other, fighting over the scraps they left us.

You get into enough of those fights, reform school is the next stop.

SACRIFICE

In the reform schools, they didn't have cells. Just a big room with a toilet in one corner. Cots all over the floor. Whichever kid had to sleep right next to the toilet, he spent his life being pissed on.

I remember the kid who slept there. When he got out, he vowed he'd never sleep next to a toilet again. He went out with a gun in his hand, got something of his own. In prison, they had cells, not dorms. The lucky ones, the ones with juice, they got a one-man cell. This kid, he did a lot of things, went high-profile, made his rep. When he went down again, he was grown. They gave him a one-man cell. With a single bunk. Right next to the toilet.

When I got out, I made my own vows. I found a basement. Mine. An older guy wanted it for his crew. I was so scared, I shot him.

That cost me a stretch in the joint. That's where I ran into the kid who'd slept next to the toilet, heard his story. The State's good at that— arranging reform school reunions.

In prison, you've got nothing but your body and your honor. Plenty who'll try and take those too. I knew a guy, had tattoos all over him. The only real estate that was his. They couldn't take that from him, he said. Made it easy to identify the body when they found it.

I didn't need time to think about what the Queen said. Even as she spoke, I knew what she meant. Who she meant. She called him a vampire—I always think of him as the Mentor. A heavy-networked pedophile, safe like rich makes you safe. I'd gone to him years ago, looking for a picture of a kid. For Strega, the Witch. I got to him through the Mole. The freak had done something . . . was still doing something . . . for the Israelis. I couldn't hurt him, the Mole told me. Came with me to make sure.

The Mentor told me his philosophy—silky voice wrapping around the lying words. Sodomizing children is love. Taking pictures of it happening was preserving that special love . . . icons to a perfect moment in time.

I was the vigilante Wolfe thought I was, he'd be dead.

The last time we talked, I'd learned something. Never put it together before last night. All freaks are dangerous, but they're not all the same.

No point calling the Mole. He'd give me the same warning. Insist on going with me again. Maybe even tell me to stay away.

The Israelis wouldn't be watching his house, but breaking in would be tough. And for this guy, the cops would use the siren.

154

I shaved carefully the next morning. Put on one of the suits Michelle had made me buy, dark gray. A pale blue shirt, dark silk tie with blue flecks in it. Laced up my shoes, gave them a final buff with an old T-shirt.

"Where're we going, mahn?" Clarence asked as he got into the front seat.

"To school," I told him, heading back to Manhattan.

It took a while, three full circuits of the cesspool. The Prof was on his cart, tiny body looking legless under the blanket, talking to a pair of hookers a block from the exit off the Lincoln Tunnel. Two young black girls, one with a blonde wig, both wearing short shorts, halter tops, high heels. One squatted next to him, listening. The other tapped her foot nervously, looking left and right. I pulled over, motioned Clarence to come with me, started back up the block.

The Prof was gesticulating wildly, his arms flapping in the oversized sleeves of his coat. Last year's Cadillac squealed to a stop, a baby-blue coupe, gold custom wheels, gold trim. A player oozed out the driver's side, a heavy-bodied man in a short red jacket with gold trim, white pants tucked into red boots. We closed the gap on his blind side.

"Get your black ass back on the stroll, bitch! You costing me money."

The blonde-wigged one looked at him cautiously. "We was just . . ."

He slapped her so hard the wig went flying. She went to her knees in the street, snatched it up, took off. Her sister went with her, moving fast.

"Hold up, brother!" the Prof said. "The Lord will punish the wicked. Do not harm these children."

"Yeah," I said from behind him. "Don't."

The pimp whirled on us. "This ain't your business, man."

"That's right," I said, reasonable-voiced, "it's not. But I don't want you thinking maybe you don't like my brother talking to your women, maybe you figure you'll catch him again someday, alone."

"Tell the little nigger stay away from my string, then."

"I can't tell him that—can't tell him nothing. It's not what I do. I'll tell you instead, okay?"

"You looking to cut in, motherfucker?" Trying for ice in his voice, eyeing Clarence. Clarence in his tangerine silk shirt, fingertip white linen jacket. "You fronting off for pretty boy here?"

"You think I want your dirty women, mahn?" Clarence asked sweetly, the pistol materializing in his hand, leveled at the pimp's beltline.

"No trouble, man," the pimp said, ice melting. Backing away toward his car.

"Put away the tool, fool," the Prof snapped at Clarence. "There's heat on the street." He unwrapped the blanket, climbing off his cart. We put the cart in the trunk. The Prof jumped lightly into the back seat.

155

"Carlos is history," I told the Prof, talking just over my right shoulder. He was draped across the back of the front seat, between me and Clarence.

"Some dreams turn to screams, bro'. Ain't no big thing."

"Yeah."

"There was a cop . . ." Clarence started to say.

The Prof waved away the explanation. In our world, "why" won't draw flies.

I made the introductions. "Prof, this is Clarence. Clarence, my brother the Prof."

"Prof?"

"Some call me the Prophet for what I preach—some call me Professor for what I teach."

"What do you teach, then?"

"Time and crime, son. Time and crime. You from Jacques?"

"Yes, mahn. He is my boss."

"You working with Burke?"

"Learning, more like."

"And what you think this schoolboy could teach you? He's still learning himself."

"From you?"

"You ever been to prison, boy? Ever been behind the walls? I met this fool, he was a crazy rookie. Gunfighter, he wanted to be, posing for bank cameras until they dropped him for the count. I taught him to play with fire, walk the wire, you understand? I'm a thief, boy. A sweet thief. Make a buy, tell a lie. No guns, son. I don't fall, been through it all."

I nodded. "The stone truth," I assured Clarence.

"You work free-lance?" the Prof asked. "Or you on apprentice? . . . Jacques gonna teach you to run the guns?"

"I'm on the payroll, mahn. But to run the business . . . Jacques has plenty ahead of me."

"Cold beats bold, son. You don't wait, you visit the State, understand?"

"Yes, I know this."

"That pimp, back there by the tunnel, the one running those scaly-leg girls . . . you'd shoot him?"

"No, mahn. I was just showing him some firepower. Playing backup."

"*Play* ain't the way, boy. Your eyes fire when he call your name, then the man knows your game. You want to scare a motherfucker, hot ain't worth a lot—ice is nice."

"He said . . ."

"Hey, *say* ain't play. Jump, and you're a chump. Man slaps you in the face, what you do?"

"I kill any man who slaps me. I'm not a woman, a man be slapping me."

"Schoolboy, what's the first two things I taught you, a man slaps you."

I lit a smoke, buying some seconds. The Prof had done the voice-over, but it was Wesley who walked it through. Years ago, on the prison yard. An iron-freak named Dayton had slapped the ice man in the face, right in front of everybody. Wesley just slumped to the ground, didn't say a word. Dayton strutted off, floating on the whispers. The cons said Wesley was a dead man—a man who won't fight when he's slapped is pussy. Free meat. They kept saying it until the guards found Dayton dead in the weight room.

I looked over at Clarence. "Smile," I said. "And wait. You're gonna come, come quiet."

The kid wouldn't let it go. He turned to the Prof. "That religion stuff I heard you run down . . . you're a preacher, where's your church?"

"You think the Lord's got nothing better to do than be sitting up there taking attendance? I got the call when I was small. Where I walk is where I talk."

"I was just . . ." Clarence's voice trailed off. I wondered if he got it, if he understood the legless man on the cart was a giant.

"You got a silencer for that pistol?" the Prof asked him.

"Yes, mahn. I mean, not with me, but . . ."

"Get one for your mouth," the little man snapped, lighting himself a smoke.

156

Limestone town house just off Fifth Avenue. I pulled to the curb. "I'm going inside," I told them. "Clarence, when you drive, watch the gas, this thing'll pull stumps. The guy I'm going to see, he's about forty-five. Rail-thin, dark hair, going bald on top. Face makes kind of a triangle, wide across the top. Thin lips, long fingers. Name's on the door, brass plate right over the bell. Come back in about an hour. I'm not here, just park anywhere on the block, wait, okay?"

"Sure, mahn," Clarence said, sliding over behind the wheel.

The Plymouth drove off. The Prof would tell the kid what to do if I didn't come out.

157

The teak door sat smugly behind a wrought-iron gate set flush in the frame. I pushed the pearl button. No sound from inside. Waited.

The door swung open. The vampire was wearing a quilted burgundy robe of heavy brocade, a black length of braid knotted at his waist. Hard to make out his features in the shadows, but I recognized the shape of his face, the hair dark at the sides. Saw the skull beneath the taut skin.

"You," he said, a whisper-hiss of surprise.

"Can I talk with you?"

"We've already talked."

"I need your help."

"Surely you know better than that."

"If you'll hear me out . . . it's something you'll *want* to do. And I have something to trade."

"You're alone?"

"Yes."

He touched one finger to the tip of his nose, deciding. Then a twisting gesture with his other hand. I heard a heavy deadbolt slide back, tugged gently on the wrought iron, and the gate came toward me. I stepped inside.

"After you," he said, gesturing toward the staircase.

The room hadn't changed. Old-money heavy, thick and dark. Only an amber computer screen marred the antique atmosphere. The screen had several rows of numbers across the top—it blinked into darkness as I glanced at it, defying my stare.

"Notice anything new?" he asked, pointing to the chair I'd used last time.

I sat down—swept the room, playing the game. In one corner, a rectangular fish tank, much longer than it was high. I got up to look closer, feeling him behind me. The fish were all some shade of red or orange, all with wide white stripes outlined in black.

"This is different," I said. "What are they?"

"Clowns. The family name is Pomacentridae. They come in many varieties. The dark orange ones are Perculas," pointing at a fat little fish near the top. "And we have Tomatoes, Maroons, even some Flame Clowns—my favorites."

The Flames had red heads with a white band just behind the eyes— the bodies were jet black. They stayed toward the bottom of the tank.

"Saltwater fish?" I asked him.

"Oh yes. Quite delicate, actually."

"They're beautiful. Are they rare?"

"More unusual than they are rare. Clowns get along wonderfully with other fish. That is, they never interact—they stay with their own kind, even in a tank."

"They don't fight for territory?"

"No, they don't fight at all. Occasionally, a small spat among themselves, but never with other fish."

I watched the aquarium. Each tribe of Clowns stayed in its own section, not swimming so much as hovering. I saw his reflection in the glass fade as he went over to a leather armchair and sat down. I took the chair he'd first indicated, faced him.

He regarded me with mild interest, well within himself, safe where he was.

"You said you had something . . . ?"

"Yeah. The last time we talked . . . when you told me your . . . philosophy. About kids . . ."

"I remember," he said stiffly. "Nothing has changed."

"I know. I listened. You told me you loved little boys then. I came because I need to see how deep that goes."

"Which means . . . ?"

"What you do, what others like you do, it's love, right?"

He nodded, wary.

"You don't force kids. Don't hurt them . . . anything like that."

"As I told you. What is wrong with our behavior . . . *all* that is wrong with our behavior, is that it is against the law. We are hounded, persecuted. Some of us have been imprisoned, ruined by the witch-hunters. But we have always been here and we always will be. You didn't come here to engage in philosophical discourse . . ."

"No. Just to get things straight."

He got to his feet, turned his back on me. Tapped some keys rapidly on the computer, too fast for me to follow. He hit a final key with a concert pianist's flourish. The machine beeped. He got up, went back to his easy chair.

"You've been logged in. Physical description, time of arrival, your code name, everything. It's all been transmitted—the modem is open."

"I didn't come here to do anything to you."

"I'm sure."

"Listen to me," I said, leaning forward, keeping my voice low. "Can we not be stupid? I didn't come here to do anything to you. But don't confuse yourself—the Israelis aren't your pals. I don't know what you did for them, what you do for them . . . and I don't care. But all they are is a barrier. A threat. Like you think I am. Somebody drops you, they aren't going to get even. Understand what I'm saying?"

"Yes, quite well. You are saying if I don't give you information you want, you'll kill me."

"That's cute. You got enough for your tape recorder now? I'm not threatening you. Not with anything. I'm just trying to tell you something . . . and you should listen. Listen good . . . maybe you don't want this on tape."

He steepled his long fingers, regarding me over the top of the spire. I counted to twenty in my head before he moved a muscle. He got to his feet, languid movements, tapped into the computer again. Sat down, waiting.

"This is the truth, okay?" I told him. "You don't have friends in high places. Not *true* friends. What you are is an asset . . . something of value. Everybody protects what they value. You know that good as anyone. You have this valuable painting, okay? Somebody steals it, you try and buy it back. But if there's a fire, all you can do is collect on the insurance. The Israelis can't protect you unless it's the *federales* who pop you. They got no reach with the locals. What I have for you, it's another barrier. Something you can't get from your friends."

He raised his eyebrows, didn't say a word.

I reached in my pocket, handed him an orange piece of pasteboard, about the size of a business card. He turned it over, held it up.

Get Out of Jail Free.

"Is this your idea of a joke?"

"It's not a joke. You got a lawyer, right? Probably got a few of them. Have your lawyer go over to City-Wide, speak to Wolfe . . . you know who she is?"

"Yes."

"See if I'm telling the truth, then."

"I'd get . . . ?"

"Immunity. Kiddie porn's the only way you're going down, right? The only risk you take. And you're not getting stung by Customs—

you don't deal with people you don't know. Only way it's gonna happen, somebody drops a dime, City-Wide does the search."

"There is nothing here."

"You're looking at the big picture, pal. And that's a mistake. What you should be looking at is the frame, see?"

He took a breath. Small, cold eyes on mine. "You couldn't deliver," he said quietly. "We know about Wolfe. People have . . . talked to her before. She's not . . . amenable . . . to . . . whatever you propose."

"Have your lawyer talk to her again. Do it first, before you do anything for me, okay? I'll tell you what I want, tell you right now, in this room. Just listen—I guarantee you it won't be against you or your people. Give me a couple of days, have your lawyer go see her, all right? Nothing's changed, you don't have to do a thing. You decide, okay?"

He steepled his fingers again. I counted in my head.

"Tell me what you want," he said.

158

I lit a smoke, centering. I'd only get one shot.

"We both know how it works, you and me. Child molesters . . ." His thin lips parted—I held up my hand in a "stop!" gesture, going on before he could speak. "I'm not talking about your people now. There's people who molest children, right? I'm talking about rape. Sodomy. Hard, stick-it sex. It happens. Don't go weak on me now. I know what you do—I know what you told me. I could play it back for you, word for word. The kids you're involved with, it's love, right? There's always a consent—you wouldn't do a thing without it. I remember what you said . . . you're a mentor, a teacher. Not a rapist. I'm *separating* you now—listen good. Those people who say child sexual abuse is a myth— we know better, you and me. I'm not saying you do it—I'm saying it gets done. People do it, right?"

"Savages do it."

"Yes. Fathers rape their daughters, it's not a fantasy. Humans kill kids, make films of it, it's not a myth."

"And you think we're all the same, you think . . ."

"No," I said, eyes open and clear, calling on a childhood of treachery for the effortless lying that they made second nature to me before I was ten. "What you do, people could argue about it, but I know you love children. Maybe I don't agree with it, but I'm not a cop. It's not my job. It's the baby-rapers who make your life hell, isn't that true? You love children. You'd be as angry about torturing them as anybody else would. Even if the laws changed, even if they eliminated the age thing, made it so a kid could consent to sex, then they'd be like adults, right? And rape is rape."

"Society calls it rape when . . ."

"I'm not talking about *statutory* rape, pal. Listen close—stand up to it now. I'm talking about black-glove, hand-over-the-mouth, knifepoint rape. Blood, not Vaseline. Pain. Screaming, life-scarring pain. A little boy ripped open, maybe one of *your* little boys . . . you like *that* picture?"

"Stop it! Stop it, you . . ."

I dragged deep on my cigarette, staying inside. "That's what I want to do. That's what you've got to do. Help me."

"I . . ."

"You know. You know it happens. They did it to my client. A little boy. They split him open like a ripe melon—he's a basket case. And they videotaped it. A group. An organized group. Satanists, they call themselves, but we know what that's about, don't we, friend?"

"I don't deal with . . ." Sweat streaking his high forehead, tendons cabling his hands, veins like wires in his throat.

"I know you don't. You wouldn't do anything like that. Or your people. I know." I spooled velvet over him, a cop telling a rapist he understands . . . *those cunts, displaying themselves, wiggling like a bitch in heat, fucking <u>asking</u> for it, right? Men like us, we understand each other.* "But freaks like that, they have to be stopped. They bring heat, and heat brings light, you know what I'm saying? You know what I do. I've never made trouble for you, right? Help me."

"How could I . . . ?"

"The computer. They raped that little boy to make a commercial product. Not like your icons—not to remember a boy as he was—pictures to *sell*. The kid was a product, and they need a market. They'll be on the board somewhere. You could find them. Your friends could find them. That's all I want."

"And . . ."

"And they'll never know. And if you should happen to slip, Wolfe will make sure you don't fall."

He searched the pockets of his robe. Found a black silk handkerchief, patted his face dry, deciding. I waited, watching the dice tumble across the green felt in my mind.

Finally he looked up. "Tell me what you know."

159

Clarence slid over as I got behind the wheel. "Where can I drop you?" I asked him.

"It's okay, 'home," the Prof said. "He'll come with me, ride the IRT."

I looked over at Clarence. He nodded.

I dropped them on the East Side. Found a pay phone, called Wolfe.

160

In the front seat of Wolfe's Audi, parked on Kew Garden Hills Road, just past the cemetery. The Rottweiler was lying down on the back seat, bored with the conversation.

"Where's the switch for the recliner?" I asked her. "I need to move this seat back."

"It's over here. I'll release it . . . move back real slowly."

"How come it's over there?"

"If there's somebody sitting where you sit, and they get stupid, I can pull this lever and the passenger seat falls straight back, into full recline." She reached into the back, patted her dog. "And there's Bruiser," she said, quiet smile on her face.

I thought about being strapped in with a seat belt, lying face up like a man in a dental chair with a Rottweiler ready to pull teeth. Nice.

"I may have a way," I said, lighting a cigarette, "to find Luke's parents. I met a guy, years ago. A networked pedophile. Does the whole trip: he's a 'mentor' to little boys, guides them along the path of sexual awareness, keeps these photographic icons as a monument to the joy they shared. You know what I'm talking about—a child molester with intellectual cover. Pedophilia—the cutting edge of sexuality—the last taboo—you've heard it all. He's a child advocate, he says. Children are being restricted by the archaic laws, what good is the right to say 'no' without the freedom to say 'yes.' All that."

"Like you said, I've heard it before."

"Yeah. Well, anyway, he's doing something for a foreign government. I don't know any more about it. Bottom line: the feds wouldn't drop him even if he fell for one of their stings. I offered him immunity if the locals ever glom on to him. Told him you'd back it up. That you'd tell that to his lawyer when you get a call."

"You told him *what?*"

"You heard what I said. It's a payoff. Not for nothing. He turns up Luke's parents, he walks next time you pop him. *If* you ever do."

"You know what you're asking me to do?"

"Yeah. Lie."

Wolfe looked straight out through the windshield, tapping her long claws on the wheel. French manicure: clear nails, white tips. I watched her blouse move with her breathing.

"I can do that," she said.

161

I wasn't going to rely on the freak. Even if I'd played him perfectly, even if he went for the outside fake, I couldn't be sure he wouldn't come up empty. Luke's parents could be anywhere. As close as Manhattan, as far away as Holland.

The Queen's image hovered at the edge of my mind. Roots. Obeah. Obey. Spirit calling. I let myself be the hunter, following the spoor.

I put out the word. Independent collector looking for videotape. No commercial products wanted. Boys only. Hard stuff. The real thing. Top prices paid. Salted the Personals columns with the right code words. Tapped into the computer bulletin boards I knew about. Checked the DMV. Two cars registered to the targets: an Infiniti Q45 and a Mercedes 380 SL. The address was a house in the Hamptons. Turned out to be a rental—they were paid up through Labor Day, but they hadn't been around for weeks. The rental agent was a cautious woman—she had a photocopy of their check against the chance it wouldn't clear. It had, though. Drawn on a corporation with a midtown Manhattan address.

That turned out to be a room full of mail slots. An accommodation address, set up for forwarding. I unlocked the code with a fifty-dollar bill. A PO box in Chelsea. That would've stopped most people, but the Prof's semi-citizen brother Melvin works in the Post Office. They'd bought the box in their birth-certificate names, and the home address was listed. The one where they found Luke covered in his baby brother's blood.

Dead end.

I started over. The neighbors in the building had already been questioned by the cops. One lady didn't mind going through it again, asked if she was going to be on TV. Far as she knew, the poor kid's parents moved away to a safer neighborhood. One where a maniac couldn't sneak in your house at night and chop up your baby. She and her husband would move too, but the real estate market was so soft now . . .

The corporate checking account was on a commercial bank. I walked in, made out a deposit slip to the account number, put it together with a check for five grand made out to the corporation. The teller took it, stamped it in, went to his machine, came back and told me the account had been closed. I told him I was worried about that—here I had this debt to pay, didn't know what to do with the check. He didn't go for the bait, told me he didn't have a clue. Don't worry about it, he told me, it wasn't my problem.

162

They wouldn't give themselves away. Humans like that have two levels of immunity—the kind you can buy and the kind that comes from the pure sociopath's lack of guilt. True evil is invisible until it feeds. They'd laugh behind their masks at a therapist, breeze through any polygraph.

Best guess is they wouldn't leave the country. Other places may treat pedophiles nicer on the surface, but nobody's got our brand of freak-protection written so deeply into the laws.

I reached out for Wesley. The tracker's spirit came like it always does . . . riding the tip of my consciousness. I could never call up his face, but I'd always know his voice.

"Where?" I asked him.

"You know. Better than me."

He left me with that. I played the tapes in my head. What I know. They always use multiple locations, move the kids around. They'd have a cave close by. And they'd need things humans need. Electricity, heat, water. Phones too.

The DA could subpoena the Con Ed records, search Ma Bell. Wolfe had probably done it already, but I wasn't going to suggest it to her. I used a cutout, an ex-cop who's got a whole string of people inside the record room. Nothing on paper . . . a few quick taps at the computer keys and I'd know if they were listed.

"You want *all* the utilities?" he asked.

"All of them," I said. "Try the gas company too. And not just the city, okay? Give me Westchester, North Jersey, southern Connecticut."

"You're talking a big tab, man."

"I'm good for it," I told him, handing him a thousand in fifties. "The rest when you get back to me."

It only took him three days. To come up empty.

163

They wouldn't be too far underground, not these freaks. Humans who prey on children lead lives of monumental duplicity. The neighbors are always shocked when a bust goes down—not *those* people. They'd be community leaders, political conservatives, but with a soft spot for civil liberties. Tight lives, tightly controlled—they'd only let go inside their evil circle.

I called my pal Morelli, a crime reporter who came up hard. Asked him to leave me alone with his NEXIS terminal for a while. He said what he always says.

"Anything for me?"

I just shook my head.

164

He came back a few hours later. All I had to show for my work was an ashtray full of butts and a legal pad full of notes. Humans indicted for ritualistic abuse who had jumped bail, kiddie-sex rings exposed . . . some of the perpetrators not apprehended. Possibilities—they always find others like them.

"Any luck?" Morelli asked.

"Goose egg," I told him. "Thanks anyway."

165

I didn't say anything to Morelli about a newsclip I'd found. Sixteen-year-old girl. A babysitter in a nice lower Westchester neighborhood, she'd been arrested for sexual abuse of two little boys. The crime had taken place last year—the babysitter's name was being withheld because of her age. Full confession.

I parked my Plymouth in the municipal indoor lot across from the Yonkers Family Court. Seven-thirty in the morning—the place was empty. I walked through the lot, down the stairs in front of City Hall. The stone steps were littered with humans who couldn't find a place to sleep on the park benches, clutching their plastic garbage bags full of return-deposit aluminum cans and plastic bottles, waiting for the recycling joint to open.

I found a pay phone, dropped in a quarter. A very proper-sounding woman's voice answered. "Family Court."

"You alone?" I asked the voice.

"Yes," she said, and hung up.

The Family Court is in a regular office building on South Broadway. Nobody's allowed on the floor until it opens. I rang for the elevator, heard the gears mesh as the car started downstairs, and stepped through a metal door into the stairwell. When I got to the right floor, I gently pushed against the Fire Exit door. It was open.

I made my way down the corridor, dressed in my lawyer's suit, carrying an attaché case. Anyone stopped me, I'd say I was looking to file some papers.

Nobody did. She was waiting in the file room, a patrician woman with a proud, erect carriage, wearing a long-sleeved dress with lace at the cuffs and the throat. The boss clerk, she always got there early and left late—a disgrace to civil servants everywhere. I bowed slightly. She held out her hand. I opened the attaché case, gave her a Xerox of the newsclip. She read it carefully, nodding slightly. Then she walked over to a bin labeled "Pending" and searched through the folders. Pulled one out, showed it to me. I didn't touch it.

She walked over to the photocopier, ran off a half dozen pages. Smoothly and efficiently, the way she does everything. I put the pages in my case. Bowed again.

She turned her back on me, returned to her work. I don't know what she thinks of me, this lady. Nothing much ever shows on her face. But she knows what I do.

166

The papers I took with me had everything I needed. The kid's name was Marianne Morgan. Lived with her mother and father, attended a private school in Larchmont.

The next day, I called a guy I know. He's a caseworker in the local child protection unit, been there for years. He's also a major-league cockhound—some guys only like blondes, he only likes them married. Five-thirty in the morning, he answered the phone on the first ring. Probably just getting back home. I told him what I wanted. We made a meet for that night—he said he was coming into the city anyway.

167

I got there first—a bar on First Avenue in the Sixties. Ordered a mineral water, shot of Absolut on the side, looked around. Mostly an after-work crowd: men and women in matching pinstripes, talking about deals.

He was only a few minutes late. Slid in next to me, grabbed the vodka off the bar, tossed it down.

"I got the Intake notes," he said by way of greeting.

"With you?"

"In here." Tapping his temple.

"How'd you get a JD Intake? I didn't think that stuff went across agency lines."

"It doesn't. It should . . . they're the same kids . . . but it doesn't. Turf bullshit . . . you know."

"Yeah. So?"

"So she was a CPS referral first. Told her guidance counselor at school she was having sex with her father."

"How long ago?"

"In late '88, just before the Christmas break. She didn't want to go home from school."

"What happened?"

"She told the investigator the whole thing. Her father was a mirror freak. She hated the mirrors. Then, when we sent her to a validator, she recanted. Pulled back on the whole thing, said she made it up because she didn't want to get in trouble for her grades."

"It got dropped?"

"Yeah. Then she called the Hot Line herself about six months later. Told them the same story."

"And dropped it again later?"

"Right."

"You think it was true?"

"Hell, yes. We get recantations all the time, especially from teenage girls. She just couldn't pull it together. The way I figure it, she got herself busted so it'd be out of her hands."

"So she's in custody?"

"No. Her parents hired a lawyer for her. See, she was fifteen when it happened . . . with the kids she was babysitting . . . so she gets tried as a juvenile even though she's over the age now. The Family Court judge cut her loose. Gave the parents of the kids some Order of Protection. She has to report to a Probation Officer once a week pending trial, that's all."

A woman walked past, a young woman with too much butt for the jeans she was wearing—she was squeezed in there so tight the little back pockets wouldn't stay parallel to the center seam.

"Keep your mind on business," I told him. "Hard to talk with your mouth hanging open like that."

He snapped out of it, refocused his glazed eyes. I ordered another drink.

"You got the name of her Probation Officer?" I asked him.

"Wouldn't do you any good, Burke. She skipped out a couple of weeks ago. She's listed as a runaway now."

I was thinking of another question to ask him when he got up, shook hands goodbye, and went sniffing after the woman in the jeans.

168

Lying with my head against some pillows piled up at the end of Bonita's bed, smoking a cigarette, eyes half closed. Bonita on her knees, facing away from me, looking back over her shoulder, admiring the dimples over her heart-shaped butt. Her body still gleamed from oil and sweat.

A long time ago, I had a girlfriend. A poet, she was. "I can always see the end of everything," she told me. Explaining why she cried when we had sex.

Things don't end for me, they loop. Same stage, new players. A homing pigeon released from a poisonous coop, hung up in the sky. Waiting for them to open the door again. Watchful for hawks.

I thought about Blossom. So truly beautiful a woman it was a pleasure just to watch her dress in the morning. How even her sweat was blonde. A flash of pink in the night before a sex-sniper went down. Hard innocence.

Fresh and new. But only for me. No plastic slipcovers on her soul.

I thought about promises.

Down here, innocent doesn't mean naive. It means Not Guilty.

Bonita was telling me something about moving to another place. A place of her own. Where we'd have more privacy. But money was tight. If she could just swing the first couple of months' rent and security . . . licking at her lips, like the idea made her hot.

Knocking at her door, I'd wondered why I'd come. Soon as I had, I wondered again.

I closed my eyes. Not sleepy. Tired.

169

Heat boiled asphalt and tempers, the summer sun fried dreams. Gunfire rattled the windows of high-rise slums from Brooklyn to the Bronx. A teenager shot a boy his own age in Harlem. "It was about a diss," he told the cops.

Another teenager was stabbed to death on the subway. On his way home from his part-time job. His neck chain and bracelet were taken. "I begged him not to wear his gold on the train," his father told the TV reporter.

On Flatbush Avenue in Brooklyn, I came out of a storefront off another cold trail, hit the sidewalk. A white Cadillac at the curb, its flanks scored with gouges from a vandal's key. An old woman walked by, saw me looking, made a sad sound with her lips. "You cain't keep nothin' nice in this city no more," she said, moving on.

170

I chased dead trails. Followed a rumor about a safe house for pedophile priests. Where they take them for therapy until the heat's off. And put them right back in another parish, never saying a word to the congregation.

If there's a devil, he's laughing at this new way to recycle garbage.

And if there's a God, somebody should sue him for malpractice.

171

I took a puddle-jumper plane up to Marcy, the state joint for the criminally insane. Sat in the visiting room listening to a psychopath who'd dissected a kid with an electric knife tell me he knew how to find any devil-worshiper in the country. Just get him out, he'd lead me right to the people I was chasing. I told him I couldn't do that . . . but maybe I could pull some strings, get some time cut off his sentence. He smirked at me—he wasn't that crazy.

172

Showed the mug shots around, asked everyone. Drew blanks at every turn. I rattled every cage I could think of, but all I got back was the snarl of beasts.

173

It was eight days before he called. Mama answered, told him I wasn't around. He wouldn't leave a message, just said to make sure I was there, same time tomorrow. Said to have her tell me it was my friend calling.

He called the next day. Heard my voice, said an address into the phone, hung up.

174

That should have wrapped it.

I waited for Max to show up, got in the car, went over to Lily's. I was going to give her the address, let her deal with Wolfe, stand back.

But when I got to SAFE, Lily took me into a back room without me saying a word.

"I got it," I started to tell her.

"It doesn't matter. Not now."

"Why?"

"There's parts I don't know. Wolfe said to meet her. She wants to tell you herself."

175

I called Wolfe. Followed instructions. Almost daylight when I pulled into her driveway. She opened the door, already dressed for work, makeup in place.

"You want coffee?"

"No, thanks."

"I'll just finish mine, then, okay?"

"Sure."

She sat at a round wood table, sipping from a white china mug. The ashtray next to her had a couple of lipsticked butts in it already, scraps of phone messages at her elbow. The Rottweiler curled at her feet, face on the floor between his paws, looking like a fatalist.

"I got their address," I told her.

"I know. I knew you would. It's no go."

"What does that mean?"

"It means I got sold out," she said. "There's no way to prosecute them for what they did to Luke—we try and put him on the stand before he's fused, he's going to split wide open. And if we wait, his story won't fly. What jury is going to go for devil-worship? That's why they use all that . . . all the trappings.

"We don't have any of the tapes. They know what they're doing— the camera angles won't have his face. Or theirs. Not theirs, for damn sure. Buyers only care what the victim looks like."

"You knew this going in. What about the . . . ?"

"Prosecuting for homicide? Yes, that was the trump card. I could get a grand jury to go for it, I'm sure. It makes logical sense. We could get in all the psychiatric testimony that way too. Then we'd have a club over their heads . . . split them up, get one to roll over, talk to us, make a statement. At least we'd have a chance."

"So? What's wrong with . . . ?"

"What's wrong is that the office won't let me go after the indictment. I heard more crap these past few days about defendants' rights than I hear from Legal Aid in a year."

"You think somebody's bent?"

"No, I think they're cowards. An indictment like we'd want, it's not a sure thing. It'd go up and down on appeal for years. They're scared . . . they're scared of all those 'false allegations' freaks . . . you know, the ones who talk about the 'myth' of ritual abuse." She lit another smoke, blew out a puff angrily, sipped at her coffee. "You want to know what's funny? They may be right, those people. I'm not sure Satanists are doing anything to children . . . you know how they say the devil can quote the Scriptures? Well, *anyone* can quote the devil. This stuff is the flip side . . . child molesters can put on the costumes, and all of a sudden, it's 'Satanic.' It's like a scam inside a scam . . . we find the kids, they tell us what happened, and we get lost in prosecuting the devil. The office doesn't want any part of it—they won't authorize the presentation. And even if I snuck in the indictment, they'd move to dismiss it themselves. They've done it to me before."

I lit a smoke of my own, buying time. "Did that guy ever send his lawyer around?"

Her smile showed up, low wattage. "Oh yes. His lawyer is a partner in one of our most respected Wall Street firms. Doesn't know a lot about criminal law, though. We made our deal."

"You gonna keep it?"

"Sure. He gets flat immunity for anything we drop him for. Limited to nonviolent offenses, of course. That's the way he presented his client—we just went along. And he throws in truthful testimony about any others involved."

"That'd get him dead."

"Yes." She made a clicking sound with her tongue. The Rottweiler sat up. Wolfe held the coffee mug steady as he lowered his snout and slurped. "It's decaf," she said, like I was accusing her of dog abuse.

"We'll take them in. Throw a bunch of charges at them, see if one'll crack even without the homicide hammer. It depends how many of them there are, how well organized, who's representing them. You know how it works."

"Yeah. Discovery motions'll get them Luke's statements. He ends up hospitalized too. And they walk away."

"Maybe next time," she said, looking right into my face. "What's the address?"

I ground out my cigarette, getting up to leave. "I didn't bring it with me," I said.

She didn't say another word. I let myself out.

176

I spent that day drifting. The building where they were holed up was freestanding, but it hadn't been designed that way—rubble from the wrecker's ball still on either side. In the South Bronx, just over the

Willis Avenue Bridge. Pioneer-yuppie territory. When real estate prices went out of control in Manhattan, every square inch of land turned gold. Yuppies charged out of the center like maggots exposed to light: Long Island City, Flatbush, Harlem, anywhere you could find dwelling space. If you could get in first, you could get in cheap. Staking out the frontier. You held the land against the natives, you could turn it over for cash, big time. The people who'd been living there first, they got the '80s equivalent of smallpox-treated blankets. Then God died on October 19 and the real estate market crashed. Some of the pioneers were cut off from the supply lines. Too late for the natives to make a comeback, though—they got tickets in the Projects lottery, sleeping on the streets while they waited their turn.

The next-nearest building was maybe twenty-five feet to the right. Six stories, abandoned. No windows in its eyeless corpse. Chain link fence all around the occupied property, glimpse of cars parked around the side. Satellite dish on the roof, all the ground-floor windows barred. A meter-reading scam wouldn't get me inside.

It was just an address—still couldn't be sure it was them. The vampire may have gotten it wrong. Or gotten me right.

177

I was still drifting when it got dark. I let it happen. Found myself on the BQE to Queens. Thought I was heading to Wolfe's when I felt the amulet around my neck. A hot spot—the kind you get from fever.

Pulled up outside the house. Turned off the engine, giving them plenty of time to notice me. Started it up again, pulled into the driveway, around to the back.

The messenger didn't seem surprised to see me.

She was downstairs, two young women with her. They stepped aside as I approached, bowed to her, and moved away. It was so dark, I couldn't tell if they were still in the room with us.

"You are troubled," she said.

"Yes."

"Ask your questions."

"I found the people I was looking for. But they're beyond the law."

"As you are."

A soft light glowed to my left—looked like flame floating in water.

"I'm not beyond the law," I told her. "They could bring me down like swatting a fly."

"Do you seek justice?"

"No."

"What, then?"

"Revenge."

"Yes, truth does not change with names. You are afraid?"

"Not of them. Not now."

"But once, yes?"

"Yes. When I was a kid."

"These are not the same people who hurt you."

"Yes, they are. You said it yourself. Only their names have changed."

"So it is not for the child you seek them?"

"Maybe. I don't know. That's the truth—I don't know."

"That is your sacrifice. To tell me the truth. A truth you have told no other, yes?"

"Nobody knows."

"You have it on you, hunter. You will never be free. Not until you cross over. Do not fear, treasure your sadness. This earth will not hold happiness for you, but your spirit will return. Clean and fresh."

"Without hate?"

"It is your spirit to hate, hunter. Your true path is to hate righteously. Guard the health of your spirit—do not endanger your soul."

"I'm going to . . ."

"I know. Any man can break the circle, but no man can prevent it from closing again. That man, the one who came to us with the baby's body. For the sacrifice. There is one who loved the baby. She still lives."

"The mother . . ."

"She is not the one. She was never the one. The mother is with child now. She will not survive the new infant—she will die in childbirth. And she who loved the baby who died will have a new child to love."

"How . . . ?"

She put her hands behind her head, arched her back like a cat, stretched. Her smile was the secret of sex. "In the Islands, in the jungles just outside the cities, people whisper. No man lives without food. Even the spirits must eat. They must mate too. I know. It is that to be Queen. Listen now: some say baby snake eggs hatch in the stomachs of those who have offended. The babies hatch, their poison kills. Then you must cut open the body to let the spirit-snake free. The inside of a bamboo stalk is many tiny little hairs, like baby snakes. In your food, the hairs cause great sickness. Some die. The spirits are surgeons, not butchers. The mother will die, the baby will live. We will make our sacrifice— I will give myself—they will come into me. It will happen."

"Give yourself?"

"The myths are true, hunter. As I told you. I can raise the dead. As you were dead, once. Tell me this is true."

I saw Candy in my mind. Bound and gagged. And deadly. Later, on her stairwell, skirt hiked to her waist, losing my impotence inside her, paying the price.

Raise the dead—for the first time, I knew what it meant.

"It's true," I said. "Do I . . . ?"

"You too, hunter. You will not find what you seek with your own sacrifice, but it is your spirit's destiny to seek. Remember what I have told you."

I stood up. Bowed. She stood too, moved close to me. She was much shorter than I'd thought. Hands reached up around my neck, pulled my face down. Her tongue was fire in my mouth. "When you come back, it will be yours," she whispered, raising the dead.

178

The gypsy cab rolled past their house, me driving, Mole in the passenger seat, Max in the back.

"You see any way in?" I asked.

The Mole ignored me, scribbling something on a notepad strapped to his thigh.

Back in the junkyard, he looked up from a drafting table. "My friends told me you visited that . . . person. Off Fifth Avenue."

"I didn't hurt him."

"You should have told me."

"Your friends, they ask you if you knew about it?"

"Yes."

"Nice to be able to tell your friends the truth, isn't it?"

The Mole took off his Coke-bottle glasses, rubbed them on his greasy jumpsuit, said nothing.

179

Later that night, Max slipped out of the gypsy cab, all in black. We were half a block away from the target, on a side street facing the back of their house.

Nothing to do but wait.

We sat in silence, Mole checking the windshield, me the back window. No smoking, a .38 held against my leg, pointed at the floor. It wasn't Max I was worried about—in this neighborhood, they strip cars with the passengers still in them.

Max moved like a squid in ink—didn't see him until he was almost on top of us.

Back in the bunker, Max made the sign of opening a door, held up two fingers. Two doors, front and back. Held up one finger, pushed forward, made a sign like turning a doorknob, put a fist to one eye, like looking through a telescope. Held up two fingers, pulled back, flattened his palm like it was gliding over a smooth surface.

The Mole sketched quickly, showed Max the house: front view, a door between two barred windows, peephole about face level, doorknob to the left. Max nodded yes. Then the back view: the door just a slab of flat metal, no peephole, no doorknob, arrows showing it opened out. Another nod of agreement. The Mole sketched a fire escape along the back of the building, running from window to window. Max shook his head, made the flat-palm gesture again. The Mole used his eraser, showed us a pure slab, windows bricked over.

"Only way in is the front," I said. "Have you got . . . ?"

"We'll look again," the Mole said.

180

I found the Prof on Wall Street the next day, working his shoeshine rag like a virtuoso. Clarence was his customer, sporting alligator loafers to go with his pearl-gray suit. I waited my turn.

"How about riding shotgun tonight, Prof?"

"Go slow, bro'. Put another quarter in, give me one more spin."

"We got to check out a building. In the Bronx. Me, Max, and the Mole. Can't leave the car alone in that neighborhood. Just a watcher's job—scare anyone away, they come by."

"If it's a score, there's room for more."

"It's no score. Just something I'm gonna do."

"Me too."

"Listen, Prof, there'll be nothing to split up, where we're going, okay?"

"It don't scan, man. But I'll do what you say, back your play. Pick us up on the pier."

"Us?"

"This boy don't take a turn, he ain't never gonna learn," nodding his head at Clarence.

181

Clarence drove the Plymouth along the back street, its muffled exhaust motorboating against the sides of the diseased and deserted cars lining the block. He pulled to a stop, the back seat emptied. He took off as we started across the empty lot to the abandoned building.

Max went first. I brought up the rear, the Mole between us. Broken glass crunched under my feet as I turned to check behind us. I could see the Mole's bulk in his jumpsuit, stumbling along, his leather satchel in one hand.

So much garbage piled up in the gully behind the building that we could step right into the first-floor windows. The smell told me we weren't the first ones to figure it out. Rats scurried. I threw my pencil flash forward, sweeping. Newspapers piled in one corner, a shopping cart without wheels, metal frame to a TV set, plastic coat hangers, rags that had been clothes once. Another corner was the bathroom. Crack vials scattered among broken chunks of concrete from the building itself. Wine bottles. Fire scars on the walls, blackened pillars. Open-grave smell.

The metal staircase was still standing, pieces of the railing missing. Max took a length of black cord from somewhere, looped it around one of the stairs about halfway up, pulled as hard as he could. It held.

We started up the stairs, testing each one. The second-floor landing was solid. I played the flash over the walls—gang graffiti, faded under dust and ash. The next floor was better. Stronger staircase, less damage.

"Basement fire," the Mole whispered. After the building had been abandoned, some wino fell asleep with a cigarette in his hand. They probably just let it burn itself out—worth more money to the landlord empty anyway.

When we stepped out onto the roof, we could see in every direction: headlights on the highway, the quiet bulk of the Plymouth waiting. Looking straight down to the target, eyes pulled to a bright light like moths. A skylight, glowing yellow-orange, set into the center of their roof.

The Mole reached in his satchel, took out a pair of night glasses, and started his scan. Max walked the roof corner to corner, leaning far out over the edge, palms out as though the air could balance him.

The Mole handed me the glasses. I narrowed in on the cars parked along the side of the building, behind the chain link fence. Five of them, parked parallel to the building. One a Mercedes coupe for sure, but no hope of getting a license number from that angle.

182

"Their roof edges make a trapezoid," the Mole told us. "No way to get a grip. The top is smooth—even a grappling hook would come loose. And if you hit the skylight, broke the glass, it might be wired. Some kind of sensors all around the building, about chest high. Maybe infrared, motion detectors . . . can't tell."

"Which leaves what?" I asked him.

"Tunnel through to the basement, punch through the front door, or land on the roof."

"It's the door, then. They have to be getting electricity in there, right?"

The Mole nodded.

"And you could take it down?"

He nodded again.

"Okay, next thing is to make sure it's them. I got their mug shots, from when they were arrested. Had some blowups made. They have to come out sometime . . . it's a tough neighborhood to hang out in, but maybe we could . . ."

"I can watch for them, mahn," Clarence said. "Just get me an old car to drive."

Max tapped me on the shoulder, pointed at Mole, touched his mouth, patted his fingers against his thumb in a talking gesture, made the sign for "what?"

I translated, standing over a silent jackhammer, digging with an invisible shovel, moved my hand in a reverse parabola to show coming up from underneath. Shook my head "no." Then I locked my thumbs, fluttered my hands like flapping wings, showed a takeoff and a landing. Shook my head again—we'd need a helicopter. Then I mimed pushing down the T-bar on a dynamite detonator, threw my hands apart in the sign for an explosion. Made the sign for "okay."

Max looked only at the Mole. Got to his feet, pointed. They walked away together.

183

"He is still missing, mahn."

"He can't stay missing for long, Jacques. He doesn't have but one way to earn a living. And Wolfe's people are on his case."

"Yes. And if they find him, what happens? He will go to jail for killing the baby?"

"Maybe. Who knows? He'll say it was an accident . . . or maybe that the mother did it. There's no sure things."

"A sure thing if we find him first, mahn."

"Yeah, I know. That's not why I came. I need some stuff."

"What, then, mahn? You have only to ask."

"Two shotguns. A semi-auto and a double-barrel. Both twelve gauge. And a Glock with a long clip. Straps for the scatterguns, shoulder holster for the Glock, butt down. Okay?"

"A Glock? That is not like you, mahn. You are my only customer who will never use an automatic—always complaining that they could jam no matter what I tell you, huh?"

I just shrugged, thinking about what I'd learned in Indiana.

"You need that much firepower, maybe you could use a couple of men, yes?"

"No, I'm okay. It's just in case, you know?"

"I know. Clarence is still working with you? Looking for that man, Emerson?"

"Yeah."

"He is a good boy. Maybe his temper is too quick, but he is young yet."

"He is that. How soon could you have the stuff?"

"Just a day or so, mahn. I will have them all tested, in perfect order. When you're done, you may leave them wherever you work, ice-cold clean, all right? Anything you want done to them first?"

"Cut down the barrels on the scatterguns."

"Of course, mahn. Modified choke, yes? Twelve-gauge, three-inch shells, double-O?"

"Perfect."

"Tomorrow night, then."

184

I was teaching Luke how to play casino when one of the pay phones rang at Mama's. She came to the table, pointed at me.

"It is her, mahn. The woman in the photo. A dead ringer."

"Get out of there. Now."

The phone went dead in my ear.

185

"How many cards left?" I asked Luke, pointing at the pile between us.

"Twelve."

"How many cards have you already collected?"

"Nineteen."

"How many spades?"

"Five."

"How many cards loose?"

"Four in my hand, four in yours, two on the table. Ten."

"How many cards have I collected?"

"Eleven."

"Okay, now what do you do when . . . ?" Max sat down next to Luke, made a "come on" gesture to me, impatient.

"We'll finish this later," I said to Luke.

The kid bounced in his seat, eyes pleading. "Can't I come too?"

I looked at Max. He grabbed Luke's belt, hauled him out of the seat like a briefcase. The kid's laughter trailed through the restaurant as Max carried him to the back.

186

We got in the Plymouth. Max made the sign for the Mole. Late afternoon. We slogged our way north on the FDR, Luke sitting between us, eyes bright with the prospect of seeing his pal.

Terry let us in the gate. He and Luke ran off together, Simba circling them, yapping like a pup. Max pulled me ahead.

The Mole was a good distance from his bunker, hunched over a U-shaped metal bracket maybe twelve feet wide. It was anchored to what looked like metal rods, running at forty-five degree angles from halfway up the bracket arms to the ground.

"What's this, Mole?"

He ignored me, looping a thick ribbon of rubber over one end of the bracket, then the other. It looked like a giant slingshot. From the bottom of the U-bracket, he unfolded a pair of metal tubes, about three feet apart. Placed them against the back of the rubber band. Then he pulled on a lever. Ratcheting noise with each pull. The rubber stretched. Stretched some more. He nodded at Max. The Mongolian picked up two sacks of dry cement mix lashed back to back, placed them in the notch formed by the rubber. The Mole pulled the switch and the cement sacks blasted off like the Space Shuttle, flying in a high arc, smashing against the top of a wrecked car maybe two hundred feet away.

"You're fucking insane," I told the Mole. He bowed. Max grinned.

"It's impossible," I said. "Max'll get killed."

"It's not impossible," the Mole said. "It's just a ratio. Thrust to weight, height to distance. It's got way too much power now. All we need is an arc, Max can float down."

"Float? You're a maniac. And he's a bigger one."

Max was pulling black silk out of a duffel bag when Luke and Terry walked over to us.

"What's Max doing?" the kid asked.

"Making a fool of himself."

"Max wouldn't do that . . . Can I see?"

The warrior climbed into his costume. He was encased in silk: a hood fit tightly over his head, Velcro closures at his wrists and ankles. Standard night-stalker stuff—I'd seen it before. Then he spread his arms in a crucifixion gesture and he sprouted wings—ribbed silk billowed from his wrists to his ankles.

"It's wonderful!" Luke clapped his little hands, delighted at the game.

"Jesus!" Terry said.

I didn't say anything.

187

The Mole carried his launch device in one hand. "Aluminum," he said when I looked a question at him.

"Why don't you just shoot him out of a cannon?"

"He's not going that far. The drop is about forty-five feet roof to roof. The launch building is much higher than the target."

Ask a lunatic a question . . .

We walked over to where junked cars were piled into a mountain about twenty feet high. The Mole slowly made his way to the top, set up his launcher. He climbed down, paced off a distance, took a can of spray paint from his jumpsuit, made a white X on the hard ground.

"About four clicks," he said. Climbed back to the top. It took a while.

Max went up the mountain like it was a ramp. Leaned back into the notch, nodded once. The Mole pulled on the lever.

"Max is gonna fly!" Luke said.

I held my breath.

A *sproong!* sound and Max was airborne. He shot straight up, jackknifed his body like a diver, popped open his wings with a loud snap. His body went up like he'd caught a gust, righted itself, and floated to the ground like a butterfly landing on a flower. Right on the damn X.

Max wasn't breathing hard. The Mole cut open his knee stumbling down from the mountain of cars.

188

"For the last fucking time, Prof, there's no money in this."

"Even you not fool enough to Rambo a house for nothing, schoolboy. I'll pay the fare, take my share."

I didn't try and talk him out of it—he knew the truth.

We all had our reasons.

I knew I wouldn't find any answers in that house. I was so lonely. Missing my old pal, Fear. I'd see him soon enough.

189

Two in the morning, the lights were still on in the front windows. Two downstairs, one on the second floor. The third story was dark.

I checked my watch. In a couple of minutes, calls would start flying into 911: Hispanic, black, white, Oriental voices. Gunfight at 138th and the Concourse, fire at a social club, man with a machete running down Walton Avenue, woman holding a baby on the top floor of the Projects, threatening to jump, bodega robbery, cop down on Hoe Avenue.

Clarence was behind the wheel of the pale blue slab-sided van, the name of some phony butcher shop painted on the sides in maroon script.

Cops see it moving through the South Bronx, they'd figure it was on its way to the meat market in Hunts Point.

"You ready?" I asked Clarence, adjusting the shoulder strap for the shotgun over my chest. I had the semi-auto, the Prof always worked with a side-by-side.

"Yes, mahn."

"We go first, okay? Nothing starts until *we* do. Don't be blasting away just to be doing it—they don't make a move on me, you take off for the spot soon as the front door goes. Listen, Clarence, listen good. *Everybody's* coming out the back, okay? The Mole'll get to the van first. He'll be okay. He can't see worth shit, but he can drive good enough, he has to. And he knows where to go. I come out first, I'm waiting for Max. He comes first, he'll wait for me. Don't waste your time trying to move him—he won't go. Anybody gets hit, we got the medical kit in the back. Let the Mole do the doctoring, you drive, it comes to that. Anybody comes out after me and Max, blow them away."

"I got it, mahn. I won't let you down."

"I know. Your mother raised a hell of a man."

His tight smile flashed in the dark. I watched the target house. Held my hands in front of me, palms down, fingers spread. Delicate fingers, they looked to me now. X-ray eyes, seeing the bones. Cold bones, icicles—they'd shatter like glass if I hit something.

I tapped the side of the plastic bottle of talc, rubbed it all over my hands. Slipped on the surgeon's gloves, warming my hands.

Then I pulled the Velcro band tight around my right wrist, checked for flex. I'd have to fire the scattergun with one hand.

I felt my heart pound, breathed until it settled down into a smooth idle. Inside, they weren't the ones. But they'd do.

On the top of the abandoned building, a tiny red light blinked. Time.

I held out my hand. Clarence took it, squeezed.

I stepped onto the street. Hands full. Started my walk.

The headlights on the van flashed into life. Blinked off. Flashed again. The signal to the Mole. In the target house, the lights in the windows went dark, electricity dead. The bolt cutters took the gate in one chomp. I walked up to the door, shotgun in my right hand. No sounds from inside—they probably figured it for a blown fuse. Flattened myself against the wall next to the door, molded the *plastique* all around the seams. Pulled the string and ran to the side of the house, rolling into a ball, soles of my boots pointed at the door. It blew off with a muffled thump, mini-mushroom of plaster dust billowing out.

I was up and running back to the entrance, crouching as I slid through the doorway, a human trip-wire, on the kill. Movement to my right—I squeezed off a blast from the scattergun. Voices screaming above me. Downstairs was empty except for a couple of couches, big television set. And a body dressed in jeans and a splattered white T-shirt, blood from waist to face.

Center staircase. I started up, crab-style, stomach flat against the left wall, leading with my right hand. A shape peered around the corner ahead of me. I fired, scrambled up behind the blast as a body tumbled down the stairs toward me, swung the shotgun around the corner, cranked off three more rounds, sweeping. I dropped the shotgun, whipped the automatic free of the shoulder rig.

"This is the police!" I yelled, concussion still ringing in my ears. "Come out with your hands up!"

Two of them staggered into the hall. Man in white boxer shorts, woman in a red nightgown, hands up, trying to say something.

I moved down the corridor. "Where's the rest?" I asked, leveling the pistol between them.

"Downstairs," the man said.

"How many?"

"Seven. We're the Nine. I . . ."

"Turn around, grab the wall. You move, you're dead."

They braced themselves like they'd done it before. I pulled a flare from my jacket, cracked it open. It glowed cold green fire at the end of the hall near the staircase. Enough light to see Max as he flowed down the stairs, a shadow of power. Something crackled like cellophane in my chest, suppressed fear released—he'd made it to the roof. I pointed ahead, stood guard as he went into the other rooms.

Three rooms and a bath on the floor, doors standing open. The man and woman had come from the one on the end. Max stepped back into the corridor, made an "all clear" signal to me. Pointed a finger upstairs, grabbed the finger with his other hand, bent it in half. One of them had been upstairs.

Time running down. "Where's the rest?" I asked them, reasonable and calm.

"We *told* you," the woman said. "Downstairs."

It hit me then—where it had all started for Luke. I stepped close to them, pulled the trigger again and again, squeezing them off the count. Charged down the stairs, flying now, feeling Max behind me.

The basement door was locked—felt like steel. I stepped aside. Max's leg shot out like a pile driver, rapid-fire hammering all around the knob. A final kick took it off the hinges. Gunfire answered, bullets whined up at us. I dropped to my belly, unhooked the baseball-sized grenade from my belt, pulled the pin with my teeth, tossed it in. A white flash just ahead of the bang. I crawled inside, flying blind.

Lights on—they must have had a generator. A bullet chipped the wall near my face. I emptied the Glock, sweeping in a Z-pattern, hosing them down, slithered back outside, snapped in a new clip.

All-dead silence now. I crept down the stairs. The far wall was cracked open from the grenade—I could see clear out to the night. Pair of heavy videocams on tripods, cross-firing at a black-skirted platform standing in front of an inverted cross. Foot-high numbers sprayed in red on the wall above: 666. The platform stood untouched by the explosion, waiting for the show to start. I walked over, looked down. The surface was gleaming hardwood, an upside-down pentagram carved deep into its face, like a butcher's drain. The pentagram stared back at me, a leering goat's head.

Two bodies down there. One wearing a black hood, peaked at the top, some weird symbols on it in white, a .45 in its hand. The other was a woman, black hair, heavy white makeup, black lipstick. They were both stitched with bullets from the Glock. I spun around to go when I saw it . . . in the corner. I made myself look. A little boy. Handcuffed behind his back, tape across his mouth, naked. Bullet holes along his spine. I turned him over with my hand, gently too late. The exit wound had taken off his face.

My mind blanked off the child's body, rejecting the image, a pure white screen with black numbers, counting: Nine, the woman upstairs said. We are the Nine. I'd taken out two with the scattergun before I dropped her and her pal. Max left one coming down from the roof. Two in the basement. The little boy wouldn't count—he wasn't one of them. Two more, somewhere. I held up two fingers to Max. He took the point to the back door. It was standing open, swinging softly in the night air. I snapped my last flare, tossed it outside, rolled out in its wake, Max right behind. We started toward the van, keeping low. I saw a woman's body lying face up in the weeds. We were about fifty feet away when the shots came. I caught one in the shoulder—a hard punch from an ice pick. White wires ripped through my arm, my eyes starbursted with pain as I went down. Max dove on top, covering me with his body. Double blast from the Prof's shotgun, snapping string of killer hornets from Clarence's automatic.

"The motherfucker's down, bro'! Run for it, we got your back!"

On my feet now, Max's arm around me bracing, trying to run. Heard the van's engine roar into life, felt myself lifted inside.

It all went black then.

190

I rested up in the junkyard. Hadn't lost much blood with the pressure bandage they'd slapped on. Got lost in the painkillers for a few days.

I was okay about it, the dead time. Talked to Terry, watched some

TV. Max fed Pansy every day, finally went back and brought her over to me. She was in heat. It took me fifteen minutes of one-handed sign language to convince him I wanted him to take the dog to Elroy's for a while.

Clarence came by, sat next to my cot in the bunker.

"I saw him take off. The Silent One. Like a skate, a devilfish flying. Right after you blew the front door. Seemed like he was up there so long, floating."

"You stand there gawking at him?"

"Oh, that is what the Prof said, mahn, I finally get around to the back door with him. I didn't even see the first one come out. It was the Prof who took her—a young girl. She was almost on me with that long knife, screaming like a mad witch, when I hear the shotgun speak. Cut her right down. I would not have thought the little man could do like that."

"Yeah. He's a fucking wonder."

"He's a man. Like I never knew. Quiet, after that. Then we hear shots from inside. And the explosion. I ask him, how long we gonna wait? He says, until you come out. I ask him, what if you *don't* come out? You know what he says to me, mahn? He says, then the cops find us when they come. And we die right there. Die like men. I wish my mother knew a man like that."

"Me too."

The bullet never touched bone. The bandage was a few inches from the Queen's amulet, still around my neck. I was healing, waiting my time. Staying inside, icing up.

When they brought Luke to see me, I started crying.

He was gone by the time I stopped.

191

In Wolfe's backyard, dark out.

"They identified the bodies," she said. "No tapes. They must have just gotten started when it happened."

"I guess."

"Storm had her baby. A girl. They named her Sunny."

"That's nice."

"And we arrested Emerson. Took him down yesterday. Hanging around outside the Welfare Center. He's on the Rock. And this is one indictment that'll stick."

"Yeah."

She threw away her cigarette. "Burke . . ."

"Yeah?"

She stood close to me, held my hand. Her kiss was soft. "You and me, it's not going to be."

"I know."

192

I stood alone on my rooftop, looking down into the zero. I never knew the name of the last sacrifice—didn't know who I was crying for anymore.

Thought about what I didn't have until the list got too long.

Clarence's voice, from long ago. "What would be justice, mahn? So the baby may sleep in peace?"

He was older now.

I can't make babies. Can't fake love. I finished with my tears. Back to what I had left.

193

At Mama's, in the back booth, drinking my soup, making my plans.

"You had call," Mama said. "Yesterday."

"He leave a name?"

"Not a man. Woman. Said to tell you Belinda called. She say you have her number."

194

They brought Silver to the attorney's conference room at Rikers. We shook hands. I felt the power of his grip all the way through my wounded shoulder.

He leaned forward, jailhouse whisper. "Helene told me. I owe you, brother."

I reached in my attaché case. Showed him the picture of Emerson, ran my thumb along the razor-sliced edge. Said the baby-killer's name softly. He'd be in the same joint as Silver, awaiting trial—Rikers holds city-wide.

Silver stared at the photo for a long minute, nodded, handed it back.

195

I'm here now. Waiting for my spirit to walk.

A NOTE ON THE TYPE

This book was set in a digitized version of Granjon, a type named in compliment to Robert Granjon, a type cutter and printer active in Antwerp, Lyons, Rome, and Paris from 1523 to 1590. Granjon, the boldest and most original designer of his time, was one of the first to practice the trade of typefounder apart from that of printer.

Linotype Granjon was designed by George W. Jones, who based his drawings on a face used by Claude Garamond (ca. 1480–1561) in his beautiful French books. Granjon more closely resembles Garamond's own type than does any of the various modern faces that bear his name.

Composed by PennSet, Inc., a division of
Maryland Linotype Composition Company,
Bloomsburg, Pennsylvania

Printed and bound by Arcata Graphics,
Martinsburg, West Virginia